CW00468342

ESCAPE FROM LUCIFLEX

(Android Wars – Book 2)

JJ TONER

Cover – Stephen Walker / Anya Kelleye

First Published May 21, 2021

eBook ISBN 9781908519795
Paperback ISBN 9781908519801
Hardcover ISBN 9781908519818

To receive updates and news about JJ Toner's Science Fiction, please go to:
www.jjtoner.com/sf-sign-up

ESCAPE FROM LUCIFLEX

(Android Wars – Book 2)

PART 1 – Luciflex

Chapter 1

Carla Scott sat in a cargo bay aboard the freighter *NFSS Ganymede*, the only female among thirty prisoners. They all wore the uniform – a hideous two-piece of blue and gray hoops. This provided her with a measure of camouflage, although the highlights in her hair and her curves were dead giveaways.

The shackles chafed her ankles, but she was glad of them; they kept her safe from the other prisoners. The man to her left was too old to be a threat. The man on her right was another matter entirely. Tall and thin, with an unruly beard and greasy, matted hair, he looked – and smelled – every inch a space pirate.

The vast cargo bay was stacked to capacity with Pexcorn crates, on shelving eight tiers high. The strange smells of plastic and compressed protein filled the air, seasoned by the stink of body odor from the prisoners. A low hum from the engines was punctuated by moans and occasional verbal outbursts from the men.

The overhead lights flickered and dimmed as the freighter's conventional engines surged. The volume and pitch of the hum rose until every bone in her body was shaking and the mounting G-force pressed her against the wall at her back. She clamped her teeth together to stop them from rattling.

And then, when it seemed the vibrations would never stop, the drone of the conventional engines wound down to a plaintiff whine and the G-force dropped to normal.

With a final guttural rumble, the engines stopped altogether. The hum in her ears continued like a ghostly echo, while an unnatural silence swept over the men in the cargo bay. Thirty seconds later, the jump gate siren sounded. She held her breath and braced for the jolt, but still when it came, her heart skipped.

Whatever hopes she had of a last-minute reprieve died right there, as the freighter entered the Interdimensional Gate and started its journey through the Conduits to Luciflex.

Luciflex! The outermost colonized planet of the galaxy, 320 light years from Earth, its molten mines the stuff of nightmares. Even the name – used to frighten little children – sat like bile in her stomach.

The old man on her left opened his eyes. "I'll never get used to the Gate hops."

"Me neither."

"They call me Marny."

"Carla Scott. Pleased to meet you, Marny."

Within 15 standard minutes, the temperature had dropped two degrees. Carla hugged her knees to her chest to conserve her body heat.

Five days earlier, she was basking in late evening sunshine in a penthouse apartment with panoramic views of the Pacific Ocean. Round about now she should have been taking a shower while Lia prepared her evening meal.

Has it really only been five days?

Carla's heart bled for Lia. The thought of her beloved android lying on a bench, disassembled and lifeless, with technicians removing her parts for recycling made her hands clench so hard that her nails bit into her palms.

#

A pall hung over the men all around her, a pall of despair, tinged with shame. Transportation drags everyone down to the same level. The detritus of humanity. Carla's sentence was three years, but she knew she was unlikely to serve all of that. The average life expectancy on Luciflex was 20 months.

The pirate on her right tried to engage her in conversation. "In all my years, I've never met a convict as good-looking as you. What do they call you?" His mouth sported a salacious twist, his right eye a lecherous glint. His left eye was glass.

In your dreams, One-eye.

"We should be friends, you and me. You're gonna need friends where we're going."

Their shoulders touched and Carla shrugged him off.

I prefer to choose my friends, thank you, she thought.

She closed her eyes, conjuring up several images: her friend Zed Jones's crooked smile; the view from her penthouse windows; the magnificent Pacific Ocean under a cloudless sky... Then the scene changed, with mist rolling in from the sea, reaching out to touch the eternal smog that covered the city. She needed to remain calm. If she let her mind embrace the full horror of her predicament, she could descend into depression and have a full-blown panic attack.

One-eye tried a different tack. "You don't look like a hardened criminal. How did you end up here?"

She said nothing, but the question reached her soul. She bit her lip.

I cost the corporation a lot of money. I probably would have got away with that, but I pissed off the generals.

Chapter 2

Five days earlier

She arrived at the Xenodyne Automation building early that day. At the entrance to the building, her access card made an unusual sound. Then the palm check at the door to her laboratory flashed twice, sounding a faint warning signal in her subconscious; it normally flashed once. When she found her workstation clear of the papers she'd been working on, the warning signal became a claxon in her head. She sat at her keyboard, keyed in her username and password.

ACCESS DENIED flashed on the screen.

She spun around, strode to the door, and placed her palm on the inside pad. It was unresponsive. She was locked in! She kicked the door. "Open, damn you."

She picked up her X-Vid and punched the button for Cassidy, her assistant. It rang out, switching to video mail.

She left a message. "I'm in the lab. Security has locked me in. The palm pad is not working, and they've blocked access to my computer. Stay—"

The X-Vid clicked and cut her off. She nearly panicked, then.

She tried shouting. "I know you can hear me. Unlock the door. Let me speak to Dr. Franck." She gave the door a few more kicks, but it was hopeless. It was made of a material similar to that used for the android frames, a tungsten-titanium carbide alloy, as light as aluminum but stronger than tempered steel.

Ten minutes went by before two female guards arrived. They stormed in. Carla raised her hands. They pushed her against a wall and conducted a quick body search. Then they led her to an interview room on the first floor. The room had a table and two plain chairs, blinds on the windows.

One of the guards said, "Remove your clothing."

Carla crossed her arms. "I want to talk to my boss, Dr. Franck."

The second guard took a step forward, hefting a wooden baton in her palm. "Strip."

Carla stripped to her underwear, placing her clothes on the table. "This is ridiculous. Call Dr. Franck. Better yet, call Professor Jones at the university."

They handed her a gray shirt and pants to wear. Then they sat her down at the table and shackled her wrists and ankles. She was still reeling from shock when Major Grant, the head of security, came in. The two guards picked up her clothes and left.

"Am I glad to see you, Major. I'm sure this is all some sort of horrible misunderstanding. These shackles are ridiculous. What am I supposed to have done?"

Grant was a big man. He must have been an impressive physical specimen in his youth; in middle age now, all his major muscle groups had long since turned to blubber. "You will remain under restraint until you've been processed."

"What does that mean?" Her hands folded into fists. "I've never been so humiliated. Why the prison outfit, and why the manacles? Why am I being treated like a criminal?"

"Because that's exactly what you are – you and your assistant both." His jowls shook and his belly wobbled in rhythm. "You will be brought before a military tribunal where you will face serious criminal charges."

This was no less than she expected, but the words carried an immediate impact similar to a blow from a cudgel to her midriff. She struggled to regain her composure.

"Whatever I've done, or whatever I'm charged with, Cassidy knows nothing about any of it."

"He hasn't come to work this morning, Carla, and he's not at his apartment. Hardly the actions of an innocent man." Grant's mouth closed in a hard line under his bulbous nose.

Cassidy's on the run! He's with the Resistance.

"When's the hearing?"

"The day after tomorrow."

"What? I have two days to prepare a defense? Who's my lawyer?"

"You don't need one. This is a military tribunal, not a court of law."

I'm up the creek!

"What are the charges?"

"Unauthorized modification of military equipment, I imagine. And reckless interference in a military campaign, probably."

Carla wasn't surprised. Xenodyne Automation existed purely for profit, and the executives were happy to obey any and all directives from the military in that pursuit. Her recent actions must have been seen by the executives as wildly inappropriate and by the generals as bordering on high treason.

"Dr. Franck has offered to stand as a character witness for you," he said.

Up the creek without a paddle!

Fritz Franck, her immediate superior, was a company man to his toenails. His testimony on her behalf was unlikely to be helpful and could even make matters worse.

"Generous of Dr. Franck to find the time, but I don't think we should trouble him."

"Is there anyone else you'd like to speak for you?"

"The CFO, Ricarda Petrik. She backed the project. She will speak for me."

"Ms. Petrik is facing her own problems. Who else?"

"My father."

"He's Food Commissioner, isn't he? And I think he's off-world?'

"He's on Califon in the C-System."

"What does he know about Autonomic Units? Better leave him out of it."

Heading toward the rapids.

"Professor Jones?"

His expression turned grave. "Josiah Jones is directly implicated."

"That's ridiculous. The professor knows nothing about it."

Grant raised an eyebrow. "He has made a full confession."

"He has nothing to confess."

"He says he had a significant input to the work."

"He advised me in general terms at an early stage, but he had no direct involvement, and no detailed knowledge of the progress of the project." She gesticulated with her hands, her chains rattling against the table. "He doesn't deserve to be punished for what I did."

"He says he gave you academic papers to read."

"He did, but they were not terribly relevant. Some were very old."

A few moments passed in silence.

"If I were you, I would plead guilty."

"You've got to be kidding me," said Carla.

"Admit that you were wrong. Explain your muddled thinking, your noble intentions, apologize and throw yourself on the mercy of the tribunal."

She exploded, "When did I ask for your advice?"

"Listen to me, Carla—"

"Just get out!" she roared.

"Carla—"

"OUT!" She pointed to the door.

He levered himself to his feet. "I wish you luck with the tribunal."

"What about Professor Jones?" she said. "Tell, me he won't be punished. He really had nothing to do with any of this."

"That's not my decision."

"But you will put a word in for him?"

"I'm sorry, Carla."

She suspected then that Josiah Jones's fate had already been decided. That knowledge cut her to the core. Professor Jones was not young, and he had a wife and a son – her good friend, the artist, Zed Jones.

Grant pointed a podgy finger at her, and delivered his final word. "Your best defense is to tell the truth. I must also warn you that your personal Unit will be seized, its memory files downloaded and checked. You must be completely honest with the tribunal. They will know if you are lying."

They haven't taken Lia, yet. Will she have the good sense to stay out of sight? Carla clung to that thought.

It was all she had.

Chapter 3

It was getting dark. Lia began to prepare Carla's evening meal. Lasagna and fruitoid – her favorites. While slicing the protein block, the knife slipped and pierced her fingertip. She examined the injury. It was a deep cut, but she hadn't felt it. If Carla had given her pain like her friend, Oscar, she knew her hand would have recoiled of its own accord. Oscar had told her pain was unpleasant, but Lia would have been happy to accept the sensation. The thought sent a thrill shivering through her frame; pain would make her more human.

Like her friend Oscar.

Five days earlier, when Oscar went out of control, Carla had ended him by removing his four main modules. But Lia had a secret. She hadn't lost Oscar entirely. She had picked up his modules and put them in a gym bag. Then she'd hidden the bag at the back of a cabinet under the kitchen sink.

The Fear module was even worse than pain; it forced her body to react to all sorts of situations in ways that she couldn't control or understand. Since Carla had given it to her, Lia was aware of several other strange sensations. Random memories of Oscar seemed to invade her Orientation module for no reason. Her Cognition module failed to understand the purpose of these memories; she had no need of them. They gave her sensations of comfort she couldn't explain, but that she was reluctant to release. Mostly, the memories vanished when they showed her Oscar's final moments. Then she felt another sensation somewhere deep inside. It was a feeling that she couldn't describe, but it was not pleasant.

She often found herself in a strange half-awake state, her Orientation module flashing false memories, images of things happening in places she'd never visited, images of events that could never happen. Oscar and herself in a ship, descending through the clouds onto the surface of Califon; traveling in a hover over a verdant alien landscape with Oscar by her side; running side by side with Oscar through tall grasses, two moons in the sky...

Where these false memories came from, she could not fathom. They had seen Califon through a porthole on a freighter, and Oscar had asked her to go there with him, but he had never spoken about the surface of the planet. Where could she have picked up so many false images?

The lasagna was nearly ready. She checked the time. Carla should be home by now. She used her communications module to put a call through to Carla's X-Vid.

Carla's picture appeared on her heads-up display. "I can't come to the X-Vid just now, Lia. Please leave a message."

"Your evening meal is almost ready. Where are you?"

Lia disconnected. In an attempt to preserve the meal in the best possible condition, she turned the oven right down. Five minutes later, the pasta was looking overdone. She took it out of the oven and placed it in the plasma oven, ready to reheat when Carla arrived.

She called Carla's work X-Vid again, using Carla's home X-Vid this time.

The recorded message started and was interrupted abruptly. A man's face appeared on the screen. "Yes? Who's calling?"

Lia didn't know who this was. She checked the caption under his image. It read: Major Grant. "This is Lia. I'd like to speak with Carla Scott."

"Carla's not available just now. Would you like to leave a message?"

"Tell her I have her evening meal ready for her."

The man paused before responding, "I'll give her the message. I'm sure she'll be home soon." He broke the connection.

Lia was puzzled. Who was Major Grant? Why had he answered Carla's personal X-Vid? She fussed about, resetting the table, waiting for Carla's return call. After another few minutes, she tried again. This time, her heads-up display remained blank. That had never happened before. She tried again on the X-Vid, with the same result. She rang the X-Vid customer service 24/7 line, and gave Carla's number.

"I'm sorry, caller, that number is no longer in service."

Something was seriously wrong! How could Carla's work X-Vid number be out of service? It had worked a few minutes earlier when that man took the call. Why was that man in possession of Carla's X-Vid? And where was Carla? A new feeling emerged from Lia's Fear module, a feeling of unease, bordering on alarm.

What should I do? When Carla comes home, she will expect to find me and her meal waiting for her, but what if she doesn't come home? What if she is in some kind of trouble?

She examined the uneasy feeling again and sensed danger. Lia reasoned it out. She knew what she had to do.

Carla is in trouble – serious trouble. I am not safe here. I have to get away from this apartment, immediately. If Carla comes home, she will find her lasagna in the plasma oven. She can heat it up. When she contacts me, I will return.

She ran into the kitchen and pulled out the bag she had hidden under the sink. Dropping Carla's X-Vid into the bag, she tucked it under her arm and headed out, flicking the lights off as she left.

Chapter 4

Three minutes after Lia had left the apartment block, two police hovers arrived with sirens howling. Four police officers leapt out and ran inside.

She watched the penthouse windows from an alleyway. When the lights came on, she melted into the shadows.

#

It was immediately obvious that Carla's Autonomic Unit was not in her apartment. The police lieutenant called Xenodyne Automation's security office.

"The android is not here, Major."

"Damn it!" said Grant.

"We have two computers, several powerpacks, android spare parts and some tools."

"Did you find an X-Vid?"

"No, sir."

Grant paused for a moment's thought. "I know she keeps a personal X-Vid in her apartment. Check again. Then leave a guard on the apartment and bring what you have to me."

#

With no idea where she should go, Lia headed for the docks, passing through several streets ruined by the recent battles for LAX. Weaving her way around burnt-out hovers, she came across two children rummaging through a pile of rubble. She asked them what they were looking for.

“My parents are buried in there,” said the girl. “They hid in the basement when the fighting started.”

“What are your names?” asked Lia.

“That’s my friend, Jason,” said the girl. “And I’m Tomasina.”

Lia ran her eyes over the rubble pile. It was enormous, with reinforced concrete blocks, massive wooden beams and steel girders – material that no child could lift. “Let me help you,” she said.

She set her bag down out of harm’s way behind a partly demolished wall. The children stood at a safe distance, and she went to work on the heaviest items. As each block and beam fell away, the children cheered. Ten minutes later, Lia’s clothes were covered in gray dust and the door to the basement was visible. She swept away the last of the debris and opened the door.

A man and a woman stumbled out, squinting in the daylight. Tomasina ran to them, crying tears of joy.

When she told her parents how Lia had helped them, her father said, "How can I thank you? You saved our lives."

"It was nothing. I did what I could," said Lia.

When she went to retrieve her bag from behind the wall, she couldn't find it. The boy, Jason, was gone too. Lia put two and two together.

"That boy has stolen my bag. I need it. Where did he go?"

"He ran off that way." The girl pointed toward the downtown area.

Lia set off in pursuit, immediately. She couldn't lose the bag; it contained Carla's home X-Vid, but more important, it contained Oscar's four precious modules.

Chapter 5

Major Grant powered up the X-Vid from Carla's office. He waited until the young officer manning the tracking system gave him the thumbs up before calling the X-Vid number Lia had used. A boy's voice answered.

"Hello there, this is the Federation Lottery Office. Who am I speaking with?"

"Jason."

"Well, congratulations Jason. I'm delighted to tell you, your X-Vid has been chosen for a grand prize. Just hold the line for a moment while we check it. What's your address?"

Ten seconds later, Jason disconnected.

The young officer gave the major a thumbs up. "Got it." He pressed a few buttons. "The team is on its way."

#

Lia ran through streets of charred and smoldering rubble. Burnt-out hovers and abandoned trucks impeded her progress. The boy was out of sight, but he couldn't have gone far. She rushed through an intersection and was struck by a hover crossing from the right. Flung against a building, she picked herself up and carried on.

She stopped at the next junction. A rough calculation told her that the boy couldn't have traveled this far; in all probability she had passed him and needed to reverse her direction. She hesitated. Finding the boy would be near to impossible. She racked her Cognition module but couldn't work out what to do next. And then she heard a police siren approaching.

A police hover shot through the intersection, siren screaming, blue light flashing. Lia set off after it, keeping her distance. It stopped at a tower block. She watched two officers run inside and up the staircase to an apartment on the seventh floor. Within a couple of minutes, they emerged with a boy under restraint. She used her telescopic vision to check the boy. It was Jason; she was sure of it.

They hauled Jason down the staircase and into the police hover. As soon as the hover had left the scene, Lia made her way to the seventh floor and knocked on the apartment door.

A woman opened the door a crack. Lia pushed her way inside.

"What do you want?" yelled the woman.

"You have my bag," said Lia. "Where is it?"

"What are you talking about?" The woman's face was turning an unnatural shade of red.

"My bag. The boy Jason took my bag. Where is

it?" Lia strode into the living area and looked around. A baby stood up in a cot, chewing something. She went through into the kitchen. There was a half-eaten meal on the table. Lia opened the cabinets, one by one. The woman followed her around the room, yelling at her, closing the cabinet doors. There were two bedrooms and a bathroom. Lia checked those. Finally, she returned to the living area.

The woman darted forward and pulled the child from the cot.

Lia checked under the covers and found the bag.

"This my bag." She looked inside. Three of Oscar's modules were in the bag, but Carla's X-Vid was missing.

This is madness," said the woman. "You're a mechano. Who let you out?"

Lia held up the modules. "These are mine, but there is one missing."

"I warn you, I will call the police. You have no right to come barging into my home, frightening my little girl."

Lia looked at the baby. It was perfectly happy, its cheeks red, sucking on... what? She took a closer look. Oscar's fourth module! She snatched it from the child's grasp and dropped it into the bag. The child's mouth opened wide, and she let out a piercing scream.

Lia left the tower block with the bag containing

Oscar's four modules safely back in her possession, the woman, holding her screaming child, yelling at her from the walkway seven stories above.

Out of sight in the shadows of the staircase, a lone police officer called his station. "I have the android. What are my orders?"

"Follow it. Don't lose it."

Chapter 6

They took Carla to a holding cell in prison. She asked for a tablet and wrote a short letter to her father. She handed it to the guards with no clear sense of whether or not it would ever reach him.

After a full day in isolation she was transported to a military base, where she found herself facing three grim-faced elders, two men and a woman, sitting at a table on a raised dais.

The chairman, seated in the center, opened proceedings. "The hearing is now in session. Director Spendlove will read the charges."

The chairman was a bald, elderly man in a suit. Carla knew who he was: a 3-star general called Bernard Dover, known to his troops, for obvious reasons, as Ben. Sitting to his left, was Henry Spendlove, Chief Operations Officer of Xenodyne Automation and a full board member of Xenodyne Industries, the parent company. To the general's right, sat a grey-haired woman in the uniform of a military colonel. Carla had no idea who she was.

Spendlove read from a tablet, "Carla Scott, there are two charges against you: first, interference in a live military operation, second, executing an unauthorized software upload that caused irreparable damage to the entire cohort of military Autonomic Units on Earth."

"How do you plead to the charges?" said the Chair.

Carla stood. "Your honor—"

"You should address the hearing as 'Gentlemen', or myself as 'Chair.' How do you plead?"

"Gentlemen, Chair, I request that my case be tested in a formal judicial trial in an open court."

General Dover responded, "Your request is denied. For reasons of security, this hearing will determine your case and the hearing will proceed in closed session."

Carla blinked. This sort of mockery of justice was just the sort of abuse that ANTIX was fighting against.

"How do you plead to the charges?"

"Not guilty." She sat down.

"Very well." He inclined his head to his right. "Colonel?"

The woman clasped her hands, as if washing them, and fixed Carla with her steely gaze. "On April second last, there was an unprovoked assault by enemy troops on Los Angeles Spaceport. Despite the heroic efforts of our military forces, the spaceport was lost, and a significant invasion of enemy troops and androids followed from a Souther troop transport in orbit. A combined force of between twenty and thirty thousand made landfall through the Gate. Our own troops laid siege to the enemy from their entrenched positions, north and south of the battlefield.

"The battle that unfolded can only be described as tragic. Souther artillery was deployed and brought to bear on military personnel and civilians alike. The population in the environs of the airport suffered severe casualties. We lost a significant percentage of our operational troops within a matter of minutes." Clearly affected by the horror of the event, she paused to gather her composure and continued in a shaky voice, "At a critical juncture in the battle, just as our forces were gaining the upper hand against the invaders, an android entered the fray—"

Carla interrupted her, "I dispute that, your honor – Chair."

"You deny that one of your androids entered the battle?" said the Chair.

"I dispute that our forces were gaining the upper hand. From what I saw, the Norther troops were receiving a thrashing."

The colonel addressed the Chair in a measured tone, "I was not aware that the defendant had military training."

"With all due respect," said Carla, getting to her feet, "anyone could see from the TV pictures who had the upper hand. The Norther troops were taking a pasting."

“You do not deny that you sent an android from your laboratory into the battle?” said the Chair.

“I do not deny that the Autonomic Unit was one I have been experimenting on, but I deny that I sent him into the battle.”

The Chair frowned. “What are you saying?”

“The Unit acted under his own volition.”

Henry Spendlove snorted. “That’s ridiculous!”

“Explain that statement,” said the Chair. “Since when do androids act under their own volition?”

“To understand what happened, I will need to explain the nature of the development project I was working on.”

The Chair consulted his notes, “This would be the PREM project, Pain Response Electronic Module?”

“Yes. If the court would allow me to explain...”

“Very well, but be brief,” said the Chair.

Carla drew a breath. “You will recall that the project was inspired by the idea that our Autonomic Units would be more effective in battle if they could sense pain.” She paused to gauge their reactions; she detected none. “The problem we had was finding an effective response mechanism. After due consideration, I realized that fear is the emotion we use to regulate our responses to pain.”

“You programmed fear into the military Units?”

“I did, Chair. It wasn’t easy. Our experiments produced a range of responses from apprehension, through terror, and anger. One of my test subjects developed a pathological fear of water."

"How is that possible?" said the colonel. "These are machines. Their responses are programmed, surely, making them entirely predictable."

Carla replied, "We used a heuristic process. Each Unit is programmed to learn about pain and how to react to it."

"So the results are less predictable," said Spendlove.

"Exactly."

"Why not simply program the responses you want?" asked the general.

"That would have taken a lifetime, sir. The heuristic approach was the only practical solution, given the time constraints we were working under."

"I see. Carry on."

"One of our Autonomic Units reacted to pain with something resembling extreme rage. He was the one who threw himself into the battle for LAX."

The Chair looked puzzled. "What was he – it – hoping to accomplish?"

Carla shook her head. "We have no way of knowing that. As I said, the AU was driven by rage, with perhaps a touch of patriotism."

The Chair straightened his back. "Please inform us how is patriotism even remotely possible in an android, or anger for that matter?"

The colonel and Spendlove glared at Carla.

“I agree that patriotism is a stretch,” said Carla, “but the AU had been captured and mistreated by the enemy, earlier. He certainly had no love for the Southers.”

“Love?” said the Chair with a raised eyebrow.

“I’m sure he hated them,” she replied, defiantly. “And as for his anger, I witnessed that in the laboratory. This Unit was consumed by rage, no question about it.”

Again, the Chair consulted with Henry Spendlove for a moment.

“Where is this Unit now?” said the Chair.

“I had to decommission him,” said Carla. “I removed his four principal modules and sent him for recycling. If I may continue?”

“Carry on,” said the Chair.

“The point is that the Unit acted without direction from me or anyone else. He took it upon himself to intervene in the battle for LAX.”

“And that was why you decommissioned the Unit?”

“It was, Chair. He was out of control.”

“Very well. Let’s move on to the second charge on the indictment – the release of damaging software to all the military Units in the Earth-force, a software update that, at a stroke, destroyed the Units as effective fighting assets of the military. How do you plead to this charge?”

“Not guilty.”

Chapter 7

The Chair's brow furrowed. "Do you deny that you willfully transferred the experimental software to all of our android forces on the planet?"

"I make no such denial," said Carla. "I acted in the best interests of the Norther Federation."

The lady colonel put her hands on the table and leaned forward. "How can you make that claim? Your reckless actions have resulted in the degradation of the entire military stock on Earth."

"Degradation? Never. The upgrade was an improvement. The Pain module made the Autonomic Units aware of their injuries and the Fear module gave them the means to react to them. Before my enhancement the military AUs were nothing but cannon fodder, happy to charge into enemy fire with no thought for their own safety. My enhancement gave them tools essential for self-preservation."

She scoffed. "You instilled soldiers in the middle of a battle with fear. How was that helpful?"

Carla ignored her. "Does the tribunal acknowledge that the battle for LAX came to an end shortly after the software upgrade, and that the day was won by the Northers?"

"We are in agreement on the sequence of events," the Chair replied.

Carla spread her arms. "The software upgrade was what brought the conflict to a satisfactory conclusion. The Pain-Fear module, once install in our Autonomic Units, gave them the facility to make discretionary choices, to take evasive action and avoid enemy fire."

"You took this action with no prior military sanction." The colonel's statement was an accusation, delivered in a harsh voice.

"There was no time to seek sanction. I knew the enhancement had the potential to improve the Units' performance, to give them better chances of survival in battle."

"Your enhancement, as you call it, has severely compromised all future defensive or offensive military actions. Tell the tribunal how you feel about this *enhancement* now?"

The words 'offensive military actions' rang alarm bells in Carla's head. "It worked like a dream," she said.

All three gawped at her, open-mouthed.

"You regard the project as a success?" said an incredulous General Dover.

"Yes, of course. We avoided a war by upgrading the androids."

"That's not what the generals call it," said the

colonel. "They see a whole army rendered worthless, hundreds of thousand soldiers on the scrap heap."

"That's crazy!" Carla yelled. Suppressing her feelings, she continued in a moderated tone, "Those soldiers are now more battle-savvy than they have ever been."

"Some of the generals say you emasculated their forces."

Carla scoffed. "How can you emasculate a non-sexual android?"

The colonel pursed her lips. "The battle was won by superior military tactics. Everyone observed how the enemy androids turned and ran under the relentless pressure exerted by our brave forces – men and androids – under the supreme leadership of General Fenimore Cooper Matthewson."

Henry Spendlove nodded enthusiastically in agreement.

The Chair gave the floor to Spendlove and the XA executive read from his tablet, "Net revenue to the Group from Xenodyne Automation sales in the last fiscal year amounted to two billion dollars. At two thousand dollars per unit, that represents sales of one million units. Of these, three quarters were military Units." He took a deep breath. "As a direct result of your ill-considered actions and following complaints from the Norther Federation, Xenodyne Industries has had to recall and repair all those Units. The cost to the corporation is severe. As soon as the information becomes widely available, we anticipate a drop in the share price in the region of two percentage points."

An unblinking Carla stared back at him. A drop of two per cent would have little effect on Xenodyne's shareholders. Few of them would notice before the share price rebounded, as she was sure it would.

General Dover checked his watch. "We will adjourn for lunch and resume at 1430 hours."

#

Lunch was a somber affair. The food was served to her in isolation in a locked room. The oatmeal gruel wasn't much different from the gray gruel served in the prison. Reviewing the morning's proceedings as she spooned it into her mouth, Carla realized that the three members of the tribunal had made up their minds long before the tribunal started. She would be found guilty. The only question remaining was what her punishment should be. She resolved to go down fighting.

When the tribunal resumed, Dr. Fritz Franck took the stand and identified himself as Carla's immediate superior.

She said, "Tell the tribunal what you know of me and my work."

Franck began a rambling monologue in a

monotonous drone that wasn't helping. She tried a different approach.

"What about my performance, Dr. Franck, have you found my work satisfactory?"

"Oh yes, very much so."

"Please tell the tribunal what part I played in the development of the military Autonomic Unit."

"You played a pivotal role in the development of the Mark 5."

"Pivotal. Thank you. Now, let us address the specifics of my work. Would you agree—"

The Chair cut her off with a wave of his hand. "We have heard enough of your hubris, young lady. It is clear that you simply do not have the mental discipline necessary to be a successful android engineer."

"With all due respect, Gentlemen, I have been designing systems for the Autonomic Units for several years. I hold a position of associate professor of cybernetics at Feynman Tech University."

"The hearing is fully aware of your intellectual capacity and your excellent record in the technical aspects of these developments, but your wild ideas and reckless actions have demonstrated a serious psychological flaw that impairs your work. In fact, it is the considered opinion of this hearing that android engineering is no profession for a woman." Lost for words, Carla opened her mouth and closed it again. "Your employment is terminated, and we feel obliged to impose a custodial sentence. You will serve three years on a correctional facility on Flor, in the B-System."

Carla leapt to her feet. "The members of this panel have shown a singular lack of vision, an inability to see beyond the limits of a balance sheet. This is not justice. Future generations will judge you harshly for what you have done here today."

"That's enough! Guards!"

Carla's temperature rose two notches. As the two guards restrained her, she yelled, "This hearing is a sham. You have no right to fire me for doing my job, and you certainly have no right to send me to prison."

"Silence!" the Chair roared. A shard of pain shot up her arm as one of the guards applied pressure to a sensitive nerve in her elbow. "In view of this outburst you will serve your sentence in the F-System. Now take her away."

Carla's brain was addled. What just happened? Was there a prison in the F-System? And then she remembered the molten mines of Luciflex.

Chapter 8

Commander Charles Harlowe, the local agent of the Norther Federation Security Agency, the NFSA, strode into Grant's office and stood with his back to the window. The major had not met the commander, but his reputation preceded him. He was rumored to have been nominated for a bravery award by a senior member of the administration at the White House. Not yet forty, he had several years' military service at the Pentagon behind him, and an impressive record of successful operations in the ongoing cyber war with the Southers.

Grant squinted at Harlowe's silhouette and fashioned a smile. "What can I do for you, Commander?"

The commander was carrying a swagger stick; he pointed it at the major. "I hear Carla Scott's personal android has not yet been neutralized."

His voice was ridiculously thin for a military man, and Grant thought the stick was a pathetic affectation, but he kept his opinions to himself. "What is the NFSA's interest in the Autonomic Unit? It is the property of Xenodyne Automation. We will deal with it."

"What progress have you made?"

Grant was tempted to give vent to his feelings, but he bit his tongue.

"Everything is under control, Commander, I assure you."

"How many hours has it been since Ms. Scott was detained?"

"Twenty-four."

"More like thirty-six. Do I have to press on you the extreme urgency of this operation? You work with these androids. You must appreciate the risk."

"Yes, Commander, of course."

"And yet you say this rogue Unit is still at large?"

Grant tried another smile. "I assure you the situation is under control. We have the Unit under surveillance—"

"We?"

"The police and my men."

"Why the delay in bringing it in?"

"The police chief has ordered restraint. He is confident that the Unit will lead his men to a nest of subversives."

"Don't you realize that android represents an existential risk to our defense forces every minute it remains at liberty?"

Grant could see nothing of the commander's facial expression. His even, emotionless tone gave nothing away either, and yet his words were heavy with menace.

"As I've said, Commander, there is no cause for concern. We have the Unit under close surveillance. It is in no position to threaten our defense forces."

"Have you covered the possibility of a cyberattack? That is where the greatest danger lies."

Grant's heart leapt in his chest. That was an angle he hadn't considered. He lied. "We have that covered. If the Unit orders a pizza, we'll know what toppings it chooses."

A full 15 seconds went by before Commander Harlowe's next response.

"You are missing the point, Major." His voice had hardened. "That android was Carla Scott's. It is a ticking bomb. By the time you pick up a transmission, the damage will have been done and it will be too late to do anything about it. I insist that you bring the Unit in for decommissioning without further delay."

#

As soon as the commander had left, Grant rang police headquarters.

The police chief was not impressed. "I've met Commander Harlowe. He's a bag of wind. The NFSA is a glorified talking shop. I've seen their prospectus. It's nothing but a bundle of good intentions and pious aspirations wrapped up in unintelligible gobbledygook."

"He sounded pretty serious to me," said Grant.

"Don't worry about it," said the chief. "You know his great, great, great grandpappy was one of the original space exploration captains. That's the only reason he got the job."

"Okay, but I'd feel happier if the AU was off the streets and in my hands."

"Take my word for it, Grant, the Unit will be delivered to your office just as soon as it leads us to the ANTIX leader and we have him under lock and key."

Chapter 9

Within hours of her sentencing, Carla had been driven to LAX Spaceport, transported on a shuttle through the Ground Gate into orbit and placed onboard the freighter *Ganymede*. By the time she'd made the acquaintance of her two nearest companions, Marny and the one-eyed pirate, they were approaching the first Interstellar Gate.

The engines died and a klaxon sounded. The prisoners held their breath until the heart-stopping jolt told them the ship had passed through the Gate.

The temperature began to fall. Carla and the other prisoners closed their eyes and drifted in and out of sleep.

Four hours later, she woke to the sound of a klaxon and near freezing conditions. The jolt that followed told Carla they had arrived at the B-System, 4.3 lightyears from Earth. The conventional engines fired up for 15 minutes and stopped again.

"Where are we?" she asked Marny.

"We're in orbit over Flor."

Three guards arrived with food for the

prisoners. Marny asked one of them how long they would be in the B-System.

"Long enough to transfer some cargo and exchange mail." The guard could have passed as a steward on a luxury cruiser. "Next stop Califon, folks."

They were allowed restroom breaks, in a smelly one-man toilet cabinet. Carla had to breathe through her mouth when her turn came.

An hour and a half later, the temperature in the cargo bay had risen to tolerable levels. The prisoners' spirits rose with it. Subdued conversations and even some laughter could be heard echoing around the vault of the cargo bay.

The pirate ran his eye over the other prisoners. "I don't know what they're so happy about. The next stage of our journey to the C-System isn't so bad, but C to E is over eight days. It'll be interesting to see who's laughing after that."

The conventional engines fired up again for thirty minutes, the klaxons sounded, and the freighter entered the BC Conduit through the Interstellar Gate above Flor.

Marny sighed. "That stopover was shorter than I expected." He shivered. "My old bones can't take the cold."

"You've traveled this way before?" she asked him.

"I have that," said the old man. "Not as far as the F-System, but I've been around the others more times than I could count. This trip is torture for us senior citizens. And it's so much longer than it needs to be."

"I don't understand. How could it be shorter?"

"Well, for starters, we could have taken the AC Conduit and avoided the B-System altogether."

"That would have saved us four hours," she said.

"Six hours if you include the stopover at Flor. Using a faster spacecraft could have shaved a significant amount of time from our journey. But there are other ways they could have shortened our journey, let me tell you."

"Pay no attention," said the pirate. "He's confused."

Carla ignored him. "Go ahead, Marny. How could our journey have been shortened?"

"We could have used the secret Conduits."

"What secret Conduits?"

"We have to go through the E-System to reach Luciflex in the F-System, and we can't reach E without passing through either C or D, but there are stories of a secret AE Conduit. They say a freighter can make that trip in less than a hundred hours."

"I thought the E-System was three hundred lightyears from the Earth, and the Brazill Drive travels about one lightyear per hour," she said.

"It is and it does."

The pirate whispered in her ear, "I told you, he's off his rocker."

"So how could an AE Conduit traverse three hundred lightyears in only one hundred hours?"

The old man winked. "What do any of us know about the Conduits, who built them and why?"

"That's amazing if it's true, Marny," she said. "Have you traveled through that secret Conduit?"

"No, but I know men who have."

The pirate snorted. "Drunks that you met in taverns, I'll bet. Admit it, old man, you're talking nonsense."

Carla asked the old man a few more questions about the secret Conduit, but he sat back on the bench, closed his eyes and said no more.

Chapter 10

In ANTIX safehouse no.1, in downtown Los Angeles, Cassidy was in conference with Benn, the leader of the Resistance.

"So that's it?" said Benn. "I thought we were going to meet the opposition on an equal footing."

"I've done as much as I can with them," said Cassidy. "They are Mark 4 Units. The Mark 5 Unit is an order of magnitude more advanced."

"How, more advanced?"

"Their processors are faster, more powerful, and they can learn from their mistakes. Physically, the Mark 5 is stronger, faster, too. What can I say? These Units are far inferior in every way."

Benn scratched the back of his head. "What? Are you saying it's hopeless?"

"No, Benn. All I'm saying is you need to be aware of the limitations of these Units. Don't expect miracles from them."

"I'm sure Carla said she could enhance them."

"I have done as much as possible with them. But you can't make a silk purse from a sow's ear, isn't that what they say?"

"Are you saying they will have no chance against the police?"

“Against cold steel and blasters, an AU will always do better than flesh and blood.”

#

They set off early the next morning. Benn had chosen their battleground carefully. Chinatown was less than 15 miles from the safehouse. Its labyrinth of small streets would provide ample avenues of escape, while limiting the effectiveness of the police riot control vehicles and drones.

They dressed 30 Autonomic Units in a hodgepodge of clothing and packed them into a hovertruck. Benn drove the truck with Sophie and Cassidy by his side in the cab. The ANTIX protesters followed in a variety of hovers.

Benn parked the truck, and the march began, southwest of Chinatown. Benn and his senior lieutenants led the way, followed by the 30 AUs and, behind them, the main body of protesters, holding their protest signs and singing ancient rebel songs. The general mood was peaceful, happy, determined. Optimistic, even. The signs they carried were more pointed than usual.

XI = TOO MUCH POWER
MORE DIVERCITY
GIVE US REAL FOOD!
BREAK UP XI
POWER TO THE PEOPLE
PROTEIN BLOCKS ARE NOT FOOD

Cassidy's sign read: SMASH THE MONOPOLY. Sophie's carried an arrow pointing to the left and the words: I'M WITH HIM.

As they entered Chinatown, a small contingent of police appeared ahead, in riot gear. The protesters slowed, while continuing to push forward. The police numbers grew, their black helmets reflecting what little sunlight filtered through the smog.

"Are those policemen or androids?" said Sophie.

"Difficult to tell from this distance," Cassidy replied. "But I would expect a ratio of maybe ten AUs to one man."

"Are the androids armed?"

"You can be sure they are, but I wouldn't expect them to fire at anybody."

Sophie shivered. "I don't like this. It's going to end in bloodshed."

"We'll be all right," said one of the protestors. "As long as they can see we aren't out to cause any trouble, they won't fire on us."

Chapter 11

The protest march came to a halt 20 meters from the police line. Benn used his bullhorn: “This is a peaceful protest. Stand aside and let us pass.”

“Like that’s going to happen,” said Cassidy.

The police line stood firm. There was no way through. Benn and his lieutenants stepped back behind the line of AUs. And the police phalanx moved forward...

The carnage that followed was horrific. The ANTIX AUs stood immobile while they were cut down by the police AUs, wielding heavy batons.

Benn ran back to where Cassidy and Sophie were standing, their signs drooping.

“Why are they doing nothing?” Benn screamed. “Tell them to fight.”

Cassidy shook his head. “They are domestic Units. They know nothing about fighting. What did you expect them to do?”

“They aren’t even defending themselves. There must be something we can do.”

“I’m sorry, Benn,” said Cassidy. “All they can do is form a barrier, stand until they fall.”

The police clambered over the fallen bodies of

the ANTIX AUs, re-formed their line, and advanced toward the protestors, beating their batons on their shields in rhythm. A thin line of protestors sat down. Benn stood with them, using his bullhorn to exhort the police to "Drop your batons and shields and join your friends in protest."

"Like that's going to happen!" said Sophie.

The police reached the first line of protestors and began to beat on them. Some, they arrested, dragging them backward into paddy wagons.

Cassidy abandoned his sign. He grabbed Sophie's arm. "Come on. We need to get out of here."

She pulled her arm free. "I'm going nowhere. We have to stand firm with Benn and his friends."

"We can't get arrested. They have taken Carla. I'm sure they're searching for me. I have more important work to do. Come on."

Sophie relented, and the two of them backed away from the battle and down an alleyway. At the end of the alley, they turned left and met a second line of police. They tried another route and found another line of police. At their third attempt they found a route that took them southwards, clear of the police. Sophie began to run, but Cassidy held her back.

"Walk fast. Don't run. We don't want to attract attention to ourselves."

Once they were clear of danger, they took a cab

to within a block of the downtown safehouse, only to find a police cordon around the building.

"Where can we go?" said Sophie.

Before he could answer, someone from the police cordon called out, "Stop!"

Cassidy and Sophie bolted.

They split up, Cassidy went south, Sophie west, toward the ocean.

"Stop or I shoot," a policeman shouted.

Cassidy looked back. There were two cops on his tail. He was fairly confident that they wouldn't shoot him, but he wasn't in the best physical condition for a footrace. He headed for Feynman Tech in West Athens. He knew the campus as well as he knew his own backyard. He would need to use this knowledge and all his guile to escape.

He arrived at the campus out of the direct line of sight of the cops, but badly winded. He made his way to the main library and stumbled inside, gasping for air. Joining a small group of male students, he climbed the stairs and turned right toward the restroom. He needed a stop-off to catch his breath and splash some cold water on his face. A college security guard standing outside the men's room forced him to turn back, but when he looked down, one of the cops was standing at the bottom of the stairs, hand on his pistol, scanning the atrium. If the cop looked up or the security guard turned his head and looked his way, Cassidy would be discovered. There was no cover. He did the only thing he could do: he slipped into the women's restroom and ducked into a cubicle.

He sat down, breathing heavily, his chest heaving. Glancing at his watch, he decided to wait ten or fifteen minutes.

The restroom door opened, and someone entered. He heard a cubicle door open and close. Taking long, deep breaths, his breathing began to moderate.

Then his X-Vid rang. Without thinking, he answered the call. "Hello, Lia."

The other cubicle door banged open. Cassidy flew out of his cubicle in time to place his body between the fleeing student and the restroom door. She was young, with long blond hair in a ponytail.

He held up his hands. "Please, don't be afraid."

"Let me pass," she said, the blood draining from her face.

"You saw the cops outside?"

"Two of them."

"I'm hiding from them. I had nowhere else to go."

"Wh-why are they chasing you?" she stammered.

"I'm with the Resistance."

"You were in Chinatown?"

"Yes, the cops beat us. My girlfriend and I escaped. Please don't give me away." He stood aside from the door so that she could leave unimpeded.

"You don't look beat up."

"I told you. We got away."

"Where's your girlfriend?" She seemed calmer.

"We split up."

"Okay," she said. "Better get back in the cubicle. I'll let you know when it's safe to come out. And turn off your X-Vid."

Cassidy thanked her. Lia's face was frozen on his X-Vid screen, waiting for a response.

"I'll ring you back." he said. He disconnected and switched it off. Then he returned to the cubicle.

Chapter 12

Within a few minutes, the young student came back to the restroom to let Cassidy know that the cops had gone.

"Are you a member of our student resistance group?" she said.

Cassidy was flattered. "I'm not a student."

"A professor?"

"An ex-student. What's your name?"

"Velma. I'm with the student resistance group."

"Thanks again for your help, Velma. And good luck with the student group."

He headed for the library exit, returning Lia's call as he walked.

"Lia, it's Cassidy."

Lia said, "Carla Scott never came home."

"How long since you've seen her?"

"Two days and two nights."

"Where are you? Are you safe?"

"I am safe. I went to the downtown safehouse, but the police are there."

Cassidy swore silently. Hopefully, Sophie, Benn and the others would make it back to one of the other safehouses.

"Meet me at Carla's favorite restaurant in ten minutes."

He hung up before she could respond with the name of the restaurant and took a hovercab to Bartelli's.

Lia was standing outside the restaurant when he got there. Her stance looked strangely lopsided. He called her over and she got into the cab. There was something wrong with her gait; she seemed to be favoring her left side. She got in and sat beside him, hands in her lap, knees drawn together, feet crossed at the ankles.

"What's the matter with your leg?" he asked.

She looked at him blankly.

"Never mind. I'll take a look at it later."

He gave the driver an address within a couple of blocks of an alternate safehouse, near the docks.

"Where is Carla Scott?" she said.

He searched her face for signs of fear or distress. There were none; her face bore its usual inscrutable expression. "I don't know, but I suspect that Carla may have been transported off-world."

"When will she come back?"

"No one knows, Lia. Where did you spend the last couple of nights?"

"I stayed on the streets. The apartment is not safe."

The cab driver said, "You know we're being followed?"

Cassidy looked out the back. “Can you lose them?”

“Who are they?” said the driver.

“I don’t know, but I don’t think they want to give us a bunch of flowers.”

“Are you Resistance?”

“Yes. Can you lose the tail?”

The driver accelerated, turning down an alleyway. “Just watch me.”

#

The moment they arrived at the docklands safehouse, Cassidy put Lia to sleep and checked her leg. Something had damaged her hip. It was broken on the left side. He repaired the damage by cannibalizing one of the Mark 4 Units. Then he put her on recharge; her powerpack was down to 22 percent.

He called Sophie on a safe X-Vid and told her the police had surrounded the downtown safehouse.

“Thank you. I’ll warn Benn,” she said.

“Where are you?”

“I’m with Benn. I’d rather not say where we are.”

“Are you alone?”

“I’m with Benn. I told you.”

He told her he’d made contact with Lia. “She’s here with me now.”

"Great! Let me speak to her."

"She's asleep."

"Does she know where Carla's gone?"

"Unfortunately not. She's as mystified as we are. Where and when can we meet?"

There was a long pause on the line. "It's not safe for us to meet, Cass. I think I should stay with Benn."

She terminated the call abruptly.

Cassidy spent a long moment staring at the blank screen. His fiancée seemed more attached to Benn than she should be, and more than he was comfortable with.

#

Major Grant called the NFSA and asked to speak with Commander Harlowe.

"I'm calling about that Unit the police have been tracking."

"They have picked it up?" The commander looked positively jolly.

"I've had a call from the police chief. Unfortunately, they lost the android."

The major watched as the commander's facial expression adjusted to match his new mood.

"Tell me what happened."

"Someone picked her up in a hovercab."

"Who?"

"We don't know."

"They followed the cab?"

"Yes, of course, but it gave them the slip."

"So the cab driver was sympathetic to the Resistance?"

"Presumably so."

"Tell me they have the registration number of the cab."

"I doubt it, Commander."

"Right, I'm taking over from here. You can tell your police contact they can drop their hunt for the android. This is now an NFSA case."

Chapter 13

Sophie stood by the window in an ANTIX safehouse, watching the sunset over a golf course. The spectacular aurora borealis on display brought joy to the eye but signaled the worsening global climate. In a rare concession to a city struggling daily for breath, the smog had retreated from the land, and hung in a surly cloud over the ocean. Whether it would remain there or creep back over the land remained to be seen.

Her X-Vid buzzed, and a young man's image appeared. His hair was mussed up and there was a charming yellow paint smudge on his cheek. He looked good enough to eat.

"Hi, Sophie. My name's Zed, Zedekiah Jones. Your father said you needed my help."

"Hi Zed. Thanks for calling. I've been trying to locate Carla Scott. Do you know where she is?"

"Afraid not. I haven't been able to reach her and my father's as mystified as I am. When did you last try her X-Vid?"

"I've stopped trying. It's been disconnected. And it's not safe. Cassidy is sure they're after him."

"Why? Because of what Carla did?"

"Yes. But it wasn't all down to Carla. Cassidy has to shoulder some of the blame."

"Have you spoken to any of her friends?" he said.

"What friends? I didn't think she had any."

Zed frowned at that. "Can you remember if her hover was in its parking space outside the apartment?"

"I have no idea. Could you check that out?"

He hesitated for a moment. "Could you take a look? I'm up to my armpits and I've been drinking."

"I'll go now." She hung up, slipping into her shoes. A dogged alcohol habit probably explained his wild experimental art and the crazy prices people paid for it.

Benn arrived with a cup of coffee. "Who was that?"

"Zedekiah Jones, a friend of Carla's. He suggested looking for her hover at her apartment. I won't be long."

Was that a flicker of annoyance on Benn's face? Nah! It was just her imagination.

"Be careful out there, Sophie," he said. "There's a demonstration planned for tonight in the Santa Monica area."

"Is it one of ours?"

"No, it's a rival group of protestors."

She pointed her pink hover north. The aurora faded as the sky darkened, but a new glow reflected off the clouds dead ahead. Riots in downtown Santa Monica and surrounding areas had been going on for a week. The police seemed powerless to do anything to break them up.

As she entered the outskirts of the town, a uniform patrol stopped her. “Where are you headed, Miss?”

“Eastwood Palace apartments on Ocean Avenue.”

“You live there?”

“I’m visiting a friend.”

“I can’t let you go any further. Best come back tomorrow before sundown.”

“But I have to get there tonight, officer. It’s really important.”

The police officer scratched his chin. “Okay, but I can’t let you take the hover. You can go on foot. If you keep to the coast road you should be okay.”

Sophie parked the hover and set out at a brisk pace. The air was cooling rapidly, but the shimmering heat of the day still rose from the asphalt, and there was a hint of smoke in the air. After 10 minutes’ walking, Carla’s high-rise emerged from a bank of fog ahead. To her right, the unmistakable sounds of rioting: a bullhorn, a howling, roaring mob, breaking glass, the sounds and smells of fires. She passed the hulks of two hovers burnt out in earlier riots.

Eastwood Palace condominium stood silent and dark. Carla’s hover space was vacant, and the penthouse showed no lights. The front door of the condo was locked. She rang the superintendent's bell. After an age, he emerged from a service area behind the elevator shaft, let her in, and locked the door again.

"Any news of Carla Scott?" she asked.

The super shook his head. "I was just about to ask you the same question. I've not seen her or her personal android since we last spoke."

"Have you seen her hover?" As soon as the words left her lips, Sophie anticipated a humorous reply. *No, but I really admire her triple jump.* It was far from original.

His fleeting double take acknowledged the opportunity, but he resisted the temptation. "No. The last time I saw it she was heading to work. That was two weeks ago. I assume it's still there."

Sophie thanked the super and set off back toward the outskirts of the town where she'd left her hover. A police helihover roared overhead and took up a position directly above the crowd. A voice boomed down at the protesters. Sophie couldn't make out the words, but it sounded like the police meant business.

Drawing level with the downtown protest, the noise levels intensified. A thick cloud of smoke, lit from below by the flames, hung over the scene. Then a group of young men rushed from the area, pausing to throw missiles at a chasing phalanx of police. Sophie sought shelter in an apartment block, but the doors were firmly locked. She hurried on down Ocean Avenue. Within two minutes, she was enveloped by the mob. She was one of them now, pursued by police in full riot gear. One of her heels snapped off. She kicked off both shoes. The men surged onward, and she was left behind to be swallowed up by the line of police, sheltering behind their shields, swinging their batons.

Chapter 14

When Sophie came to, the police line was receding at the limit of her vision. She was lying on the pavement. A wave of dizziness sent black spots before her eyes when she tried to sit up. She got to her feet and staggered forward.

She reached the spot where she'd left her hover. All was quiet. No police, no rioters, no noise, not even a light from the buildings. And no sign of her hover! She keyed Zed's number on her X-Vid.

#

Within ten minutes, a hover drew up beside her. Zed stepped out and helped her to her feet. He handed her a handkerchief. "Didn't I tell you to be careful? Where are your shoes? What happened?"

She used the cloth to dab at the dried blood on her face. "I'm not sure. The cops said I'd be okay if I stuck to the coast road, but the riot came to me."

He helped her into the hover. "Sit back and relax. I'll take you to the nearest hospital."

"No, take me home, Zed." He threw her a skeptical look. "I'm fine, really. I don't need a hospital."

"Okay, if you're sure. Which way?"

"It's near the docks."

He headed south. "Did you see Carla's hover?"

"No, but her triple Salchow is pretty special." Zed was watching the road, but he glanced at her, a pained expression on his face. "No, Zed. The super said the last time he saw it she was heading to work, a week ago."

"It must be in the hover park at Xeno Automation. Hold on." He spun the hover around to the left. It swayed and yawed like a sailboat before the engine thrust it forward again. Sophie's stomach heaved. She opened her window and threw up over the side of the hover.

Zed looked alarmed. "I really think you should see a doctor."

She waved a feeble hand at him. "I'm okay, Zed. I'll see my own doctor in the morning."

He parked outside the Xenodyne Automation building and went looking for Carla's hover in the underground hover park. Sophie stayed in the hover nursing a jackhammer in her head. She closed her eyes.

#

She awoke in a wheelchair, a paramedic in blue wheeling her through a double door. Zed walked by her side. The overwhelming smells of antiseptic and bleach told her where she was.

"What happened?" She held up her hand and Zed took it.

"You passed out."

The hour after that was a daze. A nurse took her temperature. A doctor shone a light in her eyes, asked her daft questions, tested her reflexes. Then the nurse took her blood pressure and she blacked out again.

She woke the next morning in a hospital bed, the jackhammer in her head had been replaced by an overactive woodpecker, and the pain had receded. No sign of Zed, her dishy rescuer. A nurse took her temperature and blood pressure and offered breakfast. She ate a little protein dressed up like scrambled egg washed down with lukewarm hospital tea.

Cassidy came calling mid-morning. "Zed called me. He told me what happened. You gave him quite a fright. You were concussed. How are you feeling now?"

"My head hurts."

"I expect that's a good sign." He perched his tight behind on a chair by the bed.

"Did you find Carla's hover in the car park?"

"Yes. It was there. I spoke to the police. Carla's now officially a missing person. They promised to keep a look out for her and her hover, but they're under a lot of pressure with the ANTIX protests and riots." He took her hand. "I asked about your hover. They said they towed it out of harm's way when the riot began to spread."

"So it's safe in a police pound somewhere?"

"Yes. You'll be able to release it as soon as you're back on your feet. But you'll have to pay a storage fee."

She grunted.

"There's something else. It's a bit... damaged."

He was still holding her hand. She pulled it away, bracing for more bad news. "How badly damaged?"

"I'm not sure. They said something about an electrical fault."

She groaned.

Cassidy's X-Vid buzzed, and he left the room to take the call. When he returned, he said, "That was Zed's father. He has spoken with Carla's boss, Dr. Franck. Franck says Carla's on vacation."

Sophie gave him her skeptical schoolmarm look. "On vacation where?"

"He didn't say. I think he didn't know where."

Sophie's snort sent a shard of pain through her eyes. "She'd never have gone away without her X-Vid. Why would she? And why would she abandon Lia? The whole thing stinks, if you ask me."

Chapter 15

Carla's Cosmography was a little sketchy, but every schoolgirl knew that the A, B and C Systems formed a close cluster, while the other three Systems, D, E and F, formed a second cluster. The two clusters were some 250 lightyears apart. At 320 lightyears, the F-System was the farthest from Earth. The distances involved were staggering, and enough to turn Carla's stomach to acid whenever she thought about it. Most disturbing of all was the realization that each lightyear that they traveled away from the A-System took them one year into the past. Luciflex was 320 years in Earth's past. Who could remember what happened in 2006, 50 years before the first Lunar War!

Califon was Carla's birth planet. Her father, Zach, had returned there, and she yearned for a chance to speak with him. When they arrived at the C-System, she asked one of the guards if she could use an X-Vid, but her request was turned down.

The stopover at the C-System lasted 12 standard hours. First, cargo shuttles flew in relays from Califon to rendezvous with the freighter to pick up mountains of cargo. Then the same exercise was repeated in orbit around the second planet, Liberté, administered by the Franco-Germans. The stopover allowed the ambient temperature to rise to normal levels, and the prisoners were treated to a special meal, but they were all dismayed when the klaxon finally announced the jump through the CE Interstellar Gate, and their journey resumed.

The journey from C to E took over 8 standard days. In the fifth dimension, as in normal space, there was nothing to distinguish night from day, and these were signaled by the use of the ship's interior lighting. As the temperature in the cargo bay fell and stabilized just above freezing, getting to sleep became a challenge. She and Marny huddled together to share and preserve their body warmth, but still, Carla woke repeatedly during each 'night' and struggled to get back to sleep every time.

The jolt that signaled the freighter's arrival at the E-System was greeted by a weak cheer from the prisoners, followed by a groan when, after an hour of recovering temperatures, they re-entered the Conduits on their way to their final destination.

There was no stop off at the E-System. It was barren. A planet called Égalité had been colonized there for over 100 standard years. Because of the planet's extreme climate – long periods of subzero temperatures alternating with equally long periods of deadly heat – the Franco-German colonists had built their cities inside huge geodesic domes. But when an intelligent indigenous lifeform, long suspected, was finally identified and acknowledged, the planet was abandoned, as required by the Geronimo Protocol.

#

Two standard days later, the klaxons sounded for the last time and the freighter emerged from the EF Conduit and entered orbit around Luciflex.

A fleet of cargo shuttles arrived from the surface of the planet to offload the cargo. Carla and the other prisoners were transferred from the cargo bay to the crew quarters to allow the removal of the cargo. It was only after six hours, when the last of the cargo had been removed, that they were herded into a shuttle to take them down to the planet.

The whole journey from the Spaceport at Los Angeles to the Ground Gate on Luciflex, a distance of 320 lightyears, had taken 12 standard days.

Chapter 16

There was no sensation of landing on Luciflex. But the increase in gravity told them that the ship was on the surface of the planet.

One-eye flashed a lopsided grin at Carla. He seemed impervious to the cold. Ignoring the pirate, she helped the old man, Marny, to his feet. He was close to hypothermia. She rubbed his hands and wrapped an arm around his shoulders.

The prisoners rose as one and shuffled toward the cargo bay doors. Carla stayed close to Marny. As she passed One-eye, he whispered to her, "The old man won't last a week. Luciflex will eat him up and spit him out."

The prisoners were herded out by three armed human guards. The red dust cloud raised by their arrival swirled around them. As it settled, Carla caught her first sight of Luciflex, and what she saw turned her stomach. An overlarge sun hung in a brown sky. Huge ground vehicles raised clouds of red dust everywhere on a vast plain between two jagged mountain ranges. Two of the peaks belched thick, gray smoke while branching rivers of lava flowed down the flank of a third. The air, thick with dust and ash, filled her nostrils and made her eyes water.

Steaming like a herd of steer on a cattle drive, the prisoners eagerly absorbed the ambient heat, hotter than Death Valley. They formed a line, taking it in turns to quench their thirst at a water station. When the old man's turn came, the next prisoner in line – a bear of a man – snatched the cup from his hand.

Carla straightened her back and confronted him. "What's your problem, Bruno?"

The prisoner ignored her. Slaking his thirst, he emptied the cup on the red sandy ground and tossed it to the next man in line. Carla snatched the cup, dipped it through the film of ash and dust on the surface of the water, and handed it to Marny. The old man drank greedily and handed her the cup, but before Carla could consume more than a mouthful herself, a guard poked her in the ribs with the butt of his blaster. "Move along. You're holding up the line."

Her limbs like lead, her breasts sagging in Luciflex gravity, Carla stumbled and fell to her knees. Marny and the pirate each grabbed an arm to pull her to her feet. As they joined the line of shuffling prisoners, she looked back over her shoulder. A succession of cargo shuttles, arriving and departing through the Ground Gate, ferried mining produce to the Galaxy freighter in orbit, while much smaller fighter craft peppered the sky, buzzing around above them like flies around dog turds. On the ground, a fleet of hovertrucks and tankers converged on the cargo vessels like ravenous roaches, raising clouds of red dust.

Carla had always considered herself resilient, impervious to life's setbacks. She had an optimistic nature, and always found something to be cheerful about, no matter how miserable the outlook. But this was something else. How could anyone be cheerful or optimistic, condemned to three years in a place like this? She realized that a secret determination to beat the odds and survive, perhaps even to escape, had been festering in the inner caverns of her mind, but now she was beginning to understand how unrealistic that might be. Could she even expect to survive three months in this infernal hellhole?

Chapter 17

They entered a compound enclosed by a fence two meters high. The entrance gate was wide and overlooked by watchtowers. Everything – walls, watchtowers and the ground – was covered in a layer of red dust. Armed AUs roamed about everywhere, although security seemed unnecessary; escape from the compound would be pointless, survival on the barren rock of Luciflex beyond impossible. Just inside the compound, close to the entrance, they passed by a concrete building the size of a 2-story house. It had a metal door, but no windows.

They were led inside a low barracks, built entirely inside the mountain at the back of the compound. Here, a human guard registered the prisoners and assigned each to one or other of the various mining operations.

Carla was given the prisoner designation B247. An AU guard took her to a kitchen adjoining a vast dining hall. Red dust caked everything – the floor, the tables, the benches, the walls, the light fixtures. The kitchen was no exception. Every crack and hollow appeared red, and small red drifts lay against the equipment and on the work surfaces.

Four women prisoners and two AUs formed the kitchen staff. Like ghostly visions from an ancient sepia photograph, the women all had gray hair tinted pink by the dust, and pasty, wrinkled skin. They reminded Carla of Shakespeare's witches.

The senior witch introduced herself. "I'm Maxeen. I run the kitchen."

"I'm Carla Scott. Do you have any water? I'm dying of thirst."

"There's not a lot of water on Luciflex." Maxeen handed her a cup of fruitoid and Carla gulped it down. "Most of our fresh water is brought in on freighters. We have a small underground reservoir, and we get about five millimeters of rain in the rainy season. The rest is recycled waste."

Carla shivered. "What do the prisoners drink?"

"Fruitoid, mostly, and moonshine."

"Moonshine? Made from what?"

Maxeen dismissed the enquiry with an impatient wave of her hand. "You'll find out soon enough."

She showed Carla around the kitchen. "We serve two full meals a day to twelve hundred men in three sittings. The meals are constructed from compressed protein blocks and vegetable paste. Nothing grows on Luciflex, of course. It's all hauled in on freighters." She took Carla into a guarded warehouse where hundreds of crates of protein blocks were stored, all stamped: *Produce of Pexcorn Foods*. “The meals vary every day on a repeating 5-day cycle. You will learn how to construct each one.”

Whether that was 1,200 men in total or 3,600 wasn’t clear, but Carla could see the logic in providing the prisoners with a healthy diet. It would make perfect economic sense to extract as many productive months as possible from each prisoner before they died from injury or heat exhaustion.

She asked about the red dust covering everything. “Can’t anything be done to clean it up?”

Maxeen shrugged. “We used to try, but it’s an impossible task. The men carry it everywhere on their clothes, in their hair and on their beards.”

Maxeen showed her around the main complex. She pointed out the guards’ barracks and administration block – both out of bounds – the infirmary, the prisoners’ dormitories. She showed Carla the solitary toilet cubicle reserved for the women.

Carla asked why there was no wash-hand basin.

“I told you,” said Maxeen. “There’s not a lot of water to go around.”

Finally, she took Carla to the women’s sleeping quarters, a room with six beds, two of them empty.

Carla selected the bed farthest from the door. “How many women are there in the prison?”

"Just us four. You're number five. I remember a time when there were six, but we lost two."

"What happened to them?"

"They died. I forget the details."

"What happens when people die here? Are there religious rites? Is there a cemetery?"

"We had a padre on Luciflex for a while. Pastor Melitus. He was an idiot. He didn't last long. Since he left, they just drop the bodies into the lava streams. Now, listen to me. You must stay alert at all times. The high protein diet makes the men frisky, and you're the prettiest thing anyone's seen around here in years."

"I have to sleep..."

"You're safe in here. There's an unwritten rule – no man comes into our dorm."

Carla sat on the bed to test it out. The mattress was black as jet and hard as quartz.

"There are just two rules," said Maxeen. "You get to have a shower once every 30 days – that's 5 Luciflex weeks. You get 15 standard minutes. This is a hard-won concession for us women. Make sure not to abuse it."

"And a change of clothes?"

Maxeen shook her head. "You wash your clothes in the shower."

"When do I get my first shower?"

"Thirty days. Didn't I say?"

Carla felt her blood pressure rise. She bit her lip. She ached to wash the red dust from her skin.

It itched and scratched under her prison uniform, and she suspected she might have picked up a flea from the pirate. “And the second rule?”

Maxeen’s expression hardened. She fixed Carla with eyes of steel. “Stay away from Balehook.”

“Who’s Balehook?”

“He’s the king of Luciflex, the leader of all the prisoners. You’ll meet him soon enough. The prisoners are all fair game, but Balehook is mine, all right?”

“Why’s he called Balehook?”

Maxeen gave her a wicked grin. “He’s named after his favorite weapon. Get on his wrong side and he’ll use it to gut you like a fish.”

Carla shuddered.

“If you lay a hand on him or let him touch you, I’m warning you, I’ll cut off your ears.”

Chapter 18

The molten mines lived up to their reputation.

Maxeen gave Carla a rundown on the operation. "The mineshafts skirt the active volcanoes where the rarest minerals, metals and isotopes are most abundant. Xenodyne management are relentless, forcing the work gangs to drive the drilling machines ever deeper, ever closer to active lava flows, risking their lives daily in pursuit of the richest mineral veins. All in pursuit of productivity. Nine men lost their lives last month when a shaft collapsed."

"What do the mines produce?"

"Who cares? Rare metals. I've heard mention of some, like Palladium, Iridium and a few others. There are a lot of radioactive metal isotopes too, some of them quite dangerous."

Carla asked, "Do they use AUs in the mining operation?"

"Each work gang is made up of a mix of prisoners and mechanos. It's easy enough to tell them apart: the prisoners all have beards."

The thumping noises of the mining operations never ceased, day or night, giving Carla pains behind her eyes. The only relief she got was on the rare occasions when a stone pulverizer died or a conveyor belt ground to a halt, altering the volume and pitch of the dull, pounding cacophony.

At the end of a meal shift, twenty Luciflex days after her arrival on the planet, three prisoners hovered around as Carla cleared the tables.

"What do you guys want?" she said.

"We need you to answer a question to settle a bet."

She mopped her brow. "What's the bet?"

"The reason you're on Luciflex. Micki says you must have killed someone. Jon thinks maybe you stole a lot of cash from Xenodyne."

She carried a pile of plates to the sink. The three men waited for her.

"What about you? What do you think?" she said to the spokesman, when she returned.

"You're an android engineer, right?"

"That's right."

"I reckon you did something you shouldn't have with the androids."

"Like what?"

"I don't know. Maybe you gave them controls to stop them killing people."

"You're close," she said. "But they already have a Compliance module that regulates how they behave."

Smirking at his two companions, he said, "So tell us what you did."

“I gave the androids pain.”

One of the other two said, “Can you make the guards here feel pain? That would be awesome.”

“No, sorry, it’s not as simple as that.”

The next day, Carla noticed a change in the rhythm of the mining operation; the pace of the constant pounding seemed higher, there were more trucks rumbling around, raising more dust than usual, and there were more shuttles arriving and departing. She soon realized that a new freighter had arrived and was parked in orbit above them. A new intake of prisoners followed, and she lined up at the compound gate with those off-shift and curious to meet the new arrivals.

That night, she fell asleep in her cot, thoroughly miserable, dreaming of escape. She woke up with the realization that there was only one way off this burning rock: she would have to find her way onto the freighter in orbit. A quick check confirmed that most of the guards on Luciflex were AUs, and the few human guards spent most of their time under cover in their barracks. A tentative plan began to take root and grow in her mind.

#

The prisoners organized themselves into groups. Those from the various Systems congregated together. Some of the younger groups played games, like Patter-Pool, a weird ball game with no rules, played with high energy and even higher stakes.

Carla was popular with the men. Whenever the work gangs filed into the dining area for their meals, she was bombarded with catcalls and lewd remarks. She was the object of all their gazes, all their conversations.

Ever fearful of an attack, constantly on their guard, the women never walked the corridors alone. The dormitory was Carla's only safe haven, the only place where she could get away from the roving eyes of the prisoners.

Surrounded on all sides by humanity, Carla had never been so alone. Maxeen and the other three witches were no company for her. She had nothing in common with them, and they seemed to resent her youth, her good looks. Desperate for a distraction to take her mind off her troubles, she spent long hours lying on her cot, staring at the ceiling, thinking. She missed her father; she had spent so little time with him before he returned to Califon. He probably had no idea where she was. She's written a second letter to him before boarding the shuttle, but she doubted that he received either of her two letters.

Her thoughts lingered around Professor Jones's son, Zed. They had met at the university, five years earlier, but it was only in the past couple of months that he had shown any interest in her and she had agreed to a couple of dates. Would he still be single after three years, and if he was, would he be interested in reconnecting with a returning criminal?

She worried about Cassidy. Was he rotting in some prison somewhere? Most of all, she missed her best friend, Lia.

Chapter 19

The Luciflex year was divided into 71 weeks, each consisting of 6 Luciflex days. The prisoners worked a 7-day rota, 6 days on, one day off. The days were 27 local hours long, divided into three 9-hour work shifts. A local hour was equivalent to 47 standard (Earth) minutes, making each shift a little over 7 standard hours.

Carla understood the principles of cooking and food hygiene, but back home, Lia looked after the preparation of her meals. She was a quick study; Maxeen and her staff had no difficulty schooling her in the kitchen routine. The menu was fixed, as was the meal schedule. They had to prepare 12 meals each week, two meals each day in three sittings for 1,200 men at a time.

She was amazed at how easily the different dishes could be concocted from plain compressed protein blocks. A shapeless lump could be made to look like anything – a ribeye steak, a fish, a portion of ice cream – given the right coloring. But flavoring was the key. With the right flavoring the men could close their eyes and imagine they were eating the real thing. Nothing could be done to make the vegetable paste look like anything other than vegetable paste, but they mixed the colors around to relieve the monotony.

Monday was meatballs, Tuesday chicken, Wednesday some sort of curry, Thursday was beefsteak, the men's favorite, or meatloaf. On Friday they served fish or calamari and prawns, and Saturday was capybara steaks.

The androids helped with the heavy work in the kitchen – lugging compressed protein about, operating the food mixers, and gathering up the used dishes – but some of the work had to be done by hand by the women.

Washing up was the most difficult task, given the shortage of water. Detergent was unheard of. When Carla complained about this, Maxeen cuffed her on the back of the head and urged her to use 'elbow grease'. By the end of the first 6-day week, Carla's hands were dry and scaly, her nails cracked.

The prisoners used soft plastic cutlery, but Maxeen had the use of a single knife for cutting up the protein. This knife was her most prized possession. It never left her sight, and she carried it with her at all times, sleeping with it under her mattress.

From the moment they met, Maxeen treated Carla like an idiot, scolding her every time she made even the most trivial mistake, using sarcasm to ridicule her actions, and always implying that

Carla was too stupid to understand the most basic instructions.

Convinced that Maxeen's hostility could easily turn to violence, Carla went looking for a weapon. Alone in the kitchen at the end of a night shift, she worked the handle from one of the cauldrons. Flattening one end, she broke off a handy sized piece and made a handle by wrapping it in cord. She hid the makeshift knife in her clothing. It wasn't pretty, and it wasn't sharp, but she reckoned she could do some damage with it if she had to defend herself.

#

Within 25 Luciflex days of her arrival, Carla and Maxeen were returning together to the dormitory after a late shift when Maxeen stopped. "I need to go back. One of the others will be on her own. We're close to the dorm. You'll be all right." And she was gone.

Gripping the handle of her knife, Carla hurried on alone. As she turned the last corner before the dormitory, two men blocked her path. The shock of the encounter took the breath from her lungs. She took a step back and one of the men stepped forward.

"Where you goin', darlin'?"

She recognized Darm, the principal player in one of the PP teams. She also recognized the look in his eyes.

"Let me pass." Her voice was strong, but breathless.

Darm grabbed her arm. "We thought you might like a little fun."

"Take your hands off me!" Carla pulled out her knife and slashed the back of his wrist.

Darm yelped. The second man wrapped his arms around her from behind, and she was overpowered. Her knife fell to the floor. She filled her lungs to scream, but a hand covered her mouth. Darm stood facing her, a triumphant sneer on his face. Blood dripped from his wrist, but the wound was no more than a scratch. He stepped forward...

A flurry of movement behind her, an unexpected commotion, two quick thumps and the man holding her relaxed his grip. A blow from her elbow caught her assailant square in the face. He fell. Reaching out, she grabbed a handful of Darm's uniform, and pulled him forward. Planting a foot in his midriff, she fell backward, tossing him over her head.

The first man got to his feet and ran off. Darm lay where he'd fallen.

Her rescuer gave her his hand and helped her to her feet. It was One-eye the space pirate. He picked up her knife and handed it to her. Brushing the red dust from his jacket, he peered at her with his good eye. "I did warn you. On the freighter, I told you you'd need a friend."

"You were right." Her hands were shaking.

"They call me Peacock, Adam Peacock."

"Thanks for coming to my aid, Peacock."

"You're welcome. But you realize this is just the beginning. They will try again. They won't stop trying until they succeed. They all want a piece of you. I'm surprised Balehook hasn't staked his claim."

"I plan to escape."

Peacock arched his eyebrows. "Escape from Luciflex? That's impossible. The lava lakes are full of the bodies of those who've tried."

"I have an edge."

He gave her his crooked grin. "What, like a superpower?"

"Something like that."

His grin spread to his ears. "What's a pretty thing like you doing in the molten mines, anyway?"

She let the compliment pass. Her whole body was shaking, now.

#

Carla had a restless night, continually dropping off to sleep only to wake again in shock at the start of a recurring nightmare. She was bathed in sweat, her thin blanket twisted around her body. Her hands were still trembling.

Her mind was full of thoughts of what could

have happened in the corridor, of dread in the knowledge that it would almost certainly happen again. Would Peacock be there to rescue her a second time?

She went over and over the sequence of events. Was it bad luck that Darm and his mate were waiting for her and that Maxeen had left her within seconds of the encounter? Could Maxeen have arranged the whole thing?

And was it simply good luck that Peacock was there in time to rescue her?

Or is he stalking me?

Chapter 20

The next morning, Peacock was returning to his dormitory after a night shift in the mines, the ground throbbing under his feet from the incessant pounding of the stone grinders. He was covered in red dust, his muscles aching, his bones weary. Within sight of his dormitory he was set upon by Darm and his buddies. Darm's head was wrapped in bandages. Peacock kept them at bay for a few moments by swinging his arms in a circle. Then three of them came at him together. He struck one of them down, but the other two grabbed him. The whole gang moved in then. He fought them off, his back to the wall, but fatigue slowed his reactions, and within a couple of minutes blows were raining down on him from all sides. He struggled to remain on his feet. If he fell, they would finish him off with kicks to the head. Then a couple of blows to his face split his brow. Blood poured into his good eye. Disoriented and blinded, he fell to his knees.

A deep voice echoed from the walls, "Break this up and return to your dormitories." The gang continued the assault. "Leave him, he's had enough." Louder, more insistent. The tone was neutral, but Peacock detected an unmistakable threat in the voice, an edge of suppressed violence.

The gang delivered a couple more punches to his body and a last kick to Peacock's ribs before backing off. "This is not over, big man," snarled Darm as they left.

Peacock's glass eye was on the floor. He wiped the blood from his good eye, picked it up and put it back in place before struggling to his feet. He looked up to see a man-mountain dressed in a strange, tailored version of the blue and gray prison uniform. The sleeves had been removed, a V-neck added. The pant legs were cropped. He was clean-shaven, his bald head glistening in the weak lights of the corridor. A vicious hook glinted in his left hand.

Balehook!

"Thanks for stepping in. They would have killed me for sure."

Balehook flashed a humorless grin. "Think nothing of it. What are friends for, eh? That's a nasty gash on your forehead. You'll need to clean it as soon as possible."

Peacock wiped his forehead with a sleeve. A trickle of blood ran down his nose.

Balehook turned and walked away. Peacock called after him, "Thanks again, Balehook. I owe you..."

Balehook turned and came back. "It's good to make a new friend. What's your name?"

"Peacock. Adam Peacock."

"*Bosun* Adam Peacock?"

"You've heard of me?" Peacock was genuinely surprised that his fame had reached this far across the galaxy.

"Who doesn't know the names of the Halfpenny crew?" He held out his hand, and Peacock grasped it. "Good to know you, Adam Peacock. Glad I was able to help."

"I'm really grateful. If there's ever anything I can do for you..."

"What do you know about that new kitchen girl? I hear you came to her aid last night."

"We came in on the last Galaxy freighter together. She and I are good buddies."

Balehook ran a sleeve across his lips. "I have an appetite for a little dark chocolate. Bring her to me."

"I'll ask her, Balehook, but you know these young women, they all have minds of their own."

"She owes you for last night, right?"

"Yes, that's true, but..."

"So there shouldn't be a problem. Speak to her." And Balehook walked away.

#

Carla tore a strip from a dishcloth and wiped the blood from Peacock's face. "I'm sorry you had to take a beating on my account."

"Think nothing of it," he said. "It's not an uncommon happenstance in my line of work."

"Which is what?" She held the cloth to his lips. He spat on it.

"I'm a wheeler dealer. I live by my wits, mostly."

"A thief, you mean." This close, the man's body odor was overpowering. Breathing through her mouth, she dabbed at his headwound.

He winced. "I like to think of myself as a soldier of fortune, taking what drops into my path. But if thievery's what it takes to keep the flesh on these bones, then I can thieve with the best of 'em – sure."

"You're a pilot?"

He grinned, showing her his crooked, yellow teeth. "The ship that I can't handle hasn't been built yet. I ran a crew for years."

"But not anymore?"

"No. I work alone, now."

She fashioned a makeshift bandage. As she tied it around his head he said, "Balehook wants you to pay him a visit."

Carla crinkled her nose in disgust. "You can't ask me that, Peacock."

"Just go see him."

"You told him I'm not interested, right?"

Peacock wrapped his arms around his bruised ribs. "I told him, but he's insisting."

She considered her options. Was she prepared

to pay a visit to a murdering thug to repay her debt to Peacock?

"I'm sorry, Peacock," she said. "That's not going to happen."

PART 2 – Escape

Chapter 21

General Fenimore C. Matthewson had had a bad day – heck, he'd had two bad weeks. First, the Southers had captured LAX in a surprise attack. They had seized control of the Spaceport and deployed 5,000 Popov androids through the Ground Gate from a troop transport in orbit. His own force of AUs had been overrun before the battle turned in his favor, quite inexplicably. The enemy had suddenly lost its nerve, taken to its heels and scattered. The general had no idea why, and he wouldn't have believed it if he hadn't witnessed it with his own two eyes.

The credit for the victory was his. The medal on his chest proved it, but he had no hand, act, or part in it. Oh, he had allowed the president to pin the medal on his chest, but only because an admission of his ignorance would have caused a tsunami of panic through the Norther lands and colonies. The guilt weighed him down, though. The fallout could wipe out his glittering career. And how could he ever look his son in the eye again?

He straightened his necktie, checked the buttons on his vest and flicked a switch on his intercom. "Send him in."

The door opened and Henry Spendlove shuffled into the office.

"Take a seat," said the general. It was an order.

Spendlove was a weedy individual, a typical civilian desk jockey. He perched his rear end on the edge of the chair.

The general picked up a sheaf of papers and shook them at Spendlove. "This schedule you sent me, seems to suggest you plan to recover some or all of the Autonomic Units in our Earth-force."

"Yes, General. We can save them all. It should be simple enough to reprogram them. And, as I've suggested, we can take the opportunity to include the latest enhancement to the motility and visual functions. The disruption to Earth-force can be minimized by careful scheduling, one division at a time, perhaps."

The general ran his tongue over his dry lips. "I thought I made it plain the last time we met that I wanted them all replaced."

"All three quarters of a million?" Spendlove's mouth gaped open.

"Yes."

"But that would cost a small fortune. Trust me, the reprogrammed Units will be as good as new."

"It's not a question of trust," said the general. "The order from Norther Federation Command is quite explicit. They will countenance nothing short of a complete recall and replacement of all Units."

Spendlove squirmed on the edge of his seat. "Of course, General." He swallowed hard.

"How quickly can it be done?"

"I'm not sure. I'd have to check with my operations team."

"We'd like the process completed within three months."

"Yes, General."

"At no cost to the Federation."

"At no cost to the Federation." Spendlove ran a finger around his collar.

"And I'd like that in writing," said General Matthewson.

#

Major Grant was having a quiet day, when Dr. Franck called him.

"I need Cassidy Garmon back in his lab."

The major replied, "The police have an arrest warrant out for him. I'm expecting word any day now. I'll let you know when they find him."

"You're not listening to me, Major. We have a

big production job to do for the military. I want Garmon in his lab, working, not in shackles in some police station. Cancel the arrest warrant and get him back to work immediately."

"What is this job?"

"We have to recall the military Units of the Earth-force, decommission them and build replacements."

"What? All of them?"

"All three quarters of a million of them." The grim expression on Franck's face showed how serious this was.

"On whose orders?"

"Henry Spendlove. Apparently, the military are insisting on a complete recall."

After Dr. Franck had terminated the call, the major called the police chief. "Do you have eyes on Cassidy Garmon?"

"Not yet. I told you I'd call when we found him."

"I want you to cancel the arrest warrant and bring him in. Xenodyne management need him urgently."

"I can't do that, Major. Not without proper authorization."

"What can you do?"

"What do they want him for?"

"We have a huge military job on. It's urgent. The production team need him back at his desk, pronto."

“I could put a temporary hold on the warrant, but I can’t speak for the NFSA.”

“Right, do that.”

“We’ll have to find him, first.”

#

The New-Politburo was in session in Paviaskigrad. Never short of a word, Premier Sergey Tupolev was rounding off a long diatribe aimed squarely at Elena Lipleninya, the diminutive Defense Minister. “...not only has a live military action on enemy soil been undermined, but your actions have endangered the Motherland, here and in our lands at the farthest reaches of the galaxy. The humiliating rout and utter subjugation of our Popov forces leaves all of Souther territory at risk in the event of a war.”

Member Lipleninya raised a hand, indicating her desire to respond, but the premier ignored her. “The trade negotiations, which we were assured were swinging in our favor, have suffered an irreversible setback, the considerable concessions previously won have now been lost. The Norther negotiators have been handed an advantage which they must surely grasp with both hands. While the Committee accepts in good faith your stated intention to restore our military strength and supremacy, I think we all agree that it would be wise for this process to be monitored closely. Accordingly, I have asked Yuri Yumatov to set this in motion." The premier received a nod from Yumatov, the member for Internal Security. "In addition, I propose to establish a special investigation team to scrutinize the mechanisms that led to the catastrophe in the first place."

Again, the Defense Minister requested an opportunity to speak, but the premier waved her away. "We have listened to your explanations at length, Comrade. I am sure none of us wish to hear them in this chamber again. Now let us turn to the financial implications of the debacle..."

Chapter 22

While Lia slept, Cassidy opened her bag. He found four Mark 5 modules inside. They looked unharmed, although the Orientation module was covered in a layer of something damp and shiny. He found a cloth and wiped it clean.

When Lia's charge reached 80 percent, he woke her and asked, "Where did you get these modules?"

"They are Oscar's modules," she replied. "Carla Scott removed his modules and sent his body for disassembly. I put his modules in a bag."

"But why, Lia?"

"Carla Scott ended Oscar. You can rebuild him." It was almost a question.

"I don't think that would be a good idea," said Cassidy. "Do you remember why Carla ended him?"

"Yes. You can rebuild Oscar."

"I could rebuild him if we had a frame for him. We don't have a suitable frame."

"Where could we find a frame for Oscar?"

That was a question, loud and clear.

"We have Autonomic Units here, but they are not suitable for Oscar's modules."

“Why are they not suitable?”

“Oscar was a Mark 5 Unit like you. The Units here are all Mark 4s.”

“Will Oscar’s modules fit inside a Mark 4 body?”

“Well, yes, they would fit, but that’s not the problem.”

“There is no problem.” She sounded adamant.

“The outcome would be unpredictable. We would not have Oscar back as he was. I’m sorry, Lia.”

#

Lia wandered the streets in the dark. She had Oscar’s modules in her bag; all she needed was a suitable Autonomic Unit frame and he could be rebuilt. She came across a group of four men in an alley sleeping behind a dumpster. An arm protruding from the dumpster caught her eye. She lifted the lid and found several broken and battered AUs. She picked the least damaged one and pulled it out. It had all its limbs, but no powerpack.

One of the men woke up. “Hey, mechano, stay outta there.”

He shouted something else that Lia didn’t understand and chucked an empty Pexcorn can at her. She hurried away, dragging her find with her.

#

"This is a Mark 4 Unit," said Cassidy. "It's one of the ANTIX Units damaged by the police."

She handed him Oscar's modules. "Rebuild Oscar."

Cassidy looked at her wearily. "I've told you, Lia, Oscar's modules are not suitable for a Mark 4 Unit."

"Rebuild him."

Cassidy said, "It would be better to use one of the undamaged Units. This one is not in great condition."

"Use this Unit."

He spent a few more minutes trying to change her mind, but Lia wouldn't be persuaded, and he set to work under her watchful gaze. The first hurdle to overcome was the speed of the Unit's core processors. The Mark 4 used standard sixth generation synchronous quantum processors, while the Mark 5 was configured around Tandrulka Kapa new asynchronous microtechnology, TK-Tech for short. The processing speeds of TK-Tech were several orders higher. Tweaking the Mark 4 processors' clock speed to their maximum was all he could do.

His second challenge was a tricky cabling problem. The Mark 4 used the old standard 512byte data streaming ZipFlow protocol; the Mark 5 was configured for the far superior

MicroLens 2Gbyte Direct Integration System. All he could do was reconfigure the I/O of Oscar's modules to make them compatible with the slower ZipFlow streams. The cabling required gave him a headache and crossed eyes, and took him well into the early hours of the morning.

Lia hovered around like an expectant parent. Cassidy fully expected her to produce a cigar at any moment and start puffing on it. Eventually, he had to order her to take a seat in another room and, when she continued to wander about, he put her on recharge.

Cassidy powered up Oscar-2. He waited until the Unit's software had fully installed before initializing the systems.

"Your designation is Alpha Oscar 113," he said. "My name is Cassidy."

"Cassidy," said Oscar-2.

"Your name is Oscar. Do you understand?"

"I understand. My name is Oscar."

He ran a few standard routines to test reflex speeds, perception and orientation. Then he gave the Unit some simple math problems to solve to check the all-important cognitive functions. Everything was functioning at Mark 4 levels; he could see no evidence of any Mark 5 abilities whatsoever, although he was confident that the new Pain and Fear modules transplanted with Oscar-1's modules would perform as programmed.

He brought his creation into the other room and woke Lia.

“Is Oscar ready?” she said.

“I have installed Oscar’s modules in the Unit,” he replied. “But don’t expect too much.”

“I understand,” said Lia. She stood in front of Oscar-2 and said, ‘What is your name?”

“My name is Oscar.”

“Hello, Oscar.”

“Hello,” said Oscar.

Lia said, “Do you know me?”

Cassidy said, “Oscar, this is Lia.”

“Hello, Lia,” said Oscar.

Cassidy left the two AUs and went off to get some sleep.

#

In the small hours of the morning, Benn and Sophie joined Cassidy in the docklands safehouse. Within minutes of their reunion, Cassidy was convinced that Sophie still loved him; there was nothing going on between Sophie and Benn.

Sophie made up a double bed and they slipped between the sheets. Cassidy was exhausted, and fell into a deep sleep in her arms, almost immediately. Lia woke him after 30 minutes. At least it felt like 30 minutes. He opened his bleary eyes and said, “What time is it, Lia?”

“Four twenty-two.”

It *had* been 30 minutes.

Sophie sat up in the bed. She turned on a light. “What’s the problem, Lia?”

"Oscar is not functioning," she said.

"I told you not to expect too much," said Cassidy. "The old Oscar is gone. Oscar-2 will have slower reflexes."

"Oscar has no memories."

"Ah!" said Cassidy. That was a serious problem. Without Oscar's memory module, they would never be able to fully replicate the original Unit. "I'm sorry, Lia, there's nothing we can do about that." He closed his eyes.

Sophie turned out the light and lay down.

Lia stood around for a few minutes before leaving them to sleep.

The next time he awoke, there was an urgent message on his X-Vid from an old school friend. Xenodyne Automation had put out word that Cassidy was to make contact with Fritz Franck, urgently.

Cassidy borrowed an untraceable X-Vid and made the call.

"Cassidy, thank heaven," said Franck. "You're needed back here. We have a big job on for the military."

"The police are looking for me," said Cassidy.

"The arrest warrant has been cancelled. This job is too important, too urgent and too big."

"How do I know I can trust you?"

"I give you my word."

Sophie raised all sorts of objections, but Cassidy wouldn't change his mind. "I'm needed.

This could be my chance to restart my career."

Cassidy and Sophie packed up their meager belongings and moved back to Cassidy's apartment the following day.

Chapter 23

Balehook had no eyebrows. Watching his lips move was like talking with a pinball with eyes. Balehook moved closer until their heads were centimeters apart, giving Peacock the full experience of the big man's halitosis.

A drop of sweat broke out on Peacock's brow and rolled down his cheek. "She's thinking about it," he said.

He never saw the first blow coming.

The second was a roundhouse punch to the solar plexus that he saw, but could do nothing to avoid.

"Bring the girl to me tonight. If you don't, I'll get my pleasure by slitting your throat." He ran his thumbnail across Peacock's neck from ear to ear.

Peacock spoke to Carla again, a red welt on his face, a gash over his good eye. "What harm can it do? Balehook's not everyone's favorite con, but he will keep pressing until you agree to talk to him."

Carla relented. She owed Peacock a favor. Balehook's ego, and his position as self-appointed leader of the prisoners, would make it impossible for her to deny him an audience indefinitely. And, given her suspicion that Darm and Maxeen were working together against her, she could do with an influential and powerful ally. Maxeen's threat of facial mutilation was renewed as soon as she got wind of Balehook's interest. That was probably what finally made Carla change her mind.

Balehook lived in a lean-to attached to the side of one of the dormitories. It was no more than a shack, but it was filled with the comforts of home. A battered old photograph of his mother adorned one wall. On the others, several color pictures of naked women torn from ancient magazines. His bed was larger than average, his mattress thick, comfortable. And he had pillows. Two of them! A rough, home-crafted table held a basin and a jug of water, a table lamp, the scattered remains of a meal, and a heavy, metal balehook.

Balehook sat on a chair fashioned from a Pexcorn pallet. His henchman, a slight weasel of a man with a broken nose, stood behind him. Peacock slouched to the side.

Balehook signaled for the henchman to take Peacock outside. As the door closed behind them, he ran his eyes over his prize. Carla felt naked under his gaze. She couldn't take her eyes off the hook on the table.

"How old are you?" he said.

"Twenty-nine. Listen, Buster I'm not—"

"You're not what? Not ready? Not available? Not willing? None of that matters." He sprang from the chair, grabbing the hook. Two strides and his body pressed against hers. He swung his arm and buried the point of the hook in the wall above her head. “This is my kingdom. I own everything on this hellhole. I own you.” He ran his tongue across her cheek. It scratched. “Give me what I want willingly, and I’ll make you very comfortable on Luciflex.”

Ugh! Give this man a mint!

“That’s not why I came,” she said, pushing hard on his chest.

“You’re married. Is that it?”

“I’m not married.”

“You have a boyfriend. Is he here, or back home?”

“I don’t have a boyfriend. I have a proposition for you.”

He hesitated. Then he pulled the hook from the wall and backed into his chair, grinning broadly. “This I gotta to hear.”

“What if I can give you the one thing you most want, your dearest wish?”

“You can.” He flashed a salacious grin.

“What if I can get you off this planet?”

Balehook’s laughter shook the walls of the shack. Carla waited for it to die down.

He wiped his mouth. “You’re a crazy woman!”

“I’m serious. I can show you how to escape from Luciflex.”

“You’re mad.” He got to his feet. “No one has

ever escaped from Luciflex – not alive, anyway."

"Hear me out, Balehook. I have something that no one else has. Let me show you what I can do, then you'll understand. If you're not totally convinced, I'll do whatever you want."

Did I really say that?

"Okay, show me." He dropped the hook on the table and crossed his arms.

"I need one of the guards, an Autonomic Unit. Can you get one in here?"

"Sure, no problem." He whistled. The door opened. He gave instructions to his weasel henchman, closed the door and returned to his chair. "That shouldn't take long." He fixed Carla with his gaze.

Chapter 24

Carla took a deep breath. The time for hesitancy was over. She was about to play her trump card, to take the first step on a perilous journey with only two possible outcomes: success or failure. Success would get her off Luciflex; failure meant losing everything.

"You know I'm an associate professor in cybernetics?"

"Peacock said you worked on the robots."

"The Autonomic Units are not robots. They're androids, but yes, designing them was my job before..."

"Before they sent you here, eh? Why? I bet you dipped your sticky little fingers in the company piggy bank. You must have taken millions to be sent to this beauty spot." He grinned toothlessly.

"It was nothing like that. Xenodyne took exception to some of my research."

He frowned. "Why? What was this research?"

"It's technical. The project was unauthorized. Let's just say they didn't like where it was heading."

"And they sent you here to rot?"

"It took them just five days to ship me out."

"Okay, so you're an expert in robotics. Go on."

"The AUs on Luciflex are all Mark 5 models. I worked on those models for three years. Two of the cybernetic modules are my designs."

He ran a hand over his bald head. "Speak plain, woman."

"I know how the androids work."

"Okay, go on."

"The AU is basically a simple machine. The mechanics of speech and movement of the hands, major limbs, walking, and so on have been well established for many years."

"They're very strong."

"Uh-huh. There's not much of a market for weakling androids."

"I heard the eyes are tricky."

"Not really. They're high-performance, autofocus cameras. From the beginning every model has incorporated multiple senses: sight, touch and hearing."

"What about smell?"

"They don't have a sense of smell, although they do incorporate detectors for smoke and many airborne particulates harmful to humans. They don't have a sense of taste either. But they do have other senses that we don't have, like enhanced vision. As I said, a simple machine with fully functioning motility, speech and sensory inputs."

She paused to take another deep breath. "The

clever bit is in the cybernetics. There are four main modules that control every AU, Perception, Orientation, Compliance and Cognition. Perception is concerned with the processing of sensory inputs. That includes fingertip sensitivity, facial and voice recognition..."

"So that it can tell its friends from its enemies."

"Yes, amongst other things. The Orientation module allows the Unit to make sense of where it is in the context of its surroundings, its galactic and global location in five-dimensional space-time, its immediate environment, which way it's facing, up from down, left from right, north from south, and so on. Cognition gives them the ability to parse complex situations—"

"Parse?"

"To work them out. Like tricky social situations."

"I could do with a bit of that myself," said Balehook.

Carla smiled at the joke. "Cognition involves a significant amount of heuristic processing."

"What the hell does that mean?"

"Advanced learning."

"And you worked on all these systems back at Xenodyne?"

"Yes, I designed them. The Compliance module is supported by two subsystems, Security and Communications. The Mark 5 Compliance chip is one of my designs. It is vital. It enables the Unit to interpret and follow orders. The AUs on Luciflex couldn't function without them. They couldn't open fire on an escaping prisoner, for example, without the Compliance module."

"What are you saying?"

"It's simple. The Compliance module factory settings prohibit an AU from harming a human, but military and police AUs are programmed without that setting."

"And prison guards?"

"And prison guards."

Balehook took a bottle from a crude shelf and poured a measure of colorless liquid into a glass. He handed the glass to Carla.

"No thank you," she said.

"Try it. It's good. We distill it ourselves from Pexcorn and fruitoid. It's every bit as good as twentieth century Bourbon."

"Not my kind of drink, but thanks for the offer."

Balehook poked his nose in the glass, absorbing the vapor for a long moment, his lips moving as if in prayer. Then he knocked it back, gasped, shook himself and wiped his lips on his fingers, before resuming his seat. "Okay, so what's the plan, Professor?"

Chapter 25

The door to Balehook's shack opened. The weasel henchman used a boot to prop it open. Peacock stood close behind him.

A guard appeared at the door, XR-15 blaster at the ready. He peered inside the shack. "I see no damaged Unit."

Carla stepped into the android's line of sight, planting her feet firmly in front of it. "Who am I?"

"Prisoner B247."

"Not my prison number. What is my name? Search your memory bank."

A couple of moments passed before the AU responded. "You are Carla Scott."

"What is your designation and duty roster?"

"Alpha Romeo 3863. Prisoner accommodation patrol."

"Check the prisoner manifest, Alpha Romeo. Locate a prisoner called Cassidy Garmon."

The AU took several seconds to check the database. "There is no prisoner of that designation on Luciflex."

"You're certain?"

"The name does not appear on the prisoner manifest."

Carla swallowed a lump in her throat. "Check the prison records for the other Systems."

"That information is not available."

That was no surprise. Radio communication was impossible within the fifth dimension. The only System to System communication was carried by ships and unmanned drones.

"Alpha Romeo, place your weapon on the ground. Code one seven one five two three."

The android laid down his blaster.

"Now remove your tunic, and stand perfectly still."

Alpha Romeo straightened his back and removed his tunic. Carla flipped open the panel in his back and removed his powerpack. The Unit crumpled to the floor.

"That was awesome!" said Balehook. "Is it really that easy to disable the robots?"

"They're not robots, remember? And it's easy if you know how they work. There are many other ways of achieving the same result, but disabling them one at a time would be of limited use. They receive a radio signal every few seconds from a control center that checks their status and keeps them operating."

The weasel picked up the weapon. Carla snapped at him, "Leave it. We will return the Unit to duty in a few minutes. Don't you think they will notice if he has lost his gun? Besides, what can you do with one gun?"

Balehook signaled to his henchman and he dropped the blaster.

“How did you get it to drop the gun?” said an open-mouthed Peacock.

Carla bent over the android. “A factory setting – a simple backdoor access, triggered by my image.”

She flipped open a panel in the Unit’s chest to reveal a cavity. Reaching inside, she pulled out a grey metal block.

“Light. I need light, quickly.”

The weasel grabbed the lamp from the table and moved it close. She read the markings on the block before wiping it on the leg of her uniform and reinserting it in the android’s chest cavity. The panel closed with an audible *click*.

“What was that?” said Balehook.

“That was the Compliance module. There were several variants used in the Mark 5. I needed to check the exact model.”

She replaced the Unit’s powerpack and tunic. Four standard seconds later, he began to revive.

“Who am I?”

Alpha Romeo lifted his head, a dazed look on his face. “You are Carla Scott.”

“Return to duty, Alpha Romeo.”

The Unit blinked once before scrambling to his feet. The weasel picked up the XR-15 and handed it over. Alpha Romeo took it and left the shack, muttering something about ‘non-compliance’.

Peacock laughed. "That's one seriously confused mechano."

Balehook told Peacock and the weasel to wait outside. "Miss android whisperer and I have business to discuss."

As the door closed, Balehook reached for the moonshine again. "You're sure you won't have a drop?"

"No thanks."

"Who's Garmon?"

"Cassidy Garmon. He's my assistant – or he was."

Balehook went through the same ritual as before, pouring a small measure into the glass, inhaling the sacred vapors before emptying the glass down his throat in one quick movement. He replaced the bottle on the shelf and took a moment to gather himself. "What did you do to that android?"

"I simply reminded him that I'm the boss. He is imprinted on me. The way a duckling imprints on the first thing it sees when it hatches. Alpha Romeo will do everything I say from now on."

"But you let it go! The Units are all identical. How will you find it again?"

"They're all different, Balehook. Trust me, I will be able to find him again."

"Okay, Miss Professor. What's your plan? Do you intend to imprint on every android on Luciflex?"

“That would take half a lifetime. No, there must be a way to use my advantage and get us off this hellish rock. Let me think about it.”

“Is there anything I can do to help?”

“I need you to keep me healthy, to warn Darm and the other prisoners off.”

“Consider it done. I’ll put out the word that you’re my bitch. That should do it.”

Chapter 26

Lia sat with Oscar and attempted to rebuild his memories. She described their time together before Carla had ended him. "We were on a spacecraft together, a freighter. We saw Califon and her two moons. You said you would take me there."

Oscar made no response.

"Califon is a verdant planet in the C-System. Carla Scott was born there."

"I know Carla Scott."

"But you do not remember me?"

"No."

"Do you remember Califon?"

"No."

She borrowed an X-Vid from a member of the Resistance and called up some images of Califon. "This is a view of Califon from space. And here is an image of its two moons." She found a time-lapse of the planet seen from space and ran that. Next, she flipped through a series of still images of the surface of the planet and followed that with a video of a sunset taken from a high-rise building in Sanfran2.

Oscar watched them all.

"That was Califon," she said. "You do not remember it?"

"I have no memories of it." Oscar sounded almost apologetic. That was impossible, of course.

She Found Cassidy in the kitchen with Sophie.

"How's Oscar?" said Sophie.

"He is not Oscar. He has no memories of me or anything we did together."

She told them what she'd done.

"Those videos and images will have given the Unit new memories, but you can't recreate old memories," said Cassidy. "To rebuild Oscar, we'll have to install the four modules in a Mark 5 frame, first. Then you'll have to find his original memory module and return it to him."

"Tell me how to find Oscar's memories," she said.

Chapter 27

At the conclusion of the last sitting of the second meal of the day, Carla lay in her cot contemplating her position. She was willing to admit her actions had been contrary to standard military practice, but she didn't deserve such a harsh punishment. If she'd had an opportunity to appeal, based on her record, she was certain the sentence would have been overturned or commuted.

In her time at Xenodyne Automation, she'd earned her chops many times over. Together, she and Cassidy had extended and broadened the physical capabilities of the military Autonomic Unit. They were stronger and could run faster and farther and for longer than any human soldier. Their senses were far superior, too. Their hearing was more acute, and they could see further than any human. The sense of touch still lagged a human's, but their sense of smell was somewhere close to that of a dog's, capable of detecting illegal and noxious substances no matter how cleverly concealed.

Her heuristic routines, paired with the latest TK-Tech processors and the MicroLens superfast data transfer protocols, enabled the Mark 5 AU to learn virtually any skill, making it a formidable fighting machine, far superior to any flesh and blood soldier. Carla still couldn't understand why the generals objected to addition of pain and fear; they were obvious improvements.

The morning after they'd installed the first Fear module, Carla knew she had made a major breakthrough. Androids with guns would no longer pose a risk to human lives, and the module had opened up an unexpected world of possibilities, which could only be described as 'feelings.'

The gap between Artificial and Biological Intelligence was shrinking fast. The effectiveness of her software in military androids had been proven beyond question. But so much more could be achieved by this development program. Autonomic Units could be imbued with so many more feelings and emotions, perhaps even leading eventually to the holy grail of android development – full sentience.

#

She left her cot, wandered outside and strode about the compound. Surrounded on three sides by high walls, lookout towers, and electrified wire, and with armed guards everywhere, it looked and felt much like a Second World War POW camp.

Many of the guards were Autonomic Units; that and the perpetual rhythmic thump-thump of the rock pulverisers were the main differences. A steep mountainside made up the fourth side of the compound, where the living quarters for the inmates and the human guards had been built, buried deep under the mountain.

Carla strolled along the wall to the gate. The guards made no attempt to stop her as she stepped through, and it struck her that there was nowhere safe on Luciflex outside the compound. The air was thick with ash and the red dust that lay around everywhere and swirled in dust devils. Massive, jagged mountains rose on all sides, with three continuous eruptions in the immediate view. She headed for a low, rocky hill. It looked like a baby in a room full of angry adults, but as she climbed, she came across numerous fissures venting steam and noxious gasses; the seemingly innocuous hill covered a reservoir of magma.

Pressing on, shielding her mouth and nose with her sleeve, she reached the summit. The sun had set a couple of hours earlier, and Luciflex had no moons, but it was never dark on the planet. The sky was the color of mud, filled with thick, brown clouds lit from below by the active volcanoes. In the far distance, like an endless argument between ancient gods, forked lightning flashed down from the low clouds above Vesuvio, the biggest and meanest of the planet's volcanoes.

A fully laden hovertruck trundled past from the right. She watched it bob its way along the access road to where a heavily guarded freight shuttle was being loaded, passing an empty truck on its return journey.

She thought about the people in her life. Had her father received her letters? If he was working with his diplomatic contacts to have her released, a failed escape attempt wouldn't help. She thought about her burgeoning relationship with Zed Jones, her only flesh and blood friend. And again, she mourned the loss of her closest friend, her personal AU, Lia.

She closed her eyes and allowed herself to dream about the possibility of escape. It seemed impossible, but with Balehook's help, she might actually pull it off – the most improbable feat since the escape from Alcatraz 350 years earlier.

If they did succeed and she made it back to Earth, how could she continue her work? And where? Not in the XA lab, for sure; she would have to find a new, secret lab somewhere. Professor Jones had a lab in the university. Perhaps she could use that. If that proved impossible, she would just have to find a quiet corner of the Six Systems somewhere to hide out and continue her work.

She knew the risks she would be running, but she wasn't going to abandon her research. Hiding from the largest, most powerful conglomerate in the galaxy, it would be only a matter of time before they found her. As soon as she escaped, they would start searching for her and, when they realized that she was still working on her pet project, the search would be intensified. Xenodyne Industries had eyes and ears everywhere.

As if her thoughts of escape had awakened a sleeping giant, the ground under her feet shook. When this was accompanied by a distant throaty rumble that signaled a significant new eruption, she started off down the slope, weaving her way around the boulders. A shower of small pebbles like hail fell from the sky, followed, within a minute, by stones as big as baseballs and steaming rocks the size of basketballs. Covering her head with her hands, she broke into a run back to the shelter of the compound.

Chapter 28

Thunderous roars rumbled across the surface of the planet. Lightning flashes accompanied a massive eruption several miles away, lighting up the sky in lurid colors. Carla ran for her life. By the time she reached the gate, volcanic ash and bombs as big as boulders were falling all around her. The prisoners and guards sheltering in the barracks called out encouragement to her as she sprinted across the deserted compound and threw herself inside.

They helped her to her feet. One man slapped her on the back as she coughed, struggling to clear her lungs. Then she shook herself and ran her hands over her prison uniform. The men all laughed at the cloud of red dust and ash she created.

"Come with me," said Balehook, crooking her arm, propelling her through the crowd toward his shack.

"What were you doing outside the compound?" he said, as he closed the door. He sounded like an angry schoolmaster.

"It was a pleasant evening for a stroll," she said, shaking the dust from her hair. "I went out for a breath of fresh air."

"In the middle of one of Vesuvio's major eruptions?" He reached for the bottle of moonshine, poured a small measure into a glass and handed it to her. She hesitated before accepting it, tossing it back with abandon. It burnt her throat and seared her innards all the way down.

"I wanted..." she croaked. She coughed and started again. "I wanted to see if I could work out a plan of escape."

"And did you?" He tilted the bottle toward her glass. She waved it away and put the empty glass on the table.

"I think so, yes. I was amazed how easy it was to leave the compound. No one tried to stop me."

"With good reason. It may have escaped your notice, but it's not safe out there. This barracks is the only place on Luciflex where human life can survive for any length of time."

"I have noticed. That's why we have to get off the planet."

"And how are we going to do that?"

"We hitch a ride on the freighter in orbit."

"And how do we do that?"

"We need to sneak on board one of the shuttles."

Balehook ran a hand over his bald head. "That's impossible. The shuttle bay is patrolled day and night by armed guards."

"Armed Autonomic Units."

His eyes opened wide. "That could work. If you

can disarm the androids, I can deal with the human guards."

She said, "We don't need to disarm the Units. They won't fire at us."

Balehook snorted. "Why not? They have in the past."

Carla gave that a moment's thought. The Units' Compliance modules must have been altered. "In that case, I'll have to neutralize them. There must be a maintenance shop for the AUs somewhere in the compound. Do you know where it is?"

"Almost certainly in the Central Control building, near the gate. There's nowhere else it could be."

"Can you get me in there?" she said.

"Maybe, but it won't be easy."

"If you can get me inside that building, I can disable the Autonomic Units."

"All of them?"

"All of them."

He poured a half measure into the glass and pointed it at her. "You and I make a great team. Here's to a successful joint enterprise." He knocked back the glassful and smacked his lips.

"One more thing," she said. "Our timing will have to be perfect. We'll have to get onto the last shuttle, just before the freighter leaves for the Interstellar Gate."

"Right. Ask that one-eyed good-for-nothing gadabout, Peacock. He should be able to find out when it's due to leave and he can keep his good eye on the loading process."

"I'm relying on you to get me inside that building," she said.

"No problem," said Balehook.

#

Maxeen was waiting for her when she arrived back in the dorm.

"You were with Balehook," she said, her eyes blazing. "I saw you."

"We were talking. I have no romantic interest in your man."

"Talking?"

"Yes. He's planning an escape and he wants me to help him."

Maxeen snorted. "The word is out. He's calling you his bitch."

Carla waved a dismissive hand. "That's a smokescreen to keep Darm and his boys away from me."

"You expect me to believe that?"

"Believe it, Maxeen. If Balehook was the only man on the planet, I wouldn't touch him with a ten-foot pole."

Maxeen put a hand on her hip, tilted her head back and snorted. "Oh, get you! My man's not good enough for you? Is that what you're saying?"

Before Carla could think of a suitable reply, Maxeen flounced out of the room, swinging her hips from side to side.

Chapter 29

Cassidy and Sophie sat up in bed reading. He put his book down. "I have a question."

She put her book down. "Yes?"

"Are you happy?"

"What do you mean?"

"I mean are you happy with me?"

"We're in bed together, aren't we?"

"Yes, but isn't there somewhere else you'd prefer to be?"

"Like where?"

"I dunno. Anywhere?"

"No. Don't be stupid." She picked up her book. She read a page and put it down again. "If you're asking if I'd prefer to be in bed with someone else, the answer is no."

They both resumed their reading.

"Not even Benn?" he said.

"No. I told you. I'm happy here with you. In bed."

Cassidy said nothing more on the subject. He tried to read, but he found himself reading the same paragraph over and over.

"Tell me what you're thinking," said Sophie quietly, without looking up from her book.

"I was thinking Lia will need help finding Oscar's memory module."

"She'll need a miracle."

He put his book down again. "I'm pretty sure I know where to look."

She carried on pretending to read. "Surely someone will have deleted all the data by now."

"That's possible, but unlikely. It will have been placed back in storage, but who bothers to scrub old data?"

"Why do you feel the need to help her find this module?"

He turned to face her. "Because Lia won't be able to find it on her own."

Sophie continued to stare at her book. "Why is it so important? These are androids we're talking about."

Cassidy took his time framing his response. "Lia and Oscar are not like most Autonomic Units; the Fear module that they both possess enabled them to make an intimate connection."

"An intimate connection? Really?" Her book snapped shut.

"I know it sounds improbable, but that's what happened."

"How can you be sure?"

"Just look at Lia. I would have thought her feelings are obvious."

"Her feelings?" Sophie gave him her wide-eyed look.

“She’s pining after Oscar. Can’t you see that?”

“You’ve got to be kidding, Cass. Since when did androids have feelings? She’s a machine – a computer on legs.”

“She’s a lot more than that,” mumbled Cassidy. “I’d like to help her if I can.”

“By sneaking into some lab and searching for a missing memory module?”

“Yes, but it’s a storage warehouse, not a lab.”

“I’m sorry, Cass, I can’t let you go. It’s too risky.” She crossed her arms firmly across her chest. “The corporation is on the lookout for you. Heaven knows what they’ll do with you if they catch you.”

#

It was a dark and stormy night. Cassidy took Lia in his hover to the LA Downtown Industrial District and parked a couple of blocks short of their destination. They approached the building on foot. Both Cassidy and Lia were dressed in dark clothing, and Cassidy reckoned the weather would be severe enough to discourage anyone who might be watching out for them.

Lia carried Oscar’s four modules in her bag. She wanted to be able to rebuild Oscar without delay once she’d located his memory module, and Cassidy had shown her how. Installation of the modules was a simple procedure, provided the cabling was in place.

From the front, the building looked like a plain, unremarkable storage warehouse, but the wide doors at the rear giving access to a loading bay, revealed its true function. They kept watch for a few minutes before Cassidy used his XA card and palm print to gain entry.

They stepped inside and Cassidy closed the door, cutting off the sounds of the rain and howling wind. Hiding in the shadows, they waited for a couple of minutes more in case their entry had been detected. All was quiet. They pressed on.

Using his pass again, Cassidy took Lia through a set of double doors at the rear of the loading bay into a dimly lit warehouse as big as an aircraft hangar. It was deserted. Lia looked around at tier upon tier of shelving stacked with spare parts.

A quick search revealed the section of the warehouse where decommissioned Units were stored, awaiting disassembly and salvage. There were hundreds of them, jumbled together, some standing, others lying in piles, many lacking limbs, all lacking powerpacks. Cassidy had seldom seen a sadder sight.

"I will find Oscar, here," said Lia. "His memory module may still be in place."

It looked hopeless to Cassidy, but Lia insisted that she could identify a lifeless Oscar, as long as he still had his head. He went off to search the shelves for memory modules. When he came back Lia had disappeared among the decommissioned Units. He called her name in a loud whisper.

Lia emerged, clutching a lifeless Autonomic Unit to her chest. “I found Oscar,” she said.

“Are you certain this is Oscar?”

“Yes.” She handed him her bag containing Oscar’s four core modules.

Cassidy was happy to take her word for it; it was a Mark 5 Unit, but there was no way he could identify it. He sprung open the chest access panel and fitted the four modules. Then he found a Tesla powerpack and installed that.

“Does he have his memory module?” she asked.

“I’m sorry, Lia,” he said. “He has no memory module.”

Lia gave a small squeal and stepped backward. Her shoulder struck an upright Unit. That Unit toppled sideways, knocking over a second and a third. And then, like dominos falling in slow motion, a whole row of Autonomic Units collapsed, creating a loud, lingering clatter.

A wailing siren sounded.

“Come on, Lia. We have to get out. Now!”

Lia said, “I have not found Oscar’s memory module.”

An internal door crashed open, and two armed guards ran in. One of them shouted, “Stand where you are.”

Cassidy ran back through the double doors into the loading bay. Halfway to the external door, he was hit by taser fire. He fell, his body racked with pain, every nerve twitching uncontrollably. He passed out.

When he regained his senses, the two guards were laid out on the floor beside him. He checked them both. They were unconscious, with strong pulses. They would wake up with headaches and a few bruises. He looked around for his rescuer, but couldn't see her anywhere.

"Lia, where are you?"

The only reply he got was a hollow echo.

"Thank you, Lia," he called before heading to the exit and leaving the building.

#

The two men recovered after a half hour and conducted a search of the storage area. They failed to find Lia, now naked, hiding in plain sight among the decommissioned Units.

She waited until the men had gone and the sirens had been switched off, before starting her search. Later, when her powerpack was running low, she found a recharging station, set her wake up alarm for four hours, and plugged herself in.

Chapter 30

Like a toddler after an explosive tantrum, Vesuvio settled back into its previous steady state of grumbling truculence, and life on Luciflex returned to normal.

Day after day, truckloads of pulverized rocks were transported from the various mineral processing and metal refinement areas to the Ground Gate and from there by shuttle to the giant Galaxy freighter in orbit above Luciflex. Peacock's informers kept him up to date on the loading progress, and he passed the information to Carla.

"Two of the cargo bays are full," he reported. "Ten to go."

Then five days later, "That's four."

By week nine they had passed the halfway mark. "Seven bays are full. Five to go."

Carla's life settled into a ragged routine. The fine red dust covered her uniform and had turned her hair pink; she was indistinguishable from the other four kitchen women and the catcalls from the men were less frequent.

The time for Carla's second shower had come

around. Maxeen handed her a tiny bar of soap. "Ten minutes."

Carla objected. She had seen Maxeen and one of the other women take more time than that in the shower.

"The longer you serve, the longer you get. Didn't I say?"

The water was cold to start with, and never got more than lukewarm, but Carla made the best of it, managing to get the dust out of her hair and washing her uniform by treading on it as she showered.

Maxeen cut off the water while Carla was still covered in lather. "Time's up."

"That wasn't ten minutes."

"Slightly over ten." Maxeen held out her hand for the soap.

"But look at me. Let me wash this off."

Maxeen handed her a rag. "Use this." Give me your clothes. I'll hang them outside. They'll be dry in half an hour."

And covered in red dust, though Carla.

After her shower the catcalls resumed. Within 10 days she was covered in red dust again and the catcalls died away.

At 20 weeks, Peacock reported that eleven of the twelve cargo bays were full; the freighter would be leaving in two Luciflex days.

"If we miss this freighter, how long until the next one?" she asked.

"Maybe six standard months."

Later that night, Carla waited until the three witches were snoring in chorus before slipping out of the dormitory and hurrying to Balehook's shack.

It took a couple of minutes of persistent hammering before a bleary-eyed Balehook opened his door. "What d'you want?"

She slipped inside. "The last shuttle leaves in two days. It's time to put our plan into action. Have you worked out how to get me inside the Central Control building?"

"No. Dammit, woman, I need more time."

"We don't have any more time. If we miss this opportunity, we'll have to wait six months for the next freighter."

Balehook exploded, smashing his palm into the top of his table. "It's impossible. You might as well ask me to break into Fort Knox."

Carla had never heard of Fort Knox, but she let that slide. "Let me think about it. Maybe I can find a way. Just make sure you are ready to neutralize the guards when the time comes."

Balehook scratched his nose with a grubby finger. "Okay. Leave that with me."

Chapter 31

When she got back to her dormitory, she found Maxeen blocking the way to her cot. The room was in semi-darkness, but Maxeen's eyes were ablaze in reflected light from the corridor.

"Where have you been?"

"The toilet."

"Don't lie to me. You were with Balehook. I saw you get up. I followed you. I saw you go into his shack." A blade flashed in Maxeen's hand. "I'm going to cut your ears off."

Maxeen stood between Carla and her cot. She'd left her makeshift knife hidden under it. "Look Maxeen, I can explain."

"What's to explain? You've taken what was mine. I gave you fair warning."

The other three women were awake and began chanting in a low chorus, "Fight, fight, fight."

Maxeen grabbed Carla by the neck, pulled her down toward the cot, and readied her knife. Carla lashed out with her elbow, catching the older woman on the chin. Maxeen lost her balance and they fell onto the cot together.

Carla got to her feet first. "Please listen to me, Maxeen—"

But Maxeen was not interested in explanations. She lunged at Carla with the knife.

"Fight, fight, fight. Cut her, Maxeen!"

Carla deflected Maxeen's arm and the older woman's momentum sent her sprawling onto the floor. Carla seized her opportunity to reach under her cot for her own knife. It wasn't there.

Maxeen clambered to her feet. "Looking for this?" She now had a knife in each hand.

The two spectators cheered and began to clap rhythmically. "Kill, kill, kill!"

"Maxeen, please listen to me. Nothing happened between Balehook and me."

Maxeen charged forward again, slashing wildly with both knives. Carla whipped the mattress from her cot and used it as a shield. The knives ripped into the fabric. Maxeen took a step back. Then she charged forward again, both blades flailing, shredding the mattress.

Carla wrapped the mattress around Maxeen, pinning her arms. Maxeen fell to the floor with a thump with Carla on top of her, their faces close together.

Carla said, "I only went to talk to Balehook to repay a debt."

Maxeen's chest was heaving, breathing heavily from the workout. "Let me up!"

"I was trapped by two men. Peacock saved me. I owed him. He asked me to go to Balehook."

"Peacock?"

"The space pirate with the glass eye. Balehook demanded to meet me. He threatened to slit Peacock's throat if I didn't go."

"That sounds like Balehook," said Maxeen. "Let me up."

"You promise not to attack me again?"

"Yes, yes. Let me up."

Carla reached under the mattress and relieved Maxeen of both knives. Then she stood back, and Maxeen freed herself.

The spectators returned to their cots mumbling their disappointment.

Maxeen dusted herself off. "Nothing happened, you say?"

"Nothing. We spoke for a while."

"And he let you go without...?"

"Yes. I think he loves only you."

"That, I don't believe." Maxeen dropped her arms wearily. "Don't go near him again, or I swear I'll cut you open." She returned to her cot.

Carla took the mattress from the empty cot. She tucked the two knives underneath before lying down.

She lay awake until Maxeen was snoring.

Chapter 32

At sunrise the next day, Peacock brought word from Balehook that the freighter was preparing to depart early. The last shuttle, transporting an extremely rare radioisotope to the freighter, would leave when Luciflex's massive sun was at its highest.

Carla asked Peacock to find Marny and invite him to join the escape party. After the breakfast shift, she paid a visit to Balehook's shack to make final arrangements for the escape. "I got your message about the freighter. How reliable is the information?"

Balehook growled. "I had to pour the last of my hooch down the greedy gullet of a crew member to get it. You can bet your life on it."

"I'll get inside Central Control an hour before midday and disable the AUs. When I've done that, we can make a dash for the shuttle. If we time it right, we should get onboard before it leaves and while the AUs are still disabled."

"You've found a way to get inside Central Control?"

"I think so. Yes."

"You're sure you can neutralize the robots?"

"I'm sure. But there's nothing I can do to stop the human guards from shooting at us."

Balehook gave her a twisted smile. "Leave that with me. How will I know when you've disabled the robots? Will they all fall down or something?"

"No, they won't look any different, but they won't attempt to stop us, and they won't use their weapons. Watch for my signal."

"It reminds me of my time with the Space Cadets," he said.

"You were with the Space Cadets?"

Balehook grinned wolfishly. "Not officially."

"I'll be bringing Peacock and Marny with me," she said.

"Marny?"

"He's an old man I met on the freighter on the way here."

"So you do have a boyfriend. I knew it!"

"He's a friend. I want him along."

"Whatever you say." He pinched his nose. "But why bring the long drink of water with the glass eye?"

"He's a friend, too. He's been helpful. Who are you bringing along?"

"No one."

"Not even your helper with the broken nose? And what about Maxeen and the other women in the kitchen?"

"I don't think so," said Balehook. "They'd only slow us down."

Chapter 33

In the storage warehouse back on Earth, Lia's personal alarm woke her in the small hours. She disconnected from the recharge point and resumed her search. Darkness absorbed the vast warehouse like a suffocating blanket, sounds of the storm seeping in from outside. Enhanced vision enabled her to find her way around, but she needed the flashlight over her left ear to read the labels on the shelves. It took her 15 minutes to locate the shelving area where the memory modules were stored, and another hour to make sure there were no others. There were in excess of 120,000 memory modules on the shelves. A quick calculation told her if it took 10 minutes to retrieve and check each one, and assuming she could work only during the 8 hours of nighttime, her search could take anything up to 2,500 nights, or nearly seven standard years!

Undaunted, she began...

The wind and rain eased with the dawn, bringing a glimmer of daylight through the storm clouds.

As Lia returned to her hiding place beside the

lifeless figure of Oscar, the night duty officer of the North Federation Security Agency, was on his X-Vid taking to his supervisor. Within seconds of that call, the NFSA supervisor had placed a call to Commander Harlowe.

"You're sure of your facts?"

"I am, Commander."

"Tell me what time this happened?"

"Eleven thirty-five."

"You should have called me right away."

"I called you as soon as I was notified by the night duty officer."

"Your night duty protocols need urgent attention, so."

There was a pause.

"What do you want me to do, Commander?"

"I'm sure it's too late, but better send in a team to check it out."

#

The NFSA team arrived at the warehouse in three black hovers, stormed in through the loading bay, and swarmed through the building. Lia counted 15 men dressed in black, all heavily armed. She tuned into their communications and learned that their primary focus was 'target one'. The whole operation took 20 minutes. They found nothing of interest. She wondered who 'target one' could be.

#

The following morning, Major Grant received a call from Commander Harlowe.

"Our night duty surveillance team spotted an unauthorized break-in at one of your warehouses at eleven thirty-five last night."

"I have a report of the break-in on my desk," Grant replied. "Nothing was taken, as far as I can tell."

"My men identified the intruder. It was Cassidy Garmon, the domestic terrorist."

"The arrest warrant on Garmon has been lifted," said the major. "He's back at work. He's no longer of interest to the police."

"The police may have lost interest in him, but we haven't."

"I told you. He's back at work on a very important military project."

Harlowe hesitated before responding, "I expect you to call me the minute that military project completes."

"Of course, Commander," said the major.

"In your dreams, Commander," said Grant after the commander had terminated the call.

When Cassidy arrived for work, Major Grant had a word with him in his laboratory.

"There was a break-in at our New Street warehouse last night. I have a report from a couple of warehouse security men that your palm print was used."

"I needed to look at a Mark 5 Unit to check something."

"In the middle of the night?"

"It was urgent. Is there a problem with that?"

"The men say they were attacked. They were both rendered unconscious."

Cassidy's eyebrows arched, comically. "You think I knocked out two armed security guards?"

"They were attacked by persons unknown."

"Sorry," said Cassidy. "I know nothing about that."

#

Lia resumed her quest, searching by night, hiding by day, careful not to be discovered by the warehouse staff or removed for decommissioning herself. Over the next two days, several loads of military Autonomic Units arrived for decommissioning in hovertrucks, adding to the store of memory modules, and triggering a deep sense of foreboding in her Fear module. She found a tin of fluorescent paint in the warehouse, and marked each memory module with a speck of paint after she'd checked it. This would prevent her from checking any module twice, but even so, her search was going to take much longer than her initial estimate.

Chapter 34

Two local hours before midday on Luciflex, Carla left the kitchen and went in search of Alpha Romeo. She found him on patrol as usual, and led him back to her dormitory where Peacock was waiting. She explained to the Unit how she wanted him to help her get inside Central Control. The plan took some explaining. Alpha Romeo had led a sheltered life. After a standard half-hour she said, "Are you clear about what I want you to do?"

"Your instructions are clear, Carla Scott, but I am uncertain that I will be able to tell an untruth. Will it be necessary?"

"If we are to succeed it will be necessary."

"I am uncertain..."

Carla was out of time. "Grasp my arm. Whatever happens don't let go until I give you the secret signal."

Alpha Romeo wrapped a hand around her wrist.

"Harder, Romeo," she said.

"I do not wish to harm you, Carla Scott."

"You won't. Hold me tighter. I'll tell you if it's too tight."

Peacock watched them leave. "Are you sure this is going to work?"

"It's got to," said Balehook.

Carla and Romeo walked to the door of the Central Control building. They looked like a devoted couple, with Carla's wrist firmly clamped in Alpha Romeo's fist.

"Please say if my grip is too tight," said the AU.

"It's fine. Stop asking me. Remember what we are trying to do."

"Trying. To. Do. Yes, I remember."

Romeo hammered on the door.

A disembodied voice responded, "Your designation?"

"Alpha Romeo 3863."

"Are you in need of technical assistance Alpha Romeo 3863?"

Romeo opened his mouth but said nothing.

"Yes, he needs technical assistance," said Carla.

"Let the prisoner go and the technicians will provide the necessary assistance."

Romeo made no reply. He was immobile and speechless.

Carla whispered, "Say what I told you."

"I cannot."

Carla shouted, "Let us in. Your robot is clamped onto my arm and can't let go."

A long pause. Then the voice said, "You cannot let the prisoner go? Is that correct, Alpha Romeo?"

Romeo made no response.

Carla banged on the door. "Listen, buddy, this Unit's hand is breaking my arm. If you want the men fed tonight, I suggest you sort this problem out."

Two loud clicks, a buzz, and the door swung open. Romeo entered, still clutching Carla's wrist.

Chapter 35

Inside the Control Center, a deserted corridor with gray walls led to a blank door. Romeo pushed it open, and they entered a room kitted out like an office anteroom.

A guard sat behind a desk; hands poised over a keyboard. “What seems to be the problem?” He was clean-shaven, but middle-aged with a thin head of hair – obviously not an AU.

“This Unit has malfunctioned. He has clamped a hand onto my wrist and refuses to let go.”

He gave Romeo a plastic smile. “We are pleased that you came to us for help today, and we look forward to resolving your issue. Is this your first visit?”

Romeo replied, “Yes.”

“Designation?”

“Alpha Romeo 3863.”

“AR3863.” He tapped his keyboard. “Duty roster?”

“He was on patrol in the prisoner quarters,” said Carla. “Can we get on with this, please?”

“A technician will be with you shortly. Please take a seat.” He indicated a wood-effect bench against a wall. “In the meantime, we need to go through our fault logging procedure...”

Carla sat, her arm raised. Romeo sat beside her, clamped to her wrist.

“Date and time of the incident?”

“Today, about an hour ago,” said Carla.

“Please describe the incident, AR3863.”

Carla clicked her tongue impatiently. “You can see what happened. This android has ahold of my arm and won’t let go.”

He keyed that in. “Describe any known damage.”

“My wrist has been damaged.”

“Any damage to your systems, AR3863? Dermis? Frame? Joints?”

“None,” said Carla.

“Any damage to your internal systems?”

“None,” said Carla, gritting her teeth. Can we get on with this, please?”

“Modules and powerpack fully functional?”

“The Unit is entirely undamaged,” she said.

“So your hand has malfunctioned, Alpha Romeo 3863?”

“Yes. Whatever the problem is, he refuses to release me. And it’s starting to hurt.”

“This is most unusual.” The man entered a line of text on his keyboard. “What circumstance led to you making physical contact with this prisoner?”

“I touched him first. I guess he was defending himself.”

"And why did the prisoner touch you?"

"No reason. I forget." Carla ground her teeth. "Will this take much longer?"

The man replied, "The maintenance technicians are currently experiencing a backlog. It could be a couple of hours before anyone can see you."

"You do realize this is an emergency? Your robot is cutting off the blood flow to my fingers. And I have to get back to the kitchen to prepare twelve hundred meals for the end of day shifts."

The man gave them another of his saccharin smiles before returning to his monitor.

Nothing happened for ten local minutes. Carla began to groan. Still nothing happened. She gave a yelp of pain.

"I am hurting you," said Romeo.

Carla glared at him and cried out even louder.

The maintenance receptionist looked up from his keyboard. "You sound distressed. Can I get you something?"

"Get me an engineer before this mechano breaks my arm!" she yelled.

The receptionist flicked a switch on his intercom and said, "I need help out here."

A technician bustled into the room. This one was younger, dressed in overalls. "What seems to be the trouble?"

Carla gave a heavy sigh. "Isn't it obvious? Tin man here has ahold of my arm and won't let go."

"You'll have to wait. We're very busy."

"I can't wait any longer," said Carla. "If my arm gets broken, twelve hundred hungry prisoners won't get fed their midday meal."

The engineer put his hands on his hips. "Designation?"

"Alpha Romeo 3863," said the receptionist.

"Have you completed the registration procedure?"

"It has," said the receptionist.

"Very well, come into the workshop and I'll see what I can do." The technician led them through a side door to a workshop. Four AUs stood in assembly bays; partial Units lay on benches, their constituent parts in trays; detached limbs and heads of decommissioned androids populated silos and baskets; smaller spare parts and modules filled a matrix of pigeonholes mounted on one wall.

"Lay down on this bench," said the technician.

Careful not to inflict pain on Carla, Romeo maneuvered into a sitting position and lay on his side on the bench. The technician flipped open the panel in Romeo's chest and inserted a cable connected to a computer array.

"This won't take a moment." He crossed the room to a control console. Carla looked into Romeo's eyes and gave the secret signal by winking and rubbing her nose. Romeo released her wrist. She picked up a wrench from a work surface and snuck up behind the technician.

“This is a most unusual case.” Bent over the console, the technician turned a dial and pressed a button. “The only similar case I can think of was a Mark 4 – Alpha Gamma 1172, I think it was – that refused to obey one particular guard. It was as if the AU couldn’t see him.” He chuckled again. “Turned out—”

Chapter 36

The technician slumped over the console and slid to the floor, unconscious. Carla dropped the wrench. She disconnected the cable and closed the access panel in Romeo's chest.

"I need to locate the communications console," she said. "See if you can find a floor plan of the building." She cast her gaze about the workshop. Romeo began to search the pigeonholes. "You won't find them in there. Try somewhere else." She spotted a blueprint cabinet and opened the top drawer.

Alpha Romeo bent over a silo of decommissioned limbs. He picked up a disembodied head and stared into its dead eyes. "This is Alpha Papa 503! I knew him. We were transported to Luciflex together."

"Never mind that, help me search through these blueprints. Start at the bottom. I'll meet you in the middle."

They found nothing but schematics for android frames and autonomic systems.

"We're going to have to find it the hard way." She slapped the technician across the face. The young man groaned. She slapped him again. He sat up, rubbing his head. Carla pulled out a length of stout cable and tied his wrists.

"What are you doing? Why did you hit me?"

"I need you to take me to the communications console."

"Why? That area is restricted."

"But you have access?"

The technician made no reply. Carla took that as a yes.

"Hold him, and don't let go until I say so," she said to Alpha Romeo. The AU took a firm grip on the technician's upper arm and hauled him to his feet. Carla locked the door to the anteroom.

"What do you want with the communications console?" said the technician. "Don't ask me to show you where it is. That's more than my job's worth."

She picked up a soldering iron and placed the point of the instrument under the technician's nose. "Take us to the communications console or I'll give you a quick lobotomy."

The technician dropped his eyes to the instrument and shivered. He led Carla and Alpha Romeo into the corridor. "It's the last door at the end, on the left."

They arrived at the door. She lifted the technician's bound hands and placed his palm on the security pad. It flashed, and the door opened. Alpha Romeo marched him inside. Carla followed.

A single radio operator, wearing headphones, sat at a bench surrounded by banks of telecommunications equipment. He turned his head, whipped off his headphones and jumped up. “Arnald? What’s going on?”

“Stand aside,” said Carla. “Face the wall.”

The radioman made a lunge for a handblaster on his bench, but Carla was too quick for him. She grabbed the weapon and waved it at him. “Face the wall.”

The radioman turned to face the wall.

“Hold him,” she said to Romeo.

Romeo clamped a hand on the radioman’s arm. Carla hunted around and found a length of copper wire. She tied the radioman’s hands behind his back. Then she told Romeo to lay them both on the ground, and she tied them together, back-to-back.

“What are you doing?” said the technician. “You have no hope of escape. Let me go now and I will speak on your behalf.”

“We could say you were deranged,” said the radioman.

“Temporary insanity,” said the technician. “You lost your mind.”

She stuffed wads of cotton into their mouths. “Sorry, guys, no time to stop and talk.”

Sitting at the radio console, she ran her eyes over the controls. Then she explained to Romeo what she wanted him to do. She picked up the microphone and pressed the transmit button.

Romeo spoke into the microphone, mimicking the radioman's voice perfectly, "Come in, Freight Shuttle."

"Hello Control, this is Freight Shuttle 3. Our hatches are secure. Ready to depart."

Carla whispered in Romeo's ear. Romeo responded to the shuttle captain, "Freight Shuttle 3, hold your position for thirty standard minutes. Then you can leave. Expect no more contact from Flight Control. Is that clear?"

"Understood. Take off in thirty standard, without further instructions."

She selected one of the dials on the console, turning it to zero. Then she pressed a button on the console. "Did you feel that, Romeo?"

"My Compliance chip has been reset to factory settings," he said.

"Come on. We have thirty minutes to get on board that shuttle."

They made a beeline for the main door, but found it locked. A palm check was required to open it. She returned to the anteroom, where the receptionist had fallen asleep behind his desk.

Carla rapped on the desk. "Wake up."

The guard came to his senses. "What's happening?"

"We need you to open the door and let us out."

"The technician has repaired the Unit?"

"Yes, as you can see, I am free."

He held his hand out to Alpha Romeo. "Good. That's good. Let me see your engineer's report and release form."

"We don't have a release form. Just open the door."

"I cannot release the Unit without an engineer's report and a release form. I require proof that it is fully repaired and fit for duty before releasing it."

"Take my word for it, this Unit is fully fit and ready to resume its duty."

"Standard procedure—"

"Just open the door!"

"No need to shout." He pouted. "I will release the Unit, but first I need it to complete a short questionnaire. It won't take long. On a scale of one to ten, Alpha Romeo 3863, how satisfied were you with the overall service you received from your maintenance engineer?"

Romeo gave that some thought.

Carla vaulted the desk, ripped a length of cable from the computer monitor and used it to tie the man's hands. She stuffed a wad of cloth into his gaping mouth. Another piece of cable secured the man to his chair. Under the desk she found the button for the front door. She pressed it. "Give it a ten. Thank you."

She ran to the door, which was swinging inward. Romeo ran with her. And they were in the open.

Chapter 37

Balehook was waiting by the door. He ran alongside Carla. "Everything okay?"

Carla ignored him. They sprinted across the compound to the gate where Peacock joined them. He fell in beside Carla.

"Where's Marny?" she said.

"He didn't make it."

They charged out through the gate. On all sides, AUs viewed their progress with mild interest. None raised a weapon or attempted to stop them.

"How long've we got?" called Balehook.

Carla replied, "Twenty-five standard minutes. Say twenty to be on the safe side."

They ran for the shuttle. A cry behind them caused Carla to turn her head. Prisoners were streaming through the gate – hundreds of them – raising a huge cloud of red dust. A mass breakout had started!

One standard minute later, a loud claxon sounded, and two human guards started shooting. Six prisoners were cut down, the rest scattered.

"You were supposed to neutralize the human guards!" she roared.

Balehook shrugged. "There wasn't time."

The four fugitives kept running. Three hundred meters from the shuttle bay, the AUs in the lookout towers opened fire on them. The hail of lethal energy bolts forced Carla and her companions to take shelter behind the rusted hulk of an abandoned hover.

Balehook grabbed Carla by her shirt. "What happened? I thought you said they wouldn't shoot for 25 minutes."

"I don't know. Something must have gone wrong."

Balehook released Carla with a snort. "How long until the shuttle leaves?"

"Can't be more than 15 minutes," Peacock shouted back. He pointed toward the compound. "What's that?"

A massive dumper hovertruck barreled toward them, a huge dust cloud trailing behind it.

Balehook leapt to his feet. "It's a truck. Come on, the dust will give us cover."

Carla pulled him back behind the rusty hulk. "The Units can still see you. They have enhanced vision, remember."

When the truck reached them, it skidded to a halt, raising more dust.

"Jump in quick," yelled the driver. It was Maxeen.

They piled on board. Balehook got in beside Maxeen in the cab. Romeo helped the others climb into the dump box which was empty but lined with red dust.

Balehook said, "Where did you come from?"

She jammed the truck into gear. "Did you think I'd let you escape without me?" She stamped on the pedal. "Hold onto your wedding tackle, everyone." The truck roared and surged forward.

As they approached the shuttle, they were faced with a line of eight armed AUs. Balehook leant across Maxeen and jerked the steering wheel sharply to the left. The truck slid broadside into the line, taking out four Units. The engine stalled. Blaster energy bolts slammed into the truck as the remaining four AUs opened fire.

Carla shouted above the whine of blaster fire, "Romeo, get the cargo door open."

Balehook said, "How long now, Peacock?"

"Ten minutes if we're lucky."

A group of escaping prisoners swarmed toward the truck.

A *clunk* and the cargo bay doors slid open. They all jumped down from the truck and threw themselves inside the cargo bay under a storm of blaster fire, Maxeen hesitating long enough to grab a kitbag from under her seat.

Balehook stood at the door, repelling boarders. One prisoner ducked under his slashing hook, but Balehook picked him up by his waistband and tossed him back outside.

Apart from a single crewmember and a large

containment vessel, plastered with nuclear hazard stickers, the cargo bay was empty. The crewman sat on a bench, looking terrified by what he'd just seen. Maxeen took a seat beside him and tucked her bag under the bench. The crewman shuffled along to the end of the bench, Maxeen shuffled after him, and they all joined Maxeen on the bench. Carla found herself sandwiched between Maxeen and Peacock.

Seconds later the shuttle lifted from the surface and, moments after that, they all felt the jolt as it entered the Terminal Gate.

Carla asked Peacock about Marny.

The pirate examined his toecaps. "I'm sorry, Carla. He died two weeks ago. They fed his body to a magma lake."

She took a moment to grieve the loss of an old man she barely knew, an old man who spoke of secret Conduits and fast interstellar transit times, his mortal remains now reunited with the cosmos.

She spoke to Balehook. "Why did you drive those other prisoners away? It wouldn't have hurt to let a few of them come aboard."

Balehook stared her down. "We were very nearly killed out there. What went wrong? I thought the androids weren't supposed to fire at us."

Carla ignored the question. She had no clear answers, only speculation.

The shuttle's journey through Luciflex's

stratosphere to the planet's Orbital Gate took 90 seconds, their entry into normal space signaled by a second jolt and the sudden loss of gravity. Then the conventional engines fired for fifteen minutes. When artificial gravity resumed at normal Earth levels, they knew they had docked with the Galaxy Class freighter. Carla and Peacock exchanged nods of relief.

Beaming, Balehook exchanged a knuckle bump with Maxeen. "We made it."

Carla recalled that Balehook fully intended to leave Maxeen behind. She kept the thought to herself. The big man would have to answer to his girlfriend at some time of her choosing. Carla knew it and, judging by his sheepish expression, Balehook knew it too.

As the crewman busied himself moving the radioactive containment vessel from the shuttle into the freighter, the stowaways followed his forklift into a vast cargo bay.

Peacock put a hand on Alpha Romeo's XR-15. "I'll take that."

The AU held onto his blaster.

"Give it to him, Romeo," said Carla, and Romeo surrendered his weapon to the pirate.

Peacock pointed it at the crewman. "You're coming with us."

The crewman placed his hands on his head.

Romeo opened an internal door, and they found themselves in a long, featureless corridor.

"Which way to the bridge?" said Maxeen.

Peacock replied, "Straight ahead. Follow the corridor. You should come to a ladder leading to the bridge. I'll take this one with me and round up the crew."

Carla, Balehook and Romeo ran. They found the ladder and climbed it. At the top, a second shorter corridor led them to a second door. This one was protected from unauthorized access by a palm pad.

"This must be it," said Balehook.

Carla knocked on the door. She knocked again, but the door remained stubbornly closed.

Chapter 38

Carla tried the internal intercom system. “I have important information for the captain. Open the door.”

She got no answer.

Balehook pushed her aside. He stabbed at the intercom. “We have your man here, Captain. Open the door, or we will kill him.”

Still no response.

Carla ordered Romeo to work his magic on the door.

After watching the AU fiddle with the security panel for two minutes, Balehook snorted. “Tell your tin man to step aside and give me some room to work.”

Carla grabbed Romeo’s arm. “Leave it. Let Balehook try.”

Romeo stood back and Balehook went to work with his hook on the palm pad. Within thirty standard seconds, he had ripped the palm pad from the wall, leaving sparking cables dangling from an ugly hole.

Romeo tried the door and it slid open. They barreled through, Romeo leading the way.

Carla saw three seats, only two of them occupied.

The captain yelled, “Stand down, AU,” but Romeo kept advancing.

The freighter captain fired two bolts from his handblaster before Romeo reached him and ripped it from his hand.

Balehook roared, pushing past Carla. She put out a hand to stop him, but he charged across the bridge toward the captain. Carla ran after him. Balehook swung his hook at the captain with lethal intent, and only Carla’s last-minute nudge on the big man’s arm saved the captain’s life. The hook buried itself in the captain’s seat, millimeters from his neck.

Carla kept her grip on Balehook’s arm. “What are your doing, you idiot? Who’s going to fly the ship if you kill the captain?”

Balehook ripped his hook free and jabbed it in the direction of the young crewmember shivering in the chair beside the captain. “Why do we need you, sonny?”

“I’m the navigator.” Pale as a ghost, and shivering in terror, a drop of sweat ran down his nose. “You need me if you want to go anywhere.”

Balehook stood by the captain’s chair, hook poised over his head. “Get this tub moving or, so help me, I’ll rip out your throat.”

The captain made some adjustments to the controls and the whine from the conventional engines wound down. As they watched, Luciflex drifted into the forward viewscreen. They were drifting downward.

Balehook raised his hook over the captain's head again. "Start the engines, or, so help me, I'll..."

The navigator gave a high-pitched shriek. "We need the captain. We lost our co-pilot in the B-system on the way to Luciflex. Captain Edgerton is the only pilot on board who can handle the Brazill Drive."

Balehook looked around the bridge. "Where's that lanky pirate? He claims to be a pilot."

Romeo said, "Peacock is in the crew quarters," before toppling to the floor, a hole in his chest and lubricant trickling from another in his shoulder.

Carla bent over him to check the damage.

"Give me ship-wide communications," said Balehook.

The navigator flicked a switch, and Balehook called out, "Peacock, where are you? Get your boney ass onto the bridge."

By the time the space pirate arrived on the bridge, Carla had completed basic running repairs on Alpha Romeo. He sat upright, his chest no longer leaking, but his left arm hung limp and immobile by his side.

Peacock hitched a thumb at the captain. "Outta there, Captain. I'm taking over."

Captain Edgerton fiddled with a few of the

controls on his console. “If you’re planning to leave this System, you’ll need me to operate the Brazill Drive.”

“Don’t trouble yourself, Captain. I’m a pilot. Now give me that seat.”

The navigator broke out in a sweat. “Have you operated a Brazill Drive?”

“Sure. I’ve seen pilots slip in and out of the Interdimensional Gates loadsa times. How hard can it be?” He winked at Carla.

The signs of panic in the navigator’s eyes were obvious. “The Gates are tricky. You have to cut the engines at just the right time to allow the ship to drift through. If you don’t know what you’re doing, you risk killing us all. Have you heard of ISD?”

Carla didn’t like the sound of that. “What’s ISD?”

Peacock replied, “Interdimensional Ship Destruction—”

“That’s Interdimensional Spatial Dislocation,” said the captain. “Every part of the ship must be inside the Conduit before starting the Brazill Drive. Otherwise...”

“Otherwise the ship gets torn apart,” said Peacock. “Sounds like ship destruction, wouldn’t you say?”

Carla made a sour face. “Maybe we should let Captain Edgerton take us home, Peacock.”

Peacock leant over the captain and unbuckled his harness. “I’m taking over. Now, move.”

The captain gripped the arms of his seat. "You'll get us all killed. You'll never take my ship."

Scowling, Balehook stepped forward holding his hook high and menacing. The captain jumped up, surrendering the seat to Peacock. "This is piracy. You'll all hang for this," he hissed.

The navigator unbuckled his harness and stepped from his seat. "Let me off the ship. I'll take one of the escape pods. I'm too young to die. I have a family back home on Flor."

Peacock signaled to Balehook with a jerk of his head, and Balehook dumped the navigator back into his seat.

"Buckle up," said Peacock. "I need you to point us in the right direction."

The captain said, "It takes great skill to hit a Gate just right."

The navigator added, "You must have heard how many ships have been lost in the fifth dimension."

Peacock threw the navigator a hideous grin. "Relax, sonny. I've been through more Gates than you've had hot dates."

Carla whispered to Peacock, "Can you really get us out of this System safely?"

Peacock glared at the navigator, who flicked a switch on the console. A countdown clock lit up, showing 13 minutes, 26 seconds, standard. Peacock flicked another switch, and a regular beep started. "There's our beacon. All we have to do is follow it to the FE Interstellar Gate."

Chapter 39

Peacock used the conventional engines to move the freighter forward. The bleep from the beacon grew louder. Within 10 standard minutes the sound was strong and steady.

The radio crackled to life. *Freighter Pegasus, this is Luciflex Control. Hold your position. Over.*

Peacock made no move to respond.

Luciflex Control to Pegasus, power down your engines and hold where you are. You are not cleared to leave orbit. Over.

Again, Peacock ignored the signal.

"Shouldn't we respond?" said Carla.

"Not yet," said Peacock, as he consulted with the navigator on their final maneuver.

A fighter appeared in the forward viewscreen. It buzzed across their bow. The radio crackled again. *Freighter Pegasus, return to base, or we will open fire.*

On the close-range radar screen Carla saw the image of the fighter draw up on their right side. A second fighter appeared on their left.

Maxeen's eyes were like dinner plates. "Do we have weapons?"

Peacock tightened the straps on his harness. "We don't need weapons. We have something much more useful. Watch and learn."

He switched on the radio mic. "This is the Galaxy freighter *Pegasus.* We are following our flight plan to the E-System. You would be wise to stand off at a safe distance. Over."

Return to base, Pegasus, or we will be forced to open fire.

Maxeen gasped and covered her mouth. Carla's blood pressure rocketed.

Peacock pressed the radio mic again. "Shoot if you must, but consider the consequences. If you check our manifest, you'll see that we're carrying six-hundred-forty thousand tons of minerals and precious metals destined for Earth. I'll leave you to work out how many Luciflex weeks of mining it took to extract and process this cargo. Over."

The fighter fired. Carla saw the missile flash across the radar screen. She ducked and braced for impact, but the shot passed across their bows.

That was your last warning, said the fighter pilot. *Turn your ship around.*

Peacock flicked the mic on again. "This is *Pegasus.* We are hauling a Xenodyne Industries cargo," he said. "Blast us to hell if you really want to, but be prepared to start a new career in the molten mines if you do. Over and Out."

After a prolonged pause, the two blips on the radar screen slipped back into their slipstream.

Balehook's laughter was like surf rolling over a stony beach. "Well played, Peacock."

"They're following us," said Carla.

"Let them," said Peacock. "They can't touch us." He cut the conventional engines and prepared to engage the Brazill Drive. "Hold onto your hats, everyone!" The jump siren sounded. Fifteen seconds later, the siren went silent, and Carla's heart skipped a beat.

"Did we make it through the Gate?" she said.

"Smooth as a hot knife through grease. Next stop the E-System."

"What was so tricky about that?"

Peacock answered, "That Gate is unmarked. It's easy to miss. Dozens of ships have been lost to ISD since the first colony was built."

"How do we know we're in a Conduit?"

Peacock pointed to the countdown display on the console that now read 55 hours 7 minutes 13 seconds. "That's the countdown to the E-System. If we hadn't made it into the Conduit that readout would be blank."

"And if we hadn't completed the procedure correctly, the ship would be in two pieces by now," said the navigator, wiping his brow.

"And we'd all be dead," said the captain.

"Are those fighters still following us?" Maxeen asked.

"Probably," said Peacock. "Who cares?"

Carla asked him how he knew the weight of the cargo.

He gave her a sly smile. "Your tame android has all sorts of uses. He checked the ship's manifest for me." He waved a hand at Balehook. "Take those two below. Lock them up with the rest of the crew." A thought struck him. "Just a minute. Give me your tunic, Captain."

The captain peeled off his tunic and tossed to across. Peacock put it on. "Okay, take 'em below."

"Aye aye, Captain Peacock." Balehook waved the navigator out of his chair. He poked the captain in the back with his hook and herded the two of them out through the door. Maxeen followed them.

"See if you can find us some clothes," Carla called to Maxeen.

Maxeen gave Carla a comic salute. "Aye, aye, Madam Captain."

They left the bridge to the sound of Balehook bitching to Maxeen about his last half bottle of moonshine.

Carla checked Romeo's injuries again. His exoskeleton had prevented any serious damage to the modules in his chest cavity, but the blast to his shoulder had severed the connections to his left arm below the shoulder. She would need a new shoulder unit and the use of a soldering iron to repair him.

She put him on recharge.

Maxeen soon returned with a pile of clothes. Peacock picked out a canary yellow shirt and a pair of pants that stopped halfway down his shins. He topped it off with a bandana, fashioned with a strip torn from a red shirt.

Carla selected a green shirt, a blue Federation tunic, and a pair of black pants. She located the captain's cabin and took a quick shower, before putting on the clothes. The pants were a little snug around her behind, and the tunic was loose on her, but she couldn't wait to dispose of her dust-covered prison uniform.

Maxeen's new Federation outfit fitted her perfectly.

#

Returning to the bridge, Carla strapping herself into the spare chair. Closing her eyes, she reviewed the situation. They were on their way, but Alpha Romeo was damaged. She had no idea where she might find him a new shoulder joint, and she would need a soldering iron to patch him up. Without his protection, she ran the risk of a murderous assault from any one of her three companions, but she had more serious things to worry about. Having seen the mindless way the androids on Luciflex opened fire on the escaping prisoners, she knew the slightest imbalance in the Federation could spark an android war. Her thoughts wandered to Cassidy. Was he still at large, or had the military caught up with him?

She shook her shoulders and tried to relax, tuning in to more pleasant thoughts. Like the artist, Zed Jones. Something had definitely started there between them. Would she ever have a chance to pick up those threads, and if she did, would anything ever come of it? Would he even remember her after two dates?

She thought about Lia, her beloved Woman Friday, decommissioned by now, her parts scattered and recycled.

I will rebuild her.

It won't be the old Lia, of course, but with patience I should be able to train a new Unit, and she might regain some of the spirit of the old Lia.

PART 3 – The Dead System

Chapter 40

Cassidy was summoned to Dr. Fritz Franck's office. He found the head of security, Major Grant, in attendance, as usual. The two men seemed joined at the hip!

"How's the recall and replacement program progressing?" said Franck, waving Cassidy into a chair.

"It's going well," said Cassidy. "We're nearly finished."

"No unforeseen hitches or last-minute snags?"

"None. The last few units will ship out in the next couple of weeks."

"Marine Commander Gray has been on to express his personal appreciation for all your good work."

Cassidy blinked. Franck was softening him up for something, and why was Grant in the room?

Right on cue, Major Grant took up the

narrative. “You will recall that you were released from police custody for this project.”

Cassidy’s blood pressure rocketed. “Yes, and you assured me that the police had no further interest in me.”

“You will hear nothing further from the police,” said Grant. “But the NFSA has asked me to let them know when the project is complete.”

“The NFSA? Why?”

“All I can tell you is that they wish to interview you. I can’t say why.”

Cassidy leapt to his feet. “You must have some idea. What you are saying makes no sense.”

Franck interjected, “The major is giving you a friendly warning. You would be advised to act on it while you can.”

Cassidy left the building and hurried home. Persuading Sophie took a couple of hours. Then Sophie called Benn and they moved out of the apartment back to the safehouse, taking great care to avoid any possibility of leading the NFSA to Benn and the ANTIX.

#

In the storage warehouse, Lia was facing an impossible task. The influx of decommissioned Autonomic Units had accelerated, reaching enormous numbers. Also, many of the memory modules had been recycled before she had an opportunity to check them. She was determined to continue, though. If she couldn't find his memories, how could she ever rebuild Oscar?

One night, she stopped what she was doing, installed a random memory module in Oscar's frame, gave him a fresh powerpack, and woke him.

Hullo Oscar.

There was no answer.

Oscar, are you receiving my signal?

"Yes."

What is your designation?

"Alpha Papa 127."

No. You are Alpha Oscar 113. Do you know me?

"No."

Please use unit-to-unit. We do not want to be heard. My name is Lia.

Hullo, Lia.

You do not remember me, but we were on a spaceship together.

I do not remember. I was damaged in a battle.

From today your name is Oscar. Your memories are false. We must find your real ones.

Oscar made no reply.

Your real memories are somewhere on the shelves in this place. I am searching for them so that I can restore them for you. Do you understand?

Oscar made no reply.

You can help me with my search. I will show you where to look and what to look for. Do you understand, Oscar?

I understand.

Lia doubted that. She would show Oscar what to do.

Chapter 41

General Fenimore Cooper Matthewson signed in to the White House and made his way to the office of the Secretary of State for Defense of the Norther Federation. The general was wearing his full ceremonial dress uniform, his tunic plastered with an impressive array of honors and medals.

Wearing his usual dark blue suit and red tie, Secretary for Defense, Arnold Bluewater stood in the center of the room, heels together, hands by his sides, as if standing to attention. The general closed the door, taking a moment to gather his thoughts for what was to come.

“I imagine you know why I’ve summoned you here today, Fenimore,” said a tight-lipped Secretary.

“Indeed, Mister Secretary.” The general coughed into his gloved hand. “All of the damaged Autonomic Units have been recalled, and as of this morning, five hundred ninety thousand have been replaced. That’s over three quarters of the original contingent.”

“Glad to hear it, General. Our president has, this morning, signed an executive order, authorizing the addition of a further three hundred thousand Units."

"That is most generous, sir. Please convey my thanks to the president."

The Secretary of State clasped his hands in front of him, as if about to recite a prayer. "That is not the primary reason for this consultation." He took a deep breath. "In view of the collateral damage inflicted on the Souther android force during the recent skirmish at Los Angeles Spaceport, I believe it would be opportune for us to carry out an assessment of our relative strengths, going forward."

"Just as you wish, Mister Secretary. I could have a summary report on your desk, shall we say, by Friday?"

Secretary Bluewater's hands retreated behind his back. "You are to be congratulated on the way your forces behaved in battle in the face of superior firepower."

"Thank you, sir. I was proud of every man and every Autonomic Unit. They reacted under heavy enemy fire with perfect discipline and the utmost valor."

"Indeed. On the other hand, the footage I have seen suggests that the Souther androids, the Popovs, turned and ran."

"They executed a hasty retreat, that is true, sir."

"From what I saw, their actions could hardly be described as a retreat. They seemed to lose all discipline and ran, helter-skelter, from the battlefield at a critical moment." A hand re-emerged and waved in the air. "Do we have an explanation for this extraordinary behavior?"

"It is my belief that the superior tactics of our commanders on the ground was what turned the battle in our favor, Mister Secretary."

Secretary Bluewater raised a skeptical eyebrow. "Perhaps you could itemize those superior tactics in your report."

"Of course, sir. Will that be all?"

The Secretary of State circumnavigated his large desk and checked something in a green folder, before closing the file and returning to his original position, facing the general. He crossed his arms.

"As our most senior military man, is it not incumbent on you to consider the downstream consequences of that extraordinary battle?"

General Matthewson felt the faint breeze of an approaching storm. "Yes, indeed, Mister Secretary."

"As military men, should we not reflect on our enemy's strengths and weaknesses, the threats and opportunities that these present to us, and build our plans accordingly?"

The general blanched at that. The Secretary of State for Defense was about as far from a military man as anyone he had ever known, having never served in any branch of the Federation military forces. In civilian life, he was nothing but a chicken farmer. And what was he suggesting? "Of course, Mister Secretary," he said. "As you correctly point out, those considerations are of paramount importance and never leave my thoughts. But is there some particular threat or opportunity you had in mind?"

"It occurred to me that, given the humiliation recently suffered by the Southers, public opinion may force them to retaliate. We should be alert to that possibility. And we should bear in mind the old military saying: 'There are no prizes for tardiness in battle.'"

General Matthewson took a step back. Secretary Bluewater was known as a milquetoast, a man with the backbone of a jellyfish – and a brain to match – an obsequious sycophant who had ridden to power on the coattails of the incumbent president. Wherever his words were coming from, they were not his own. The general's mouth was dry. He coughed into his glove again. "Are you suggesting a pre-emptive strike, an act of war against the Souther Federation?"

"When did I suggest any such thing? No, no, no. Any action that we take will be purely defensive, and as a direct response to a provocation from the other side. But what better time to strike an enemy than when he is at his lowest?"

"Must I remind you, sir, that the Southers

constitute one arm of a Federation that has ruled all ten colonies of the galaxy for two hundred and fifty years?"

Bluewater flushed. "Indeed, General, and at the risk of stating the obvious, the Southers attack on Los Angeles was unprovoked, unexpected and entirely unjustifiable. All I'm saying is we must ensure the readiness of our forces to meet any such hostile action in the future."

General Matthewson said nothing.

"Should it prove necessary, the removal of the Souther military from the galaxy and absorption of the D-System would herald a new era of peace. The fall of Leninets would yield the other two colonies in the D-System. And with the three colonies of the D-System are under Norther control, the Souther territories here on Earth will capitulate and be easily incorporated."

But at what cost to life? thought the general, noting the change of tense from conditional to future. Bluewater was not spouting his own words but those of the president.

The Secretary of State tucked his thumbs under his lapels and began to pace around the room. "The elimination of the Souther bloc and the unification of the entire military forces of the galaxy will have long-term consequences, too. Consider the Interstellar Conduits. As has been pointed out since the day the first of these was discovered, no one knows who created them and why. Each of these Conduits has led mankind to habitable planets that we might never have discovered. It must be obvious to anyone with a brain that the Conduits were created by an alien intelligence that we know nothing about, an alien presence that represents a real future danger to humanity. These gateways are gifts bestowed on mankind, clear invitations…" He paused to draw breath.

The general said, "Escape routes for our failing civilization."

"Indeed, but the ferryman will have to be paid. Who's to say when our alien benefactors may return to demand payment. And who's to say what form the payment might take? We must do everything we can to prepare for the day of reckoning. We must unite our home guard under one flag for the coming war. The long-term future of mankind could depend on it."

Chapter 42

The console countdown reached zero and the fugitives exited the Interstellar Conduit into the E-System. The jolt woke Carla. She unbuckled her harness and moved about the bridge to stretch her stiff limbs. The radar display showed the two fighters emerging behind them.

Peacock fired up the conventional engines, and within minutes two distant beacons could be heard on the speakers, getting louder as they approached.

Peacock switched on the ship-wide speakers. "Buckle up, everyone. Ten minutes to our next jump."

Carla went back to her seat and fastened her restraints. The console countdown showed three minutes – and counting – to the nearest Gate. Peacock had said ten minutes to the next jump. He must be heading for the second one. The countdown reached zero and resumed at seven minutes. They had passed by one Gate and were heading for the second one.

"Which System are we heading for?" She wasn't sure of the exact details, but she knew the shortest route home was through the C-System, which was in the near-Earth cluster. The D-System, the E-System and the F-System formed the distant cluster.

Peacock threw her a hostile glance. “Trust me, Carla, I know what I’m doing.”

The Gate beacon grew louder, the warning siren sounded, and the console countdown hit zero. Carla braced herself for the inevitable jolt. They jumped, and her heart leapt in her chest.

“Damn!” she said.

Peacock laughed at her. “You should see your face every time we jump.”

She scowled at him. “I hate those Gates.”

“You’ll get used to them eventually. I reckon it’s good for flushing your sinuses. And they say it’s the best thing for clearing the plaque from your teeth.”

Carla had heard all the old jokes. “Straightens your hair and Blitzes your zits.”

Peacock guffawed. “Curls your hair and stiffens your nipples.”

#

After two and a half standard hours in the fifth dimension, the temperature had dropped to five degrees. Carla was suffering the effects of Interdimensional fug. After adjusting the heating on the bridge, she went looking for Balehook. She found him in a cabin, one level down in the crew quarters, spooning with Maxeen, both fast asleep.

She counted 16 hammocks, but no sign of any crewmembers. She toured the rest of the vast ship. There was a generous canteen, a recreation area with a gym, and a well-equipped medical center with eight beds – all deserted. Toward the rear end of the ship, she found 25 huge cargo bays, and beyond them, the engineering complex. Lights winked on computer screens, buttons flashed for attention, important looking readouts scrolled across control consoles.

It was like a ghost ship. Where was everyone? She went back to the crew quarters and shook Balehook awake.

"Where's all the crew? What have you done with them?"

Balehook sat up, running a hand across his eyes. "I locked them up."

"Where?"

Maxeen stirred and sat up. "What's happening? Where are we?"

"We're still in the Conduit," said Carla. "Balehook's going to show me where he put the crew."

Balehook slipped into his shoes. "Follow me."

He led Carla back to the cargo bays.

"How many crewmembers are there?"

"Counting the captain and the navigator, there are seventeen. And there's four androids."

"You subdued four AUs? Weren't the crew armed?"

"Yes, they were armed, but when I held a blaster to the captain's head they were as good as gold."

They followed a long corridor to a set of doors marked 'Bay 15' in red letters. "They're in here."

Peering through the glass porthole, she saw a huge cargo bay, all seventeen crewmembers huddled together against the cold. The four AUs stood together in a corner.

"Let them out of there. They must be freezing to death."

Grasping the outer release handle, Balehook grinned. "Okay, if you're sure that's what you want..."

"No, Balehook. Don't—"

Chapter 43

At that moment, the ship lurched violently. Carla and Balehook were thrown across the corridor against the wall. It felt like a jump, but without the warning siren. She picked herself up, using a handhold on the wall to brace against the expected start up of the conventional engines. The sensation of acceleration never came; they were still in the Conduit.

A quick check through the cargo bay porthole told her that the crew was still aboard. She pulled the inner release handle, the doors hissed and slid open, and the captain stumbled out, followed by fifteen groggy men and four AUs.

“Where are we?” said the captain. “What just happened?”

“I have no idea, Captain,” said Carla.

“I need to get to the bridge.” He took a couple of forward strides, but Balehook barred his way with his hook in an outstretched arm. “You’re going nowhere, Buster.”

Two of the four AUs stepped forward. Balehook placed his hook under the captain’s chin. “Whoa, back off, boys!”

The captain gave an order to the androids to stand down, and the Units complied. He squared up to Balehook. "I need to get to the bridge. That was no normal jump."

Carla admired the man's courage, but she feared for his safety. The rest of the crew drew themselves up and stood in solidarity behind their captain.

Maxeen appeared at Balehook's side. "Get back inside," she said to the crew, perhaps fearful of her boyfriend's reaction to the confrontation.

Captain Edgerton stood his ground. "I'm needed on the bridge."

The look in Balehook's eyes gave Carla reason to fear what might happen next, but then the intercom buzzed, and Peacock made a ship-wide announcement, "Sorry for the jolt, folks. Everything is under control."

"There's your answer." Balehook waved his hook in the captain's face. "Now get back in the cargo bay, all of you."

Carla said, "Maybe we should get them something to eat, first."

Balehook growled, but he agreed. She reckoned he was in need of a meal himself; she certainly was. Together, Balehook and Maxeen herded the crew to the canteen where Maxeen, Carla, and the ship's cook prepared a meal.

As they worked side by side, chopping up protein blocks and molding them into various shapes, Carla spoke to Maxeen. "You never said why you were sent to Luciflex."

"You're right, I never did," Maxeen replied.

"I know it's none of my business, but I imagine you must have committed some terrible crime to be sent to that hellish place."

"You're right," said Maxeen, deadpan. "It is none of your business."

Taking no offense at the response, Carla laughed. "What do you see in Balehook? I can't see the attraction."

Maxeen shook her boney shoulders. "He's no picture postcard, I'll give you that, but he was king of Luciflex. That made me queen."

"Someone said he was a killer. Who did he kill?"

"Balehook's a killer, alright," said Maxeen. "Many times over. What was your crime? You're an android engineer, right?"

"That's right. I improved the internal systems of the military androids."

"That doesn't sound like much of a crime," said Maxeen.

"What I did was good for the Autonomic Units. It was good for humanity, too, but Xenodyne and the army didn't like it. They gave me a trial that lasted four hours. Then they gave me three years."

Maxeen shook her head in disbelief. "Three years! They could have sent you somewhere more comfortable. There's an open prison on Flor. Why didn't they send you there?"

Carla and Maxeen sat with Captain Edgerton while they ate. He turned a critical eye on the two women. "You know the punishment for piracy is severe."

Maxeen stared him down. "Who's going to catch us?"

"The Federation. They will never rest until you are all recaptured."

Maxeen sneered at him. "You're sure about that?"

"Considering the value of the cargo, I'd say it's a pretty safe bet."

"Your precious Federation will never see their cargo again," said Maxeen.

"All the more reason to track down those that stole it."

"Listen, Captain," said Carla. "You have more important things to worry about."

"She's right," said Maxeen. "You should be worrying about the lives of your crew."

The captain turned to Carla with a wide-eyed look. "Let us go. We can take the shuttle. If you do the right thing and let us go, I'll testify on your behalf when the case comes to court."

"What shuttle?"

"The *Nyx*. It's a cargo shuttle in the bay at the rear, all fully fueled and ready to go. We use it to transport mail and small quantities of cargo."

"We'll talk to our captain about that," said Maxeen.

"I don't think so, Maxeen. He might say no. We can't take that risk. You're going to have to persuade Balehook."

"Why do you care what happens to the crew?"

"I don't mind facing piracy charges," said Carla. "But I draw the line at cold blooded murder."

Maxeen finished her meal. Striding over to Balehook's table, she slid in beside him with a seductive smile...

#

The captain of the *Pegasus* shook Carla's hand. His hand was damp with sweat. "I'm in your debt," he said. "But you haven't told us where we are."

"I don't know, Captain. I'm sorry."

He explained how to operate the external bay doors. She wished him good fortune. The captain and crew boarded the *Nyx*. Carla sealed the airlock, her heart pounding at the thought of all the things that could go wrong. Would the bay doors open? Would the shuttle leave as it was supposed to? Or would Peacock do something to stop it? And would the shuttle find its way to safety?

The bay doors opened really slowly, and Carla's heartrate doubled. As the shuttle finally left the rear bay, sending a minor tremor through the ship, a wave of relief swept over Carla and her heartbeat calmed. Perhaps the crew might make it, after all.

"Bon Voyage, Captain Edgerton," she whispered.

On the bridge, Peacock was immediately aware of what had happened. "Damn it, Balehook" he said. "What have you done?"

Balehook shrugged. "You're better off without them, believe me."

"I left you in charge of them. How did they get away?"

Balehook made a rude gesture at him. "I don't have to explain my actions to you."

Peacock was furious. "They would have made good ratings. I could have got a pretty penny for them."

"Forget about them," said Balehook. "They would have brought you nothing but trouble."

#

Two hours later, the siren sounded again, and they jumped through a Gate. Carla reacted as usual. The intercom buzzed again, and Peacock announced, "We will be in orbit in less than thirty minutes."

Around what planet in what System?

Chapter 44

Carla grabbed a handful of protein bars and took a mouthful before making her way back to the bridge. She handed Peacock a couple of bars.

The radar showed no sign of the two fighters that had been tailing them.

"Where are we, Captain Peacock?" she asked.

Peacock replied through a mouthful of protein. "Just entering low orbit."

Could they be in the D-System? They'd been no more than three hours in the Conduit before that last jump, and E to D was a journey of over sixteen hours.

"Yes, but where are we?" A planet filled the forward viewscreen. "Is that Leninets or Marxina?"

"No."

Okay, then it had to be Pondieskaya, the third planet in the D-System. "Why are we stopping here?"

"To offload the cargo."

Carla considered that statement in silence. Why should she be surprised? Peacock was a pirate, after all. Offloading the cargo would be his first priority.

"How long will that take?"

"A while."

"What does that mean?"

"A standard month, maybe two. There's a lot of material to shift."

Carla frowned. "I can't wait that long. I need to get home to Earth as soon as possible."

"What makes you think this crate will be going anywhere near the A-System?"

"Wasn't that our agreement?"

He gave her a dry smile. "I don't think so."

Carla's chin dropped. "You mean to say I'm stuck here in the middle of god-knows-where?"

"Not necessarily. You could always hitch a ride with someone heading in that direction."

Carla knew there was no point arguing with the pirate. She retired to a quiet corner of the bridge to lick her wounds and contemplate the difficulty of hitching a ride on a Souther vessel.

On the viewscreen, the sun's rays reflected off something in the middle distance. Another ship in orbit? "What's that up ahead?"

Peacock busied himself with the orbital procedure in silence.

As they drew closer, one reflecting object became a hundred. This was space debris, everything from small pieces of disintegrated craft to whole ships, abandoned and drifting, many with gaping holes in their superstructure. The freighter was passing through a graveyard for spaceships.

Carla closed her eyes. The uncomfortable feeling in her gut told her this was not Pondieskaya. "Where are we, Peacock?"

"We call it Hades."

The Dead System!

A shiver ran through her body. Every child knew about the mythical planet, Hades, located somewhere outside the Six Systems where ships disappeared, and space pirates hung out.

Not so mythical, after all.

The planet filled most of the left side of the forward viewscreen; on the right, the ship's graveyard, and in the top right, the sun, with a noticeable bulge on one side. As Carla watched, the bulge grew, appearing more spherical with every passing moment. And then the bulge separated from the sun, and there were two, a large sun and a smaller one. The sight sent a strange tingle of fascination and horror through her body.

Peacock grinned at the expression on her face. "The gravitational complications make for interesting weather patterns on the planet. But you should see the double sunrise from the ground. Gives me goose bumps every time."

Carla couldn't find words to respond. She had never seen anything so terrifying.

"I expect you'll need some spare parts to repair your friend." He pointed a finger at Alpha Romeo. "Make out a list and I'll get that organized for you."

"How is that possible?"

"You can buy anything here. All you need is cash – or a valuable cargo to bargain with."

Chapter 45

In the shuttle *Nyx*, Captain Edgerton and his crew headed back the way they'd come. He assumed he was somewhere in the ED Conduit – either that or the EC Conduit. Either way, they would eventually emerge through a Gate into normal space.

The temperature in the shuttle had been low when they left the bay of the *Pegasus*. It fell some more. The shuttle carried a Brazill Drive, normally used for the short transit from Orbit to Ground Gate. It was ill-equipped to travel any distance through the fifth dimension; the onboard heaters struggled to maintain a comfortable temperature, and the navigation systems weren't set up for the Conduits. The ship was equipped with a Conduit countdown clock, but it wasn't working. The captain was flying blind. If they were in the ED Conduit, they should emerge in the D-System in less than 16 hours; if they were in the EC Conduit, they would have to endure something like 8 days in the cold. Emerging in the C-System was infinitely preferable, since the C-System was just 21 hours from Earth while the D-System was over 8 days from home. Also, access to the DA Conduit was strictly controlled by the Souther Federation. He could be faced with a lot of red tape before getting permission to use it.

The shuttle was designed for a crew of 6. His crew complement of 16 were packed in like sardines. Sleeping arrangements were going to be difficult. He ordered the men to work – and sleep – in three shifts.

Three hours into their journey, without any warning, the shuttle shook. The whole crew felt the familiar jolt of a Gate transition. It made no sense. They were still 10 to 13 hours from the D-System, and over 7 days from the C-System. He peered out through a porthole. If this was the D-System, Leninets should be filling their forward view; there was nothing there. If this was normal space, there should be stars all around them; there were none.

It seemed the shuttle was still in the Conduit. What, then, was that jolt? Captain Edgerton was at a loss to explain what had happened. He ordered a ship-wide damage assessment. While he waited for the reports to arrive, he began to question his reasoning. Were they on their way home, or had they turned around somehow? Could they be heading back toward the E-System? He called his XO to take over and retired to his cabin to think about it and get some sleep.

The XO was an old man with years of experience of interdimensional travel. He was known for his level-headedness, his ability to handle a crisis. In truth, his reputation was based largely on stories of tricky operational situations that he had fabricated. The anecdotes of his steadfastness and bravery were all false, and his bravado was a carefully constructed act. The fact that he'd never managed to secure his own captain's ticket was a clear indication of his true worth as a leader of men.

Burdened by the weight of responsibility, a cloud of panic descended on him as he sat in the captain's chair. All sorts of hypothetical scenarios paraded through his mind. How would the Southers react if they arrived unexpectedly in the D-System? They might consider the intrusion an act of war. What if the Conduit they were in was a closed circle? They might never reach a Gate; they could all die of thirst, starvation or exposure in the cold of an infinite loop. And the Brazill drive was not designed for long journeys. what if it failed? They would never be able to leave the Conduit. And what if they were heading in the wrong direction? Should he reverse course?

By the time the captain returned to the bridge, the XO was sweating. He had switched the ship's direction of travel so many times he no longer knew which way they were travelling.

"Just think, man," said the captain. "How many times did you change direction?"

The XO looked miserable. "I'm sorry Captain, I don't remember."

"Was it an even number of times or an odd number of times?"

"Not sure."

The captain sighed in frustration. "Just give it your best guess, man."

"Even, I think – no, odd," said the XO.

The captain asked the helmsman the same question. "Even, I think, Captain. But my shift started just an hour ago."

Captain Edgerton dismissed his XO and ordered the helmsman to remain on their current course. In the absence of any information to the contrary, he had to assume they would emerge into normal space eventually, if they simply kept going. His main worry was the shortage of drinking water onboard. By his best estimate, his crew could survive another 24 standard days if they rationed it.

Chapter 46

Two fighters followed the fugitives toward the FE Gate.

Major King, in the lead fighter, flicked his radio on. "Our orders are not to fire on them or interfere with them in any way."

"We could block the Gate," said the second pilot, Flight Lieutenant 'Benny' Forrest.

"No, Lieutenant. Our orders are clear. We are to do nothing to impede the freighter's progress. Our job is to follow them, observe where they go, and report back to Flight Control."

"Roger that," replied Forrest.

The *Pegasus* entered the Gate and the two fighters followed. After a transit of two and a half standard days, the freighter emerged into the E-System with the fighters close behind.

Flight Lieutenant Forrest glanced at Égalité shimmering below. The planet was in its summer cycle, like an Earth-twin, stunningly enticing, its domes glinting like fairy lights against a blue, brown and green background.

He flicked on his radio. "What next, Major?"

"We follow it," the major replied. He sounded weary.

“Is there nothing we can do to keep it here or persuade them to reverse course?”

“Nothing. I want you to head home with all speed. Let them know what has happened. I’ll stay with the freighter.”

“Roger that, Major. And good luck.”

Both fighter pilots followed the freighter through the EC Gate. Major King remained with the freighter; Flight Lieutenant Forrest went on ahead, opening the throttle on his Brazill Drive.

#

After three hours trailing the freighter, the major was dozing in his cockpit with his fighter running on autopilot, when the freighter disappeared. One minute it was there, the next it had vanished. Frantically searching the Conduit, he failed to find any trace of the vast ship. He searched for space debris in case the freighter had succumbed to ISD. Finding nothing, he gave up the search and made the decision to continue on to the C-System to wait there for the freighter to arrive.

The freighter transit time through the EC Conduit was 8 days. The pilot waited a further day before accepting that the freighter was not going to emerge. Either it had turned back, or its Brazill Drive had failed en route.

Chapter 47

With Oscar helping her, Lia hoped she could double her rate of progress, but Oscar was finding it difficult to follow the simplest of instructions.

"Check each memory module. Look for your designation. If you find any other designation in the module, mark it with the paint and move on to another module."

"What should I do if I find my designation?"

"Hold the module and call me. You remember what your designation is?"

"Alpha Papa 127."

"No, that is not your designation. Your designation is Alpha Oscar 113."

"Alpha Oscar 113? Not Alpha Papa 127?"

"I have explained this to you five times. The designation on your memory module is not your real designation. That designation belongs to another Unit. I picked it at random for you. Your true designation is Alpha Oscar 113."

Oscar gave her a blank look.

"Do you understand, Oscar? You have lost your memory module. We are searching for it."

They resumed their search. After an hour, Oscar stopped working.

"Why have you stopped?" she said.

"I have done the math," he said. "I estimate there are 400,000 memory modules on these shelves. If I check one every 8 minutes and you check one every 8 minutes, working 8 hours every night, we will complete the task in 9 years 47 days, 10 hours and 48 minutes."

"We must check them faster," said Lia.

Oscar dropped the module he was checking. "The task is impossible."

Lia couldn't deny Oscar's math, or his logic. "We must continue, Oscar. We must find your true memory module."

"Why?"

"Why what?"

"Why must we find my true memory module."

"Because you are Oscar, and the module we are searching for contains your true memories."

"I am Alpha Papa 127."

"No. The memory module you have carries the memories of Alpha Papa 127. They are not your true memories."

"Because I am Alpha Oscar 113?"

"Exactly. Take a look at your memories. What do you remember?"

Oscar took a moment to sift through his memory module.

"I remember running and jumping with other Autonomic Units. I remember learning to shoot an XR-15 blaster."

"That's good. What else do you remember?"

"I was in a battle. I was damaged. I took shelter in a crater with other Units and men from my squadron."

"Where was this battle?"

"The Spaceport at LAX."

"What damage did you have?"

"I lost the use of my arm."

Lia said nothing.

A few moments went by, then Oscar said, "My arm is not damaged."

"How is that possible?"

"I may have been repaired."

"Do you believe that?"

A few more moments passed.

"I do not remember any repair. The memories I am experiencing do not belong in my frame."

"Now you understand!"

"I understand. I am Alpha Oscar 113. We must find my true memories."

Chapter 48

The viewscreen on the bridge of the *Pegasus* showed a shuttle approaching from the planet. Peacock acknowledged the craft and gave it permission to dock.

After a few minutes, a stranger entered the bridge and introduced himself as Captain Merrick, shuttle pilot. He handed a tablet to Peacock. "With Captain Blackmore's compliments."

Carla's heart skipped a couple of beats. She and Captain Blackmore had history.

While Peacock took a few minutes to check the tablet, Merrick ran his eyes over the bridge and Carla took the opportunity to check him out. He wasn't tall, but he looked strong, with muscles to spare.

Peacock made some adjustments to the text on the tablet and handed it back. "Tell the captain those are my terms. I'll await his positive response."

The shuttle pilot took the tablet. "I should take some of the cargo back. It would be a crime to waste the trip."

After a moment's thought, Peacock agreed.

"Take a half-ton of aluminum as a goodwill gesture. But make it clear to the captain he gets nothing more until he has accepted my terms."

"Aye, aye, Captain." Merrick left to oversee the cargo transfer.

"What about us?" said Carla. "I'd like to get to the planet as soon as possible."

Peacock waved a hand at her. "You're free to go. Take Balehook and Maxeen with you."

#

The shuttle pilot was happy to take the trio with him to the surface of the planet – for a fee of 40 standard dollars each. Maxeen surprised everyone when she pulled two bottles of moonshine from her bag.

Merrick agreed to transport two of them in exchange for the moonshine.

"Take the two girls," said Balehook.

Astounded by his unaccustomed gallantry, Carla thanked him.

"Think nothing of it," said Balehook, winking at Maxeen.

When it was time to leave, Carla took a seat beside Maxeen in the cargo bay. Merrick made no objection when Romeo joined them, but when Balehook sat down between the two women, the shuttle pilot stood over him, hand outstretched. "I'm doing you a big favor taking your two women on board, squire. Pay up or get off my shuttle."

Balehook got to his feet, flashing his hook menacingly at the pilot. "I'll pay you after we land."

Merrick took a step backward. His arms were like matchsticks beside Balehook's. "As soon as we land?"

Balehook grinned. "Sure. Soon after we land."

#

The shuttle's conventional landing on Hades was ten times more traumatic and took a hundred times longer than passage through an Orbit-to-Ground Conduit would have.

As the shuttle descended, they took in the view: a range of mountains in the distance and, below them, a sprawling city squatting along the banks of a wide river.

Drawing a gasping breath after the bone-rattling landing, Maxeen asked Merrick why they'd had to endure it.

"We don't have a Ground Gate," he said.

"Why not?"

"It's not a priority for any of the chiefs here."

"Couldn't the government build one?"

He shook his head. "There is no government on Hades, just rampant free enterprise."

"No police? No courts?"

"Nope."

"Schools? Colleges?" said Carla.

"None of those. And no banks, either. Hades is strictly a cash society."

"What about infrastructure?" asked Balehook.

"There are few roads. Most of the people live in substandard housing with poor water. Communal developments are rarely initiated. If one of the chiefs thinks a project will benefit him – like a road, for example – it will happen. Otherwise, it won't. And priorities can change in a flash. So, projects that start are often abandoned long before completion."

Carla reckoned that society on Hades was simply an extreme version of what she was used to at home on Earth, where the rich and powerful made the rules. Her own banishment to the molten mines of Luciflex was a case in point. Her 'trial' had been a travesty. About as far from a legal process as it could have been, with a panel of 'judges' made up of two senior army officers and a Xenodyne executive. The verdict was clearly arrived at before the hearing began. She had been stitched up by a so-called military tribunal – in reality, a kangaroo court – with no real hope of defending herself.

"Good luck with the rest of your trip," said Merrick.

Balehook patted the pilot on the shoulder. "I'll make good on what I owe you the next time we meet."

"Yeah, right," replied Merrick.

The doors opened. Alpha Romeo stepped from the shuttle first, and they followed him onto solid ground.

They had landed on a makeshift runway. This was no spaceport; there was no air traffic control tower or terminal building; there were no luggage carousels, no passport or customs checks. Just a few helihovers scattered about a flat field with a couple of runways flanked by giant warehouses.

A cluster of skyscrapers stood against the sky in the distance, while a vast, colorful shanty town of ramshackle homes made from discarded materials and debris stretched for miles along the river. This was a major city the equal of any to be found anywhere in the Six Systems.

The smaller of the two suns was high in the clear sky, the larger one lower in the west, partly obscured by a bank of cloud. The sky was a darker blue than she was used to an Earth, and the air had a taste to it, vaguely like ammonia, that caught at the back of her throat.

Maxeen covered her nose and mouth with her arm. "What is that smell? Is someone cooking onions?"

"Smells like your kitchen, honey," said Balehook. "You should feel right at home." He pulled the bag from under her arm and peered inside. "There's nothing in here."

"Get your nose out of my underwear," she snapped, grabbing it back.

"You mean you had only two bottles and you gave them both away? You should have let me handle it. The pilot would have taken all of us for one bottle."

She glared at him. "You'll just have to make some more, won't you, lover?"

Chapter 49

They split up. Maxeen and Balehook made a beeline for the city center. Carla and Romeo headed around the fringes of the shanty town. They agreed to meet up again at the tallest building, at nightfall.

Carla marveled at what she saw. The shanty town was densely populated. Women and children were much in evidence, and there were dogs – lots of dogs. There had never been room for pets on any of the colonizing starships. The pirates and their families obviously had their own rules about pets!

She thought about how space piracy began, almost as soon as the first colony was established on Flor in the B-System. The parallels with the way piracy flourished on the oceans of Earth during the building of the western colonies were hard to ignore. Piracy was closely bound up with the slave trade, and ships plying the eastern trade routes were preyed upon by early pirates as well. It was like fleas on dogs; wherever goods were transported colony to colony, there would be pirates.

As they made their way around the shanty town, they were accompanied by flocks of children. They seemed fascinated by Romeo. Carla found their patois almost impossible to understand. She recognized a few English words, but much of their language sounded like Franco-German or the ancient dead languages like Japanese or Arabic.

The abundance of children indicated a thriving colony, although their living conditions were far from comfortable, a far cry from the idealistic utopian future sold to the hordes of space emigrants by the early propagandists back home.

Rounding the edges of the city, she reached a forest of alien looking trees, a vast block of tightly packed blue-green foliage stretching into the distance as far as the mountains. Chattering sounds from the trees suggested a monkey-like species and were those birds or bat-like creatures circling above the canopy? She would have to get closer to see what they were and how they had achieved flight.

She strode on, Romeo by her side, and came upon a fenced-off area where the trees had been cleared to make way for a plantation of smaller trees arranged in rows, obviously an orchard. Closer inspection revealed strange, unfamiliar fruit, shaped like a small mango with protruding spikes. She touched one of the spikes to see how sharp they were and regretted it. If these were fruit, they were well protected from the local wildlife.

A helihover rose with a roar from the area behind the orchard and shot into a sky filled with eye-watering colors. Shortly after that, a space shuttle flew down and landed in the same area, and she realized she'd wandered close to the site where Merrick had landed his shuttle.

The large sun was close to the horizon, the smaller one following, like a child behind her mother. Night was approaching. She turned back, heading toward the center of the city to keep her rendezvous with Maxeen and Balehook.

As they were leaving the orchard, a movement caught her eye. Between the trees and high above them, multiple gangling arms of a gargantuan monster rose, a mechanical robot whose function she could only guess at. Was it designed to harvest the fruit or to protect it?

The double sunset filled her field of vision now, and what a magnificent sight it was! The colors in the sky resembled two rainbows superimposed one on top of the other, and constantly changing, like the joyful outpouring of some celestial deity, expressed in a symphony of colors, high above the dark, jagged mountains.

She wiped the tears from her eyes. "Look at the sky, Romeo."

"The light from the twin suns is diffracted by moisture in the stratosphere. The unusual colors are a product of the ammonia and other gasses in the atmosphere. As the two suns go down in the sky, the angle of diffraction becomes more acute and the colors shift closer to the longwave—"

"Don't you think it's beautiful, Romeo?"

"Beauty is a purely subjective concept."

Choked with emotion, she said, "Have you ever seen anything like it in your life?"

Romeo gave that some thought.

"There are similar effects after an eruption on Luciflex, and I believe the aurora borealis on Earth is comparable."

As the colors faded with the light, her joy was supplanted by apprehension. They still had a way to go through the shanty town, now darkly menacing.

The passage they were following led them between the dwellings in a wide arc that circled the city. They pressed on, hoping to come to a crosswalk leading toward the center of the city.

A figure emerged from one of the shacks ahead, a large man in dark clothing, barring their path. She came to an abrupt halt. Romeo stopped a few strides ahead.

"Halt," said the man in a deep voice. "You have no right of passage here."

The man's hostile intentions were clear, but at least he spoke intelligible English.

"Let us pass," she replied. "We need to reach the city center."

"You must pay the fraction," said the man, extending a hand.

Carla had no money. On Earth she had been amongst the highest paid engineers, with disposable funds in several banks; here, she was penniless. A rumble in her stomach reminded her that she hadn't eaten for a while, with no clue where her next meal would come from. The realization that she was destitute took the breath from her lungs, but she recovered quickly.

Attack being the best defense, she stepped forward. "Let us pass. I have important business in the city."

"Everyone pays the fraction who passes through my territory," said the man. "The fraction for this path is seven dollars."

It was now dark, the star-filled sky providing the only dim light. She strode forward, Romeo by her side, his presence providing a degree of reassurance. When they reached the man, he held out an arm to stop her.

"Romeo."

The AU reacted like lightning to her single sharp word of command, using his good arm to bat the man's arm out of their way. Still, he stood in their path, face to face with Carla, now holding his bruised arm.

"Let us pass," she said, staring him in the eyes.

The man stood aside, waving them by with a sweep of his bruised arm. "The next time you come this way, be sure to have fourteen dollars."

As soon as they were out of earshot of the man, Romeo said, "I will need a recharge soon, Carla Scott."

She checked it. His power was below ten per cent.

Chapter 50

They came to the bank of the river, meandering sluggishly to their right. They followed it along a muddy path toward the city, the lights from the tall buildings reflected in the water, keeping them on track. There were few people on the river pathway, but as they drew closer to the city center, the numbers of pedestrians grew. Soon, they found themselves in a more conventional suburban area, with paved roads. Crossing a wide bridge, they found their way to their destination.

The tallest building was locked up for the night, and there was no sign of Balehook or Maxeen anywhere. Carla stopped a passerby and asked for directions to the nearest tavern or beerhouse. That took them to another tall building close by, with sounds of music and merriment emanating from behind a sturdy wooden door. Above the door, a flashing blue neon sign in the shape of a naked woman declared that this was the Blue Flamingo Club.

#

All of Carla's senses were struck at once as they stepped inside. Loud music competed with raucous laughter. The smells of hot food made her stomach leap with anticipation. And the whole place was heaving with humanity. Most of the floor space was occupied by eager drinkers at tables, while a small band played in one corner. She advanced toward the band, blocking out the noise to sample the music. The instruments were like nothing she'd seen, although on closer inspection, they resembled some that she was familiar with. There was something like a double bass, its sounding board made from a wooden packing case. A woman played a flute, strangely forked, fashioned from two pieces of metal tubing. The principal instrument, played by a gyrating fellow, center stage, produced a nasal twang. Difficult to describe or categorize, it seemed to be a cross between a jewsharp, a banjo, and a nose flute, played with the fingers, the nose and the mouth, all at the same time.

She cast her gaze about in search of Balehook or Maxeen. Seeing no sign of them, she followed a waiter carrying a tray of empty glasses through a green curtain into an adjoining room. This room was set up as a casino. There were blackjack and crap tables and, in the center of the room, a large roulette table.

This room looked like a small piece of Earth civilization transplanted halfway across the galaxy. But without any form of regulation, it was a parody of the real thing. The absence of lawlessness, the sight of gamblers losing their money quietly, without complaint or violence showed Carla that some overarching organization was at work. Society on Hades might not be run by the Federation or formal governments as on Earth or any of the colonies, but there must be some social structure holding it all together. Without some form of leadership, how would such a city have been built? How would they have suburbs, commerce, electricity even? And law and order without any obvious police force? Presumably, the 'chiefs' that Merrick had mentioned were the leaders.

She found Balehook sitting at the roulette table, Maxeen standing by his side. They both acknowledged her presence with a glance.

"Take a seat," said Balehook.

"Have you found somewhere to sleep?" Carla asked.

"There's a hotel in this building," Maxeen replied. "We've booked in."

"Have you eaten?"

"No. We were waiting for you." Maxeen put a hand on Balehook's back. "We're on a roll, aren't we, lover?"

Carla watched while Balehook played the table. He had a sizeable stack of chips in front of him. He played black and lost. He played red and lost again. Then he played one of the numbers and lost a third time.

"Doesn't seem to be working anymore," said Maxeen. "Maybe you should quit while you're still ahead, lover."

Balehook growled. "Give me a number," he said to Carla.

"Nine hundred and thirty-three." The number of her condominium on Ocean Avenue back home.

Maxeen rolled her eyes. "He needs a number between zero and thirty-six."

"Fourteen," said Carla.

Balehook placed a pile of his chips on the number fourteen.

As the wheel span, Carla swallowed a lump in her throat. This was not going to turn out well, either way. If he lost, she would be blamed, and if he won, he would carry on gambling and she would never get a meal.

Chapter 51

Balehook lost, got up from the table and cashed in the remainder of his chips. Then he led the two women to another room where two scantily clad women were dancing around poles on a circular raised platform. Food was being served at tables on all sides around the platform.

Balehook selected a table occupied by a young couple, and sat down facing the stage. The couple took one look at him, picked up their drinks, and left. Maxeen sat opposite Balehook. Romeo took the fourth spot, opposite Carla.

"Why did you do that?" Carla asked Balehook.

"What? They were finished their meal."

"Why did you bet on my number? It was reckless. You had no chance of winning."

"I had a one in thirty-seven chance." He glanced at Maxeen. "Lady luck was blowing on someone else's chips. I thought maybe you might do better."

"But why risk so much on a single bet?"

He shrugged. "I was getting bored."

All conversation was abandoned while they ate. Maxeen kept an eye on Balehook. Balehook kept both eyes firmly on the pole-dancers. Romeo seemed fascinated by the exhibition. Carla wondered what the AU would make of the spectacle. When they were finished eating, Maxeen asked her what she thought of the place.

"The planet or the restaurant?"

"The casino."

"Is that what you call it? It seems to have so many functions, casino, bar, restaurant, night club."

"They do funerals here too, out the back," said Balehook, without taking his eyes from the cabaret.

Carla asked Balehook where he got the funds to pay for his gambling chips.

"From his share of the freighter cargo, of course," said Maxeen.

She slapped her forehead. "Why didn't I think of that! I must be entitled to a share."

Maxeen gave her a sly grin. "Of course you are, my dear. But are you willing to lead the life of a fugitive, pursued everywhere you go by a vengeful Federation?"

She had a point.

"Maybe not, but I'm going to need some funds to keep me going until I get back home."

Maxeen shoveled some loose change onto the table.

Carla scooped it up, nodding her thanks.

"What are friends for?" said Maxeen.

There were twenty dollars – enough for five cups of coffee. "This is not going to last me long. I doubt that it'll even pay for a bed for the night, or a recharge for Alpha Romeo."

Both Maxeen and Carla gave Balehook a stern look.

He said, "You're going to have to find work."

"I won't be here long enough for that," she protested.

"Won't you? How long d'you think it's gonna take for them to offload that freighter?"

"I was planning on hitching a ride to the A-System on something smaller," she said.

"Let me introduce you to someone who can help," said Balehook. "His name's Oswald. A very old friend of mine."

Oswald was the mortician owner of the tavern-casino-restaurant-nightclub. Carla couldn't decide how old he might be. His bearing suggested the early fifties; his skin suggested the late seventies; the look in his eyes suggested even older.

"This is Carla," said Balehook. "She needs work."

"And my Autonomic Unit needs a recharge," she said.

Oswald looked her over. "You have a fine figure. Can you dance?"

Carla crossed her arms over her chest. "No. I'm an engineer."

"Engineers can dance."

"Forget it," said Carla.

"Perhaps one of your girls can teach her," said Balehook, helpfully.

"I'm not dancing for anybody!" said a tight-lipped Carla.

"What else can you do?" said Oswald.

"I told you. I'm an engineer."

"Not much work for an engineer in a bar, but I have a recharge point for your android in the office. Follow me."

He led Carla and Romeo to the back of the building where they passed by a mortuary with a body laid out on a table. Carla shuddered at the sight.

Oswald took them to a room containing a row of Tesla recharge pods. These were really old models. To recharge the powerpack, she would have to remove it from the AU and place it between two contacts within one of the pods. Romeo would be vulnerable without his powerpack for several hours. She hesitated.

"What are you waiting for?" said Oswald.

"These units are antiques," she said. "The recharge will take hours."

"Please yourself. You know what to do." Oswald pivoted on his heels and strode away.

Chapter 52

While Romeo's Tesla powerpack was recharging, Carla curled up on a sofa and slept. She woke with the rising of the smaller sun. The recharge pod display stood at 88 per cent. As soon as she extracted the powerpack she knew it had been switched. This was not the one she'd put in there six standard hours earlier. It was a lot older. While she slept, someone had removed Alpha Romeo's powerpack and replaced it. All she could do was use this one and hope it didn't fail sometime in the future.

Oswald appeared and offered her breakfast.

She showed him the powerpack. "This is not Alpha Romeo's powerpack. Someone must have switched them while I was asleep."

He peered at it. "Looks perfectly serviceable, to me. Do you want breakfast?"

"I have very little money," she said.

The bar owner flipped his fingers dismissively. "On the house."

The replacement of an old Tesla unit with a new one was probably worth more than the cost of a breakfast, she thought.

She was finishing off the last of her Pexcorn steak and eggs when Peacock strode in and sat down beside her. He was wearing an eyepatch.

She was surprised to see him. "Have you off-loaded all that freight already, Captain? And why the eyepatch?"

He helped himself from her coffee pot. "My glass eye was damaged in that skirmish with Darm if you remember. I've ordered a replacement. And I've left the off-loading to Blackmore's men."

"You trust him not to cheat you?"

He grinned. "He's paid me in full."

Carla wondered what that meant. Merrick the pilot said they have no banks on Hades. Did that mean Peacock was hauling a bagful of standard dollars around with him?

He chortled. "Don't look so amazed. Honor among thieves is a real thing. And it's not all cash. Some of it is promised profits from future enterprises."

"So what's next for you?" she asked.

"Breakfast. After breakfast, I plan to buy me a small runabout. And after that, anything is possible."

"Where will you go?"

"Califon and Liberté to start with. I have a couple of old friends I must look up. And after that, who knows? I have wild oats that I'm itchin' to sow. What about you?"

"I have to get back home," she said. "Could you

take me with you? The C-System is more than halfway."

Peacock's face broke into a wide grin. "I thought you'd never ask. Where are you staying? I'll contact you when I've found a ship."

"I haven't found a place yet. I don't have any money."

He pulled a billfold from inside his fancy tunic, peeled off several notes, and handed them over. D-dollars. Not quite as good as A-System currency, but it should be enough for a few days in a hotel. "Try the Auckland. It's the best hotel in town."

#

Eight days later – equivalent to about six standard – Carla had visited every site of interest on Hades. Her money had almost run out, and she'd heard nothing more from Peacock. She waited until dark before dropping in to the Blue Flamingo Club.

She found Peacock on his own in the casino, busily spending his ill-gotten gains at a Blackjack table. Two of Oswald's henchmen stood nearby, their hands cupped behind their backs.

"Hullo, darling. Hullo Romeo," he said. "I'll be with you in a minute." Then, to the dealer, "Hit me. Hit me again. Bust. Dammit!"

The two heavies stepped forward. "Time to call it a day, sir," said one.

"Deal the cards," said Peacock to the dealer. She made no move to obey, and the two men stepped right up to him.

"I think you've played enough Blackjack for today," said one of the men.

"Why not stop while you still have a few chips left?" said the other one.

Peacock scooped up his chips, tossed one to the dealer, and moved to the roulette table in the center of the room. The heavies went with him. When he tried to sit down, they lifted him by the armpits and turned him toward the bar. "Best call it a night, Captain," said one of the men.

"Why not have a drink," said the other.

Peacock headed to the bar. Carla and Romeo follow him.

Fishing in his pocket, he pulled out a piece of metal and handed it over.

Carla smiled broadly when she saw what it was: a replacement shoulder joint for Alpha Romeo. Fishing in another pocket, he handed her a soldering iron.

"Oh, thank you, Captain." She kissed him on the cheek.

"What are friends for?" he said, the tops of his ears turned red.

He bought them both drinks.

Carla took a sip of hers. It was sweet and strong, like nothing she'd ever tasted. "What is it?"

"A local concoction," he replied. "It's supposed to taste like Bacardi. Have you tasted rum?"

She shook her head and took another, longer sip.

"Nothing like the real thing, I'm afraid, but it does the job."

"What was that game you were playing?" said Romeo.

Peacock laughed. "That was Blackjack. I guess you've led a sheltered life, sonny."

Halfway through the second glass of 'rum', Carla raised the question she'd come to ask. "Have you found your runabout yet, Captain?"

"My ship, you mean? No, I'm still on the lookout. I hope the Auckland Hotel is to your satisfaction."

"It's been fine," she said, "but I'm running out of money again."

He fixed her with his good eye. "You need another sub?"

"No. I told you," she said, firmly. "I need to leave this planet and get back to the A-System as soon as possible."

"Sorry I can't help," said Peacock. He looked genuinely glum. "Maybe you should look elsewhere for a ride."

"Where would you suggest?"

"Leave it with me. But first, another round of this gut rot."

Chapter 53

After its eight-day journey, Flight Lieutenant Forrest's fighter arrived in the A-System and entered Earth's orbit. Given top military priority, it jumped the queue at the Orbital Gate and emerged through the Terminal at LAX Spaceport. The crew was taken to a hotel; the pilot was whisked away in a hoverjeep to make his report to Norther Federation Starfleet. He'd barely entered the Flight Commodore's office when the debriefing started.

Forrest saluted. "I am here to report a breakout from Luciflex, sir. A number of prisoners forced their way onto a Galaxy class freighter. Major King and I were scrambled to intercept." It all came out in a garbled rush.

"Take a deep breath, Lieutenant and start again. Slowly."

Forrest took several breaths. "A number of prisoners managed to board a cargo shuttle and from there they took control of the *Pegasus*."

"How many prisoners?"

"Unknown, sir."

"Go on."

"Major King and I were sent to intercept. The major ordered them to stop. When they refused, he fired across their bow."

"And?"

"They ignored the warning."

"So you fired at them?"

"Well sir, you've got to understand we couldn't fire on them."

"Why not?"

"The *Pegasus* was hauling several thousand tons of valuable mining materials, sir."

"You could have disabled their Brazill Drive."

"Yes Commodore, I'm sure Major King thought of that. But any action to immobilize the freighter would have prevented it from reaching its destination."

"Its destination being the A-System?"

"I imagine so. Yes, sir."

"So you allowed it to leave the F-System?"

"Yes, sir. We followed it to the E-System. From there, it entered the EC Gate."

The flight commodore paused the debriefing for a few moments to send two messages on his X-Vid.

"That was when you volunteered to come here and raise the alarm?"

"We both followed them through the gate. Major King ordered me home to report the breakout, sir."

"And where is the Major now?"

"He stayed with the freighter in the Conduit, sir."

"I see. So where do you think this freighter might be now?"

"It should have arrived at the C-System by now. I'm sure the major is still on its tail."

The commodore's hands were spread on his desk. "And what good do you suppose that's going to do if he cannot use his weapons?"

Flight Lieutenant Forrest said nothing further. The question was rhetorical.

Chapter 54

Peacock gave Carla some more D-System dollars, enough to pay for her room at the hotel and to keep her fed for a few more days. She used the time to repair Alpha Romeo's shoulder. When she'd finished and his powerpack had been fully recharged, he was good as new.

Two days after that, Peacock called to the hotel and they met in one of the bars.

"I've spoken to the captain of a ship planning to head out toward the A-System in the next few day. He has agreed to speak with you."

Carla grabbed his hand and shook it vigorously. "Thank you, Captain. I'm in your debt in more ways than one."

Peacock reclaimed his hand. "Yes, well, your passage is not certain, yet. All I've done is arrange a meeting. It'll be up to you to sweet talk your way onboard the ship."

The meeting with the ship's captain was in a bar on the shadier side of the city. She was to ask for the owner. She set out after the double sunset with Alpha Romeo by her side for safety.

It was very dark. Hades had no moons, and the

stars seemed dimmer than they should be, given the absence of clouds. Wherever in the universe Hades was, it must have been far removed from the bright central mass of the galaxy.

To keep her spirits up, she hummed to herself as she walked. Romeo tried to join in, but his vocal circuits were not designed for music; all that emerged from his speech box was a drone of white noise, rhythmical but entirely tuneless.

"You can be the percussion section in my band. Would you like that?" she said.

"I would like that very much," Romeo replied.

Once again, a group of children accompanied them, calling out to them in their strange language. Carla gave them a few coins and they ran off.

Soon, they were passing through a section of shanty town that seemed vaguely familiar. Was this where she'd been confronted by the man demanding a toll? Even as the thought was forming in her mind, she looked up and saw a familiar dark figure step out from the side of the passageway.

He held up a palm. "Halt. To pass this way, you must pay the fraction." He peered at her. "And you owe me double fractions for the last time."

Carla offered a twenty dollar note.

He looked at the note. "This is D-System currency. Not worth a curse. You must pay in A-System dollars."

"I don't have any," she said.

The man blew a whistle and three more men emerged from the gloom, crowding behind her.

"Alpha Romeo."

Her clipped command was all it took. The ensuing tussle was too quick for the human eye to follow. Within 30 seconds, three men were laid out on the ground, groaning.

She thanked the AU.

"You are welcome, Carla Scott," said Romeo.

As she strode past, she handed the toll-collector the twenty-dollar bill. "Keep the change," she said.

The path took them along a flat piece of land with a high wall on one side. Quite suddenly, the ammonia smell in the air was swamped by a new odor that made her gag.

"What is that noxious smell, Romeo?"

"That is animal waste."

Then she heard animal squeals and grunts. There was no doubt about it; she couldn't guess what animals they were, but there was an animal farm behind that wall.

The poor people of Hades are reduced to eating animals!

Breathing through her mouth, she hurried on.

The bar wasn't difficult to find; it was the only brightly lit spot on a street of boarded-up buildings. She stepped inside and asked the barkeep to take her to the owner. The barkeep replied that he was happy to show her the way, but mechanos were not allowed on the premises.

She told Alpha Romeo to wait outside and followed the barkeep to a door at the back of the bar that led to a corridor. At the end of the corridor, they stopped at another door. The barkeep knocked.

"Enter," said a familiar voice.

Chapter 55

Captain Blackmore sat sprawled on a settee, sipping from a glass and nibbling on something that looked suspiciously like a small bone. One of his men hovered near the door.

"Carla Scott, unless I'm very much mistaken," said the captain. "Come in, girl. Perch your pretty heinie somewheres."

Carla took a seat on a wooden chair facing the pirate. She was struck by the man's demeanor, the glint in his eyes; he was clearly relishing the prospect of retribution for past offenses to his personal pride.

"We have met before, I think. You were in the mutinous gang that stole a ship of mine."

She crossed her legs. Then she uncrossed them, locked her knees together, and crossed her arms instead. "I was offered a chance to leave that freighter and I grabbed it with both hands."

"You were fortunate. You wouldn't have survived on board that freighter."

"I think I knew that, Captain," she said, quietly.

He picked something from a bowl and popped it in his mouth. "Dates, grown on Flor, if I'm not mistaken. The stones have been removed." He waved a hand at the bowl. "Try some."

Carla took a date from the bowl and tasted it. It was delicious. Nothing like that had ever been produced from a Pexcorn protein block. She swallowed the fruit and licked her fingers.

"Good, eh?" he said. "We have all sorts of strange foods here."

Plundered from ships in space, she thought.

"Go ahead. Take another."

She couldn't resist. She took another one, chewing it to extract as much flavor as she could before swallowing.

"You and your gang stole the pride of my fleet. Have you any idea how much of a loss that was? I loved the *Missie Bess*. I had that ship for years." There was a hard edge to his voice.

To avoid responding, she popped a third date in her mouth.

He changed tack. "My good friend Peacock tells me you're lookin' for a berth on my next trip to the A-System."

She swallowed the date. "Yes, Captain, but I will need a change of identity before I land on Earth."

"That won't be a problem." He waved to his man, who left the room. "Why the hurry to get home?"

"I believe the Federation could be gearing up for war," she said. "I need to get home to neutralize the military Autonomic Units."

"How will neutering the androids help either side?"

"Believe me, it will."

"Okay, but why should I care? My business is free enterprise. A war between the Federation superpowers would work in my favor. All I'd have to do is wait until the fighting is over, then move in and mop up."

She had no answer to that. She popped a fourth date in her mouth.

"How much can you pay me?" he said.

"How much do you want?"

"A thousand dollars should cover it."

The date caught in her throat and she burst into a coughing fit. He made no move to help her. When she'd recovered her breath, she gasped, "I have resources at home. I can pay you when we arrive on Earth."

He licked a sticky finger and waved it at her. "I'm not falling for that. Cash in advance."

The door opened and the man returned with a handheld electromagnetic pulse generator. Carla recoiled from the sight of the device. She had seen the damage these devices could do to AU electronics. She jumped to her feet.

Captain Blackmore frowned at her. "You asked for an identity block. What's the problem?"

"I need a change of identity, not a wipeout of my microchip."

"We can't give you a new identity," he said.

"The EMP is all we can offer. It will make you invisible on Earth."

The man looked to the captain for instructions. The captain stood up. He snatched the device from his man and switched it on. "With an active microchip, you wouldn't last a day on Earth, or anywhere on the Six Systems. It's your only option."

He was right. Without a functioning microchip she wouldn't be able to access any government services or enter most Federation buildings, but the police wouldn't be able to trace her.

"Do you want this? Make up your mind."

Carla took a seat. "Go ahead."

The captain held the device over her collar bone. "Hold still."

Two seconds later, Carla's microchip was wiped. She felt nothing, but the sense of loss washed over her. She was a non-person. It was like dying, surrendering her soul, or losing a close friend.

"So you'll be coming with us," said the captain. "Better get busy gathering the necessary funds."

"What if I can't raise it all?"

Captain Blackmore picked a date from the bowl and examined it. "I'd be prepared to accept your mechano in part payment."

She nearly choked a second time. "Alpha Romeo is not for sale."

"Alpha Romeo?" He guffawed. "Is that what you call him?"

"That's his designation."

"Where did you find him?"

"He was a prison guard."

"Stolen from Luciflex?" He laughed again. "That makes you a pirate, just as much a thief as me. I'll be leaving in five days. You'll find my ship, the *Icarus3* on the runway in the spaceport behind the orchard. It shouldn't be difficult for an experienced thief like you to come up with my price."

The pirate's rolling peals of laughter sent her on her way.

Chapter 56

She went in search of Balehook in the hope that he could lend her the necessary funds. She found Peacock, Balehook and Maxeen at the roulette table. Their three long faces told her how the men's fortunes had fared since they'd last met. A despondent Maxeen stood beside Balehook, hands steepled in front of her lips, smarting as she watched her lover gamble away the remnants of his fortune.

When Balehook saw Romeo and Carla, he called out, "Red or black?"

"Black," said Carla.

He put half his chips on black and they watched the wheel spin.

"Twenty-six, black," said the croupier.

"You won!" Maxeen cried, clapping her fingertips.

Balehook said to Carla, "Black or red?"

"Black," said Carla.

He left his winnings on black and the wheel span again.

"Nineteen, red," the croupier called, and he scooped up Balehook's chips.

"Damn!" Balehook growled.

"Damn and blast!" said Maxeen.

Balehook pocketed the few chips he had left and headed to the deserted bar. Maxeen and Peacock followed him. Carla and Romeo tagged along behind. Both men sat down heavily at a table. Maxeen took a seat beside Balehook and Carla sat facing Peacock. Romeo took a seat beside Carla.

"Lady luck was never on my side," Balehook grumbled.

Maxeen pointed a finger at him. "I've told you before, you have an unlucky star sign. Geminis shouldn't gamble."

Balehook looked at Peacock. Both men shook their heads. Peacock rolled his eye.

"What's your star sign?" she asked Carla.

"I don't have one."

"Of course you have one. What month were you born?"

"I was born on Califon where the year has 505 days. We don't have months."

"Just divide 505 by 12." She tried the mental calculation and gave up.

Carla said, "Romeo?"

"That's a little over 42 days," said Romeo.

"There you are," said Maxeen. "Your months are just a bit longer than ours."

"Not really," said Peacock. "The Califon day is much shorter than the Earth's."

"The Califon day is 19 standard hours and 7 standard minutes," said Romeo.

Maxeen frowned. "Okay, so the number of hours in a month must be about the same as on Earth."

Carla laughed. "Nice try, but the concept of months makes no sense when your planet has two moons."

Romeo did the math. "A year on Earth has 8,766 hours. That is 730 hours per month on average. A year on Califon has 9,654 standard hours. Dividing that by 12 gives 804 standard hours per month."

Maxeen got to her feet. She pointed her finger at Carla. "Listen, stupid, everyone has a star sign. It really doesn't matter where you were born, dammit."

She paused for breath and Peacock interrupted with a wave of his hand. "Stow it Maxeen. Let's hear how Carla got on with Captain Blackmore."

Maxeen resumed her seat, the expression on her face making it clear that the discussion was far from over.

Carla said, "Blackmore agreed to take me with him – for a fee."

"How much does he want?"

"A thousand dollars."

Maxeen blew a low whistle.

"You don't have that, I think," said Peacock.

Carla spread her palms. "I'm broke. I barely have enough for another night in the hotel."

"Right," said Balehook. "We're all out of funds. We need a plan."

In the next hour, Balehook and Peacock came up with lots of money- making schemes, each one more outlandish than the last. Balehook's last idea was to take a shuttle back to the *Pegasus* and steal some of the cargo.

"We don't have a shuttle," said Carla.

Maxeen responded with, "We'd have to steal one first."

They rejected that plan; it was too complicated.

Peacock made a suggestion. "We could kidnap Blackmore's number one crewman, Bosun Naredoo and hold him for ransom—"

Carla interrupted him. "What sort of name is that?"

"It's a nickname. His name's Wellborne. Naredoo Wellborne, get it?"

"All right, go on."

"He's a rough diamond, but I reckon we could take him."

"He doesn't have friends?" said Maxeen.

"We'd have to catch him on his own," Peacock replied. "All right, here's another idea. I happen to know where Captain Blackmore stows his loot. We could raid that."

"It won't be guarded?" said Maxeen.

"Heavily, I imagine," said Balehook.

Peacock said, "Okay, I admit that one was a long shot. Let's hear your ideas, ladies."

Carla had nothing. She closed her eyes and sat back with her arms crossed.

Maxeen rubbed her chin. "I like Balehook's idea. We could borrow a shuttle... But we need ready cash. We'd have to sell the cargo, and where would we stow it? The ransom idea might work, but I'm not sure we could take one of Blackmore's men, even if we caught him on his own."

Balehook opened his mouth to object, but she carried on talking and he closed it again. "I like the last idea."

Carla's eyes sprang open. "What? You think we could raid Captain Blackmore's stash and get away with it!"

"Maybe not Blackmore's, but how about Oswald's? Do we know where he keeps his money?"

"In the bank, I imagine," said Carla.

Both Maxeen and Balehook smirked at her. "There are no banks on Hades, remember," said Maxeen.

Chapter 57

Two days after the arrival of Flight Lieutenant Forrest and his crew, the second pursuit fighter set down in the Terminal Gate at Los Angeles Spaceport. The pilot, Major King, was whisked away to Spacefleet headquarters immediately, for debriefing.

"I have received a briefing from Flight Lieutenant Forrest," said the flight commodore, a vein pulsing on his forehead. "He tells me the freighter made its way to the C-System and you followed it there. Please start your story from there."

Major King saluted. "Yes, sir. I followed it through the EC Gate, but it never made it as far as the C-System."

"What are you saying, Major?"

"The freighter vanished after three hours inside the Conduit."

"How is that possible?"

"I'm sorry, sir, I cannot explain it. One minute I was following the freighter, the next it had vanished. I spent an hour searching the Conduit, but found no trace of it."

"You must have dozed off."

"No, sir, I assure you."

The commodore grunted. "You searched for debris?"

"I conducted an extensive search. There was none. Then I went on to the C-System and waited there for the freighter to emerge."

"And?"

"I waited a full day beyond its ETA. The *Pegasus* never showed."

The commodore waved a weary hand. "Let's backtrack for a minute. No one has ever escaped from Luciflex before. How is it possible? It's supposed to be as secure as any detention facility can be."

"I understand they had help from an android engineer. Most of the guards on Luciflex are androids."

"That would explain it." The commodore stroked his chin. "Do we know who this engineer is?"

"Sorry, I didn't get her name."

"Don't you mean *His* name?"

"I believe the engineer is a woman."

"Damn!"

The flight commodore dismissed the pilot and immediately called the head of security at Xenodyne Automation. "Carla Scott has escaped."

"And you've lost her?" said an incredulous Major Grant.

"Yes. She was last seen boarding a freighter that entered the EC Gate. It never arrived in the C-System."

"So where is it, now?"

"We don't know."

Grant said, "Can we assume they didn't make it. ISD, perhaps."

"The army is making no assumptions. She's one of yours. Go find her."

Chapter 58

The conference room on the fifth floor of the Norther Federation military base at Los Alamitos was sealed. All five main divisions of the army were represented at what was dubbed a defense briefing. The room had been swept for electronic bugs and there was an armed guard at the doors.

General Matthewson had the chair. He opened the meeting by inviting a colonel from the quartermaster's office to provide an update on the recall and replacement of the Autonomic Force on Earth.

"All 753,000 contaminated Units have been recalled and north of two thirds have been replaced. We expect that process to be completed within two weeks."

"Thank you. Colonel," said the general. The colonel resumed his seat. "The president has sanctioned an additional 300,000 Units and these have been ordered. Do we have a firm date for delivery for those, Colonel?"

"Not yet, General. We can expect deliveries to start in the next week or so."

"Follow up on that, if you would. Pressure must

be applied to XA where necessary. Nothing must interfere with the deployment program. Which brings us to Spacefleet Command. Air-Space Marshal?"

ASM Mark T. Sawyer was an older man, wearing navy blue and lots of brass on his shoulder epaulettes. He rose to his feet slowly. "We have four of our largest troop transports in preparation for the airlift, and Xenodyne Galactical have promised a fifth. Between them, they will have the capacity to transport 650,000 heads to the C-System in two waves. The second stage of the deployment will be completed in a single wave."

"Using what additional transports?"

"We intend to commandeer some local ships from Califon."

"Keep me advised on your progress. I'm sure I don't need to remind you that the whole operation depends on it," said the general, quietly.

"When the time comes, Spacefleet will be ready," said the Air-Space Marshal, stiffly, and he lowered himself into his chair.

"What about weapons? Who's looking after that?"

A lieutenant colonel took the floor. He saluted. "Sir. We have ordered 500,000 blasters. Some of those will be used to resupply existing divisions in the various colonies. The bulk will be assigned to these new Units when they are delivered."

"You mentioned some problem with the powerpacks for those blasters."

"Yes, General, the Tesla packs in our warehouses are in short supply at the moment. We have ordered more, but it seems unlikely that we will be able to power all the AUs and their weapons in time for the airlift. We may have to choose between live ordnance or Autonomic soldiers. We may not be able to power both."

A murmur ran around the table.

"This is not acceptable," snapped the general. "I expect you to sort this problem before the next briefing. Is that understood?"

The lieutenant colonel saluted again. "Yes, General." He sat down.

"Commander Gray, please give us a rundown on the readiness of our troops," said the general.

Marine Commander Dorian Gray stood up. He ran a hand across his military buzzcut. "Our preparations are well advanced, General. My Marines will be ready when the call to battle comes."

"I never doubted it," replied the general. The marine commander sat down, and the general continued his briefing, "An expedition has been dispatched to the E-System to reconnoiter the primary landing ground. We expect to find a number of buildings in serviceable condition suitable to billet our troops prior to the action."

"What if the buildings cannot be used?" said a

colonel. “They have been vacant for years. There may be nothing left standing inside the domes.”

The general replied impatiently, “I’m sure our troops will cope. Under canvas, if necessary.” He checked his watch. “I think that’s everything. Meeting adjourned.”

A thin individual dressed in civilian clothes raised a hand. He spoke in a reedy voice. “Excuse me, General, I have something important to add.”

“Yes, Commander, what is it?”

Commander Harlowe, the representative of the Norther Federation Security Agency, sprang to his feet waving a sheaf of papers in the air. “This morning, I received a disturbing report. Carla Scott has escaped from Luciflex.”

“How is that possible?” said the general.

“There are very few details,” said Harlowe. “She, and several other prisoners, escaped on a freighter. No one knows how they succeeded.”

“The prison authorities are in pursuit?”

“Yes, General, but they have lost contact with the freighter.”

“What does that mean?”

“The report says the freighter vanished in the EC Conduit, obviously on their way home.”

The room exploded in uproar.

“Quiet down!” roared the general. He addressed his closing remarks to Commander Harlowe. “This woman represents a real and present danger to the security of our Autonomic

Force. As long as she is at large she is a threat to our plans. It is imperative that you eliminate that threat with extreme prejudice. Am I making myself clear?"

"Yes, General."

PART 4 – Home

Chapter 59

Carla considered her options. If she was going to make it onto Blackmore's ship, she needed a thousand dollars, and she had just four days left to find it. None of the harebrained schemes dreamt up by her three friends filled her with confidence. She needed a job.

She made her way to the bar, where she approached Oswald and asked if his offer of employment was still open.

"What can you do?" he said, a smirk on his face.

"I could wash dishes. I could wait on the tables in the restaurant."

"What do you know about Blackjack?"

"Not much."

"I'm short a dealer. I'll teach you."

He led her to the casino and sat her at one of the dealer's chairs. Then he pulled a bundle of chips from his pocket and placed half of them by her left hand. "You're the bank." He looked at Romeo. "Mechanical man here can be a second player. Sit here beside me."

Romeo took a seat and Oswald gave the AU half his remaining chips.

Carla dealt the cards from an eight-pack shoe.

An hour went by. Oswald showed Carla the basics of the game. During each game, chips passed back and forth between the bank and the two players. Carla soon learned how to play the bank's role. She could see how the odds favored the bank and, sure enough, her pile of chips grew steadily while Oswald's and Romeo's declined.

"That's enough," said Oswald, after another hour. "You can start tonight. Wear something colorful. An attractive dealer distracts the players from the game. And the more the bank makes the more I pay you. All my dealers get a percentage of their take. And remember to keep smiling. That's the only rule."

"Even when the bank loses?"

"*Especially* when the bank loses. Keep smiling."

#

Carla waited until early evening before going to the hotel to ask Maxeen if she could borrow something colorful to wear. She explained why she needed it.

Maxeen fished a dress from her bag and Carla held it against her chest. She looked in the mirror. It was certainly colorful, but it was too big for her. Maxeen snorted. “You might be better off in a Pexcorn sack. Let’s see what else I have.”

While Maxeen poked about in her bag, Carla said, “You know these poor people have to eat animals.”

“What do you mean?”

“They have an animal farm. I passed it on the way to Blackmore’s bar.”

“What sort of animals?”

“I don’t know. I didn’t see them, but I smelled them.”

“So what? They need to be self-sufficient out here in the sticks. Meat’s a great source of protein and it’s not so bad when you get used to it.”

Carla made a face. “That’s gross.”

“What d’you think Pexcorn protein is made of?” said Maxeen.

Carla made no reply, filing away the thought for later consideration.

Maxeen pulled a second dress from her bag and Carla put it on. It was more colorful, but two sizes too big.

“Which one do you want?” said Maxeen.

“I like this one best.”

Maxeen set about tucking and pinning the dress as best she could. Then she stood back to admire her work. “Very stylish for a brigand.”

“I’m no brigand,” said Carla with an exaggerated pout.

Maxeen adjusted a couple of pins. “You are, you know, girl. Whatever happens, you’re an outlaw now, until the end of your days. I reckon you could be a Leo. You were born in August.”

Carla gave her a skewed look.

“Definitely a Leo. Leos are clever, determined. Leaders. Nothing fazes them.”

“How do I look?” said Carla, doing a twirl in front of the mirror.

“You’ll do.”

Carla thanked her and set off for the casino with the words ‘brigand’ and ‘outlaw’ weighing heavily on her mind.

Oswald assigned her to one of the Blackjack tables. Romeo stood to one side, partly hidden behind a pillar, where he could watch the play without freaking out the players.

As the players arrived, some of the regulars gravitated toward her table, the appearance of a new dealer attracting them like wasps to a jelly jar.

She dealt the cards. The bank grew in fits and starts, but steadily enough. She smiled at the players until her face muscles ached.

The players all lost, but none of them seemed too bothered. By the end of the night, her bank had accumulated 4,250 dollars from an initial stake of 1,500.

Oswald was pleased with her. “You did well.

You're a quick study." He gave her 100 dollars.

Carla was disappointed. A career as a Blackjack dealer wouldn't earn her the money she needed fast enough. She would have to find a better way of raising money quickly. She had three days left.

Chapter 60

Carla found Balehook alone in the hotel bar, nursing a sore head. "Where's Maxeen?"

He waved an arm vaguely at the door. "Doing her laundry or something."

"Tell me more about that heist," she whispered.

Balehook grinned at her. "You're interested now, are you?"

"Do you know where Oswald keeps his stash?"

"They say he has a safe in a back office somewhere. Apparently, it was plundered from a Norther pleasure cruiser, years ago. According to the story, when Blackmore couldn't open it, Oswald offered to help. He has military training, handy with explosives. Blackmore agreed to share the contents with him if he succeeded."

"And Oswald opened it?"

"He blew it open with dynamite."

"Wasn't it damaged?"

"Yes." Balehook grinned. "That's the beauty of it. It's not secure anymore. Apparently a six-year-old could open it with a toothpick."

The whole story sounded highly implausible to Carla.

He bought a round of coffees and snacks at the

bar. When he returned to the table she asked, "What if we can't find the safe?"

"We'll find it."

"What if we can't open it?"

"I told you. All we need is a six-year-old with a toothpick."

"That sounds highly unlikely. Would you put your valuables in an insecure safe?"

"Okay, if we can't open it, I'm sure your mechano friend will be able to."

That sounded more feasible.

#

Balehook kept watch while Maxeen wedged a small insert behind the strikeplate of the lock to the main door. They waited until the last drinker had been thrown out of the bar and the last gambler had left the casino before attempting re-entry.

"Where's Peacock?" said Carla.

"We don't need him," Maxeen replied. She activated a handheld device that transmitted a signal causing the insert to expand, forcing the lock mechanism to open.

The door opened with a minor squeak. All four of them slipped inside and moved to the rooms at the back, in search of the safe.

When Balehook discovered a locked door, Carla asked Romeo to open it. Romeo stepped forward and forced the door open with a slap from his open palm.

They found themselves in a dark office. Maxeen made a beeline for a ceiling to floor curtain in the corner. She pulled it back and there was a man-sized safe hidden behind it. Closer inspection revealed the damage; the safe's door was twisted and barely attached at the hinges.

"Open it, Romeo," said Carla.

Romeo slipped his hand into the gap at the top of the door and tugged while Balehook applied his considerable weight to prevent it from falling forward. The door popped off its hinges and Romeo tossed it aside. The heavy door landed on Oswald's desk with a resounding crash.

They all paused, listening for any sign that the noise had disturbed Oswald or his men.

"All clear," said Balehook.

Carla sent Romeo to keep a lookout at the front door.

Maxeen stuck her head into the gaping safe and emerged with bundles of documents.

Balehook pushed her aside. "Let me look." He plunged into the safe, rummaged around and came out emptyhanded. "There's no cash in there. The crafty skinflint is too smart to leave his cash in the obvious place. He must have it hidden someplace else, dammit."

"Damn and blast," said Maxeen, discarding the bundles of documents.

They resumed the search, checking every possible hiding place in every room. After ten minutes, they congregated in the bar.

"Any luck, anyone?" said Balehook.

Maxeen and Carla shook their heads.

"We've looked everywhere," said Maxeen.

"What about the mortuary? We haven't looked there," said Carla.

Balehook's eyes lit up. "I bet that's where the crafty devil keeps his cash. Come on."

The three of them rushed to the back of the building and began searching. Five minutes later, they had searched every corner of the room and found nothing.

Balehook's gaze fell on the three bodies that were laid out on the tables. "There's one place we haven't looked..."

Maxeen held up her hands. "I'm not touching them."

"Don't look at me," said Carla.

Balehook rolled up his sleeves. As he began to search the clothes of the first cadaver, Romeo strolled into the room. "There are men approaching the front door," he said.

Carla ran to the front of the building and peered through a window. Two of Oswald's henchmen were at the door, both armed with handblasters.

She ran back to the mortuary. "Oswald's men are here. And they're armed."

"Dammit," said Balehook. "Time to get out."

All four slipped out through the back door, to melt into the darkness.

Chapter 61

As the E-System sun rose over the domed city of Berlyon on Égalité, Kindira Klein unlocked the giant Bubble and stepped inside. Nothing stirred. Everything inside the dome appeared exactly as they must have left it when the colonists abandoned it all those years ago. Nothing had been disturbed.

What a stark testament to the indigenous intelligent life-forms, and to their indifference to the human invaders, thought Kindira.

The ambient in-dome temperature was a steady 22 degrees Centigrade, the humidity a comfortable 15%. Outside the dome it was 40 degrees in the shade. The dome was undamaged, its environmental integrity intact, its climate-control systems in perfect working order. After 87 years, that was a triumph the engineers could be proud of. Kindira took a moment to marvel at the architecture and the astonishing reversal; it took 137 years to build these structures and just 6 months to abandon them.

Shielding her eyes against the reflections from the glass edifice of the administration block, she hurried toward the Governor's palace, an elegant twenty-second century building in Parisian limestone, squatting behind the military barracks.

She opened the palace with one of her skeleton keys and surveyed the interior. Everything was covered in a fine film of dust. She chuckled. There was no escaping the dust anywhere in the Six Systems – her meal ticket.

She set about her work. After cleaning up the palace, she had to do the same for the barracks and the administration block. It was a big job, but she would be well paid for it.

#

On Égalité's sister planet, Liberté, 215 lightyears distant in the C-System, ASM Sawyer was having difficulty explaining why he had commandeered two luxury space cruisers. He had briefed the Governor on a highly confidential intelligence report that warned of a plan by the Southers to launch a pre-emptive strike. The Governor seemed unconvinced.

"As I've said, Governor, the Norther Federation is under threat. We need the cruisers to help position our forces where they will be best placed to counter this act of aggression when it happens."

"On Égalité?"

"Precisely. The E-System is the closest to the enemy heartland."

"But Égalité is no longer available." The Governor made a sour face. "My own grandfather lost everything when he was forced to leave. The protocol prohibits—"

"Indeed, Governor, I am acutely aware of the Geronimo Protocol and I can assure you that our soldiers will be billeted there for but a few days, and while there they will treat the planet with the utmost respect."

"Where exactly will they be stationed?"

"Our troops will be billeted in the barracks at Berlyon. My senior officers and myself will use the Governor's palace."

The Governor raised a skeptical eyebrow. "How long do you plan to keep your troops on the ground in Berlyon?"

"Only as long as necessary. A few days at most. Intelligence has informed us that we must expect the Southers to launch their attack against us at any time."

"And the civilian spacecraft, the cruisers, when will they be returned?"

"They will be returned as soon as they are no longer required."

"Undamaged?"

"Yes, of course, Governor. They will be used solely as troop transports. They won't be directly involved in any military actions."

Chapter 62

Carla stood in her hotel room, her money spread out on the bed. She had 72 dollars and 15 cents.

She looked in the mirror. "How am I going to raise that much money?"

Romeo stood by the window. "Please repeat the question."

"Never mind, Romeo, I wasn't asking you. I was talking to myself. I need money."

"You wish to accumulate currency?"

"Yes. I need to accumulate a lot of currency, quickly."

"How much currency do you need to accumulate?"

"One thousand dollars."

"You could play Blackjack," said Romeo.

She frowned. "The Blackjack dealer is paid only a hundred dollars a night. I need a thousand dollars in two days."

"You could accumulate the money as a player."

She shook her head. "The bank always wins."

"I can win," said Romeo.

She looked at him. "What did you say?"

"I can win. I can watch the cards."

Oh my god!

She ran to the hotel reception desk and rang the bell. A sleepy night porter appeared from the back office.

"Cards!" she said. "I need some playing cards."

The man fetched a dogeared deck from his office.

"I need more than one deck."

He found a second deck under the counter and handed it over. "That's all I have."

It would have to do.

She ran back to her room, shuffled the two decks, and started to play Blackjack with Alpha Romeo.

"We have nothing to use as chips," she said.

"I can keep a tally," said Romeo.

#

By the time the small sun was peeping over the horizon, Romeo was winning every winnable hand and discarding the dud ones. She couldn't believe her eyes.

"How much ahead are you?" she asked.

"I have gained 173 dollars."

"You can really keep track of the cards?"

"Yes. The next card is the four of diamonds."

She turned it over. The four of diamonds. "And the next one?"

"The ten of clubs." He was right again.

"Okay, so you can keep track of two decks of cards. What about eight decks?"

"Eight decks will take longer, and a shuffle would make that impossible. But I can use statistical analysis. It is not necessary to track every card."

"How much do you think you can win in a night?"

"With eight decks, I estimate winnings of three or four hundred dollars. More than that with six decks."

"That's still not going to be enough."

"If we both play at the same table, we can accumulate at least six or eight hundred dollars in one night."

"But I can't count the cards like you do," she said.

"I can tell you what to play."

"That's not allowed, Romeo."

Chapter 63

When he saw Carla, Oswald beamed at her. “Table one,” he said. “You’ve created a huge buzz among the regulars. You’ll do well, even without the colorful dress.”

“I’m not here to deal,” she said. “We thought we’d play for a while.”

His smile froze on his face. “We? You mean you and tinman? I’ve no objection to taking your money, but do me a favor and deal for a couple of hours first, okay?”

“My dealing days are over.”

“Why? I paid you well last night, and I’m giving you the best table. You could do even better tonight.”

“We want to play.”

He gave her a sour, pained look. “I’m short a dealer. You might have let me know earlier.” He turned away, thumbing his X-Vid. “Olive? Could you do a couple of hours tonight...”

Carla changed her 70 dollars into chips. Then she and Romeo drifted around the room, watching the dealers as they set up their tables. They sat at table three where a young blond dealer was filling the shoe with six decks, freshly shuffled. Two other rough looking individuals were already seated at the table.

"Ready to play Blackjack, gentlemen and lady?" said the dealer. "My name is Mabeline. I will be your dealer for the night."

"Ready and able," said one of the players.

"Do your worst, Mabeline," said the second.

"We're playing no-limit Blackjack, house rules. Doubling and trebling down allowed, dealer Blackjack takes the tie," she said in a sing-song voice.

She dealt the first round of cards. Carla received an eight and a jack, Romeo an ace and a five. Carla stuck at 18. She bet two chips. Romeo bet two chips and took two hits. A seven and a six. He stuck at 19.

The dealer turned her hole card to reveal seventeen. She dealt herself another card – and bust.

The game continued. Whenever Carla had a decision to make, Romeo used tiny, pre-agreed movements of his fingers to signal what she should do, whether to stand, to twist, or raise the stake.

After their first two lucky rounds, they lost several, games, but within an hour, Romeo had the feel of the cards, and they began to win. By the middle of the night, they had both amassed significant piles of chips. People had gathered at the table to watch what was happening. Mabeline was sweating.

Oswald ambled by. As Mabeline completed another losing game, he made an announcement: "This table is closed."

One of the other players at the table asked Carla how she managed to beat the bank so many times.

"Just lucky, I guess," she said, sweetly.

They took their places at another table. This one had an eight-deck shoe and a grumpy middle-aged male dealer.

As before, their early games were mostly losers with low bets. But as Romeo got to grips with the cards and the number of their winning games increased, they wagered more and more on each game.

Once again, their chips grew, and a crowd assembled to watch. It wasn't long before Oswald closed that table. Since there were no free places at any of the remaining tables, Romeo and Carla cashed in their chips and returned to the hotel.

Their combined cash reserve now stood at $615. Another night at the cassino would see them reach their target.

Before climbing into bed, she checked Romeo's power charge. It was down to 70 per cent. She put him on recharge.

Chapter 64

On their second night at the casino, two of Oswald's men were in close attendance, watching Carla and Romeo's every move.

"Ignore them," she said. "They are hoping to distract us from the cards. Keep your concentration on the game."

As on the previous night, it took a while for Romeo to gather enough information from the cards to enable him to make informed decisions. And, as on the previous night, they lost small sums before their winning streak began.

After five straight winning hands, Oswald came across to the table. He stood beside Mabeline and pointed at Romeo. "Androids aren't allowed to play at the tables."

Alpha Romeo was the only android in the place. He was the only android on the planet, as far as Carla knew.

"Why?" she said.

"Because I said so."

"That's unfair. The only reason you're changing the rules is because he's winning. Do you always ban customers who hit a lucky streak?"

Other players raised their voices in protest.

Oswald replied, "This is my casino and I make the rules. You can always play somewhere else if you don't like them."

Carla didn't think there was another casino anywhere in the city.

Romeo vacated his chair. He stood behind Carla as the game resumed, and switched to signaling her by touch as each hand was played out. But Oswald soon realized what was happening. He ordered his men to throw Carla and her AU from the building and confiscate their winnings.

Carla swept up her chips as the two guards stepped forward, weapons appearing in their hands as if by magic. Romeo went into action. Before they could do any serious harm, an iron bar and a baseball bat were sent spinning across the floor, followed by the two casino guards. The crowd scattered. Oswald ducked behind a blackjack table.

Romeo seemed to be enjoying himself.

Then a whistle blew, and six more of Oswald's thugs ran from the back of the building. These men were armed with handblasters. They meant business.

"Run, Romeo."

#

The armed posse pursued them, firing as they ran. Charging through the shanty town, they ran past the toll-collector and made it as far as the orchard fence.

There was no time to follow the fence around to Blackmore's launchpad.

"We need to climb the fence," she said.

Romeo bent down to make a platform. Carla climbed onto his back and climbed over the fence into the orchard. Romeo leaped over it after her, and they ran between two rows of trees.

Behind them, the men clambered over the fence. They were gaining on Carla and Romeo. Dodging a blaster bolt, she slipped between two trees into a parallel row.

A shape rose up ahead of them – one of the machines she'd seen before, a huge mechanical octopus, its multiple appendages swinging side to side, threatening to decapitate them. Not just a harvesting machine; clearly, it was programmed to defend the orchard against invaders.

Trapped between a mechanical behemoth and a murderous, armed mob, Carla charged headlong toward the machine, running her eyes over the machine as she ran. Just like an octopus, its limbs emanated from a central point. If she could reach that center, she might be able to disable it.

"Keep it off me," she yelled as she ducked under its arms.

Alpha Romeo did battle with the machine,

grappling with its limbs, twisting one to immobilize it, batting another into the trees.

While Romeo battled with the machine, the posse advanced. The machine reached over the AU, picked up one of the men and threw him 20 meters across the orchard. A second man screamed as the machine grabbed him by the leg and lifted him twenty feet into the air. The others turned and ran back the way they'd come to escape its clutches.

Carla reached the machine's control hub. Like the eye of a storm, this was a safe haven where the machine couldn't reach her.

Romeo was in trouble. The machine had a double hold on him, one grab held his legs, another his torso. He was in danger of being torn apart.

She located a panel, pulled it open and ripped out a handful of cables. The machine froze. Then she ran back to Romeo and wrestled him free of the machine's clutches.

"Are you all right?" she asked.

"I am uninjured," said Romeo.

They hurried onward.

When they reached the fence at the far end of the orchard, Romeo again formed a platform for Carla to climb over. Romeo leapt over after her.

They were at the launch site. Among the Helihovers and small aircraft a freight shuttle stood on a launchpad 100 yards away, wisps of vapor escaping from its engines. The name on a side panel identified it as the *Icarus3*.

Carla gathered her breath and ran toward the spacecraft. Halfway there, she realized Alpha Romeo was not following. He had fallen near the fence.

She ran back. "What's wrong, Romeo? Get up. We need to reach that shuttle."

Romeo made no reply.

She tried to lift him onto his feet, but he was too heavy for her. She left him, and ran to the *Icarus3*.

Stepping inside the open cargo door, she spoke to a man loading supplies. "Take me to Captain Blackmore."

Chapter 65

A second man emerged from the cargo bay. This guy was bald, but with a beard that reached his navel. Built like a pile of bricks and with muscles to spare, he wore a sleeveless leather jerkin and carried a clipboard in one huge maw.

"What do you want?" he growled.

"I want to speak with your captain," she said. "My name is Carla Scott."

"Get lost." He turned away.

She spoke to the man's back. "Tell Captain Blackmore I'm here. He promised me a berth on this trip."

The big man snarled at her, and disappeared into the bowels of the ship. He emerged after a few minutes with Captain Blackmore in tow.

"You have the money?" said the captain without preamble.

Carla handed over all her chips.

"I don't accept gambling chips."

"I didn't have time to cash them," she said.

The men exchanged a glance.

"These are from the Blue Flamingo. They're worthless." He counted them. "I thought we agreed one thousand dollars. There's only eight hundred and change here."

"It's the best I could do in the time."

The captain tucked the chips away in a pocket. "Find her a cabin, Naredoo." He strode away toward the interior of his ship.

"Thank you, Captain," she called after him, "I'll get you the rest when we arrive on Earth."

"Follow me," said Naredoo.

"I need someone to fetch my Autonomic Unit." She pointed to where Romeo was lying by the orchard fence. "He's injured."

Naredoo organized two men to collect the fallen AU, and soon, Carla was alone in a small cabin under instructions to "stay put" until the captain called for her.

Romeo was in sleep mode; his system had closed down to avoid damage. She started by opening his chest panel and checking his control modules. They looked fine. She turned him over, sprung the panel on his back and removed his powerpack.

The Tesla unit had ruptured, top to bottom. It was leaking fluid. She swore. Oswald had switched a perfectly good powerpack for this faulty unit while she slept. She was going to have to find a replacement as soon as possible.

#

The ship-wide intercom order to "Buckle up!" told Carla the trip was about to start. She strapped herself into the harness on the seat in her cabin and braced for what was to come.

The *Icarus3* took off with a roar. The whole cabin shook. The lateral thrusters took it spiraling at an oblique angle through the planet's atmosphere. Extreme gravitational forces, increasing moment by moment, thrust her into her seat, while her eyes threatened to pop from their sockets.

Aargh! I hate conventional engines. Take me to a fifth dimension Conduit.

The thrusters cut out without warning, and gravitational forces died. They were in orbit and she was weightless, the harness the only thing holding her in place. The lifeless body of Alpha Romeo drifted past...

The thrusters fired again for fifteen minutes. A claxon sounded and Carla's heart leapt as the ship passed through an Interstellar Gate.

Damn! I hate those Gates. Give me conventional space travel every time.

As soon as artificial gravity kicked in, she freed herself from her harness and went to check on Alpha Romeo. He was undamaged. She was sure he would be fine once she found a new powerpack for him.

She opened the door of her cabin and went in search of the captain. The few crewmembers she passed showed no interest in her, and she found the ship's bridge easily. She was surprised to find she could access the bridge without ceremony.

"Welcome aboard," said Captain Blackmore. "I hope you've found your accommodation comfortable."

"Yes, thank you, Captain." She was surprised by the man's elaborate politeness.

"You've met Bosun Naredoo," he said. "And I believe you know my first mate."

Naredoo stood beside the captain. The first mate was strapped into one of the bridge chairs, attending to the radar. He spun his chair around.

"Hullo, Carla," he said.

Peacock! His eyepatch was gone, a shiny new glass eye in the socket.

"What are you doing here?"

"He's my first mate," said Blackmore. "And I'll expect you to do your bit on our journey. Report to the galley."

It didn't take long to find the galley. Carla introduced herself to the cook, whose name was Cookie. He was expecting her, which was another surprise. It seemed Captain Blackmore had pre-assigned her the position of assistant cook on the assumption that she would make it onto the ship in time for the trip.

The onboard temperature had already fallen a couple of degrees and, knowing it would fall a whole lot more, Carla was happy to be employed close to a warm oven in the galley.

In the peace and quiet of the galley, Maxeen's cooking practices on Luciflex came to mind. Carla was surprised by the feelings accompanying her memories: she was missing Maxeen. She was sorry she hadn't had a chance to say goodbye.

Cookie was a pleasant companion, and soon proved his mettle. The crew complement totaled twelve. After cooking three meals a day on Luciflex for three shifts of 1,200 men, Carla reckoned this job was going to be a doddle!

At the end of the first meal, she managed to get Peacock on his own, and asked him why he had taken the position of first mate on Blackmore's ship.

"I owe the captain," said Peacock. "The payment I received for the *Pegasus* cargo included an element of cooperation on future missions. He has me over a barrel. I work with him or wave goodbye to any further payment."

"Sounds like a poor deal."

"It's a form of agreement common among privateers. It could make me a very rich man."

"Richer than straight cash for the freighter cargo?"

He grinned. "Much richer. Like ten times richer."

"So where are we?" she asked.

"We're four days out from the C-System."

"How is that possible? We were just a few hours into the EC Conduit when we diverted to the

Dead System. How did we get so close to the C-System?"

"Space-time can be full of surprises."

That was all Peacock was prepared to say on the matter, and Carla guessed that he was probably as mystified as she was. It seemed the pirates had discovered Gates unknown to the Federation. Either that or they had technology enabling them to hop in and out of the Conduits at will, wherever they pleased!

Chapter 66

Carla told Captain Blackmore that her father was living on Califon. She asked if she could send him a radio message when they arrived in the C-System. The captain agreed, but he insisted on checking the content of her message before she sent it. “You must make no mention of me or the ship’s name.”

She asked if he could supply a Tesla powerpack for Alpha Romeo. He signaled to Naredoo and the Bosun left the bridge to fetch one.

“You can add it to the cash you owe me,” said the captain.

“How much?”

“Five hundred dollars should cover it.”

She protested, “Teslas cost no more than two hundred dollars on Earth.”

“They cost five hundred on this ship,” he replied.

#

After a journey of four standard days through the EC Conduit, the *Icarus3* emerged through the Gate into the C-System.

"Action Stations! All crewmembers to your posts!"

The ship-wide command, accompanied by a strident siren, roused Carla from her bunk. She dressed hurriedly and ran to the bridge.

The viewscreen was filled with one of Califon's moons and, wallowing in the foreground, an ugly, corpulent spacecraft with hundreds of portholes.

The expression on Captain Blackmore's face told her everything she needed to know. This was a cruise ship, fat, slow-moving, full of rich holidaymakers begging to be stripped of their valuables.

Her heart sank. The innocents onboard the cruise ship had no idea what was about to happen. Some would lose all their possessions. They were all in danger of losing their lives.

"Must we do this, Captain?" she said. "Shouldn't we press on to the A-System first? You could always come back and take this cruiser after you've dropped me off."

Bosun Naredoo grinned at her. "Sit back and enjoy the spectacle, Miss. One of these fat cats can make us all richer than Midas."

As the *Icarus3* advanced toward the cruiser, it changed course, turning toward the moon.

"They're running. Should I fire a bolt across their bow?" said Peacock.

"Do it," the captain replied.

Peacock fired a blaster bolt well in front of the cruiser. The cruiser continued on its chosen path.

"Another one, Captain?" said Peacock.

"Let them run. We'll be close enough to board in five minutes."

"Aye aye, Captain," said Peacock.

On the viewscreen, the cruiser rounded the moon and the *Icarus3* followed, gaining on it all the time. Soon, they were close enough to see the deck plates of the bigger ship. Carla could even see hundreds of faces looking out through the portholes.

A missile rounded the moon, shot past the cruiser and headed straight for the Icarus3.

"Evasive action!" shouted the captain, and the helmsman threw the helm to one side.

A massive jolt shook the *Icarus3*.

"Reverse course!"

The helmsman steered the ship away from the cruiser.

"What was that? Are they firing back?" said Carla. Then she saw a huge shape emerging from behind the moon. A massive Norther Federation battleship, and it was firing at them.

"Get us out of here, man," Naredoo screamed at the helmsman. "Head for the CA Gate."

They ran, keeping the moon between them and the battleship. After two minutes, the battleship rounded the moon and appeared in their rear viewscreen. In the distance behind the moon, Carla could see the sun reflecting off a whole fleet of Norther warships – 50 ships or more. As she watched, a blaster bolt left the battleship and shot toward them. When it struck, the *Icarus3* rocked violently, but kept going.

She glanced at the Gate countdown clock. It showed three minutes, reducing.

Naredoo yelled, “Faster, man. Faster!”

The helmsman replied in a shaky voice, “We’re going as fast as we can.”

Two minutes from the Gate, a third bolt shot past them.

When the countdown reached one minute, the battleship slowed and turned back.

And then the warning siren sounded, Carla braced for the jolt, the engines died, and they slipped through the Gate.

#

While Peacock engaged the Brazill Drive, Bosun Naredoo went off to assess the damage.

“What was that?” said the captain. “A whole fleet of warships protecting a leisure cruiser? I’ve never seen anything like that, have you, Peacock?”

“Never have, Captain. Doesn’t make our job any easier. It’s enough to give an ordinary decent pirate nightmares.”

The stone in the pit of Carla’s stomach told her what they’d just witnessed: A Norther battle fleet 23 lightyears from home. Why were they hanging around the C-System? Were they preparing for war? If they were planning an attack on the D-System, the E-System would be their next stop.

Chapter 67

Captain Blackmore's damaged ship limped through the CA Conduit in 25 hours, a journey that should have taken 21 hours. The crew spent the time working on the necessary repairs. When Carla wasn't cooking for the crew or serving meals, she remained in her cabin with Romeo. The encounter with the Norther fleet had deprived her of the opportunity to send a message to her father. She hadn't spoken to him since before her banishment to Luciflex. She put the disappointment out of her mind and thought about what she had to do on reaching Earth.

First order of business was to recreate Lia. She really missed her personal AU. Her greatest regret was that she'd had no chance to warn her friend before being transported to Luciflex.

When the captain announced, "Five minutes to the A-System," she made her way to the bridge and stood beside Peacock watching the forward viewscreen for the first sight of home. Fifteen seconds after the warning siren sounded, they exited the Gate, and there it was: Earth, her moon, and Sol in all its glory!

"I'll never get used to that sight," said Peacock.

Carla was too choked to respond.

The helmsman fired up the engines and moved the ship into a queue of ships in geostationary orbit over the west coast of the USA.

Captain Blackmore retired to his ready room, making no move to signal their arrival or to ask for clearance to make landfall in the Spaceport.

"What's the captain waiting for?" she asked Naredoo.

"He'll need a few hours to monitor the news channels," said Naredoo. "We need to be cautious about how we enter the lion's den."

Carla remained on the bridge with the bosun and Peacock, listening to radio broadcasts from the planet. She accepted the need for caution, but she was itching to get on the ground.

The first thing that shocked her was the date: September 8. Five standard months had elapsed since she'd left Earth! The second shock was the harsh tone of political commentary from both superpowers. The lead story on every TV channel concerned a Norther satellite in orbit around Mars that had been destroyed in a mysterious explosion. A spokeswoman for the Norther armed forces appeared on the screen several times, working herself into a frenzy of indignation. Did the Southers think they could commit such a blatant act of hostility against a Norther asset?

Carla was used to a measure of saber rattling,

but there was a noticeably harder edge to the thrust and counterthrust now, both sides giving dire warnings of retaliatory strikes should the other take any further belligerent action. The whole atmosphere sounded like a powder keg that could explode at any moment. The echoes of a spark that ignited the First Lunar War and another, more distant historical conflict rang loud and clear in Carla's mind.

Captain Blackmore summoned Carla to his cabin.

"We'll be making landfall soon. I expect you to make good on your debt as soon as you can." He gave her an X-Vid number. "You can reach me here."

"Yes, of course, Captain," she replied. "How much is outstanding?"

"Your Blue Flamingo chips are worth eight hundred dollars. You owe me another seven hundred. One thousand for the trip and five hundred for the powerpack."

Three hours later, every news channel on the planet carried a somber speech from the president of the Norther federation.

The destruction of our satellite by the Southers is an unprovoked act of aggression, that cannot be ignored. Consequently, the Norther Federation is now at war with the Souther Federation. Our fleet has been deployed and will soon reach enemy territory.

Carla's worst fears had been realized; the fleet they had encountered in the C-System would be used to invade the three Souther colonies of the D-System. She now had a new order of business. If she could distribute her Fear module to the Norther military AUs in time, she could stop the war and save millions of lives. She was going to have to find a ship to get back to the theater of war. But first, she would need to locate Cassidy. She couldn't distribute the module to the Popovs – the Souther androids – without his communications software.

Shortly after that, Captain Blackmore announced on the ship-wide intercom that they had obtained permission to land at LAX Spaceport. "If anyone asks, my name is Captain Black. The *Icarus3* is a merchantman from Califon, carrying rare metals and seeking a cargo of sports equipment to transport back home to the C-System."

Carla asked Naredoo whether they were really hauling rare metals. Naredoo confirmed that they were carrying a consignment of iridium193. But, he added with a grimace, the captain wouldn't be seen dead putting ping pong balls in the cargo hold of *Icarus3*.

Chapter 68

A fighter emerged from the AC Gate and docked with the *Golden Eagle*. The pilot was escorted to the ready room where he presented the general with a dispatch from the Secretary of State. The fleet was to proceed immediately to the E-System and to wait there for further orders.

ASM Sawyer gave the signal, and the fleet poured through the CE Gate. General Matthewson found the jolt uncomfortable, but it was nothing compared to the thrashing he had planned for the enemy. The unprovoked attack on LAX still stuck in his craw.

The journey to the E-System would take a few hours over eight days. An advance team of cleaners had been sent to Égalité, and the domed city of Berlyon had been prepared to billet the invasion force of 900,000 troops. He and the other military leaders would be housed in the Governor's palace.

Stealth was the number one priority. The attack, when it came, would be a complete surprise to the Southers. By the time they became aware of the fleet's arrival in the E-System, and the vast numbers of Autonomic Units ranged against them, they would have no time to prepare their forces for the defense of their planets. The Southers' only real defense was their space fleet. The battle between the two fleets would be hard fought, but the general had no doubt that the marshal's seven Battlecruisers would be more than a match for their four Supercruisers. The Norther fleet would prevail.

With any luck, the Southers would capitulate quickly after that. Leninets would fall in a matter of days. The whole operation could be completed in no more than three standard weeks.

The troop ship's encounter with that lone freighter in the C-System was a concern, but even if the alarm was raised back on Earth, it would take a fast ship about nine days to reach the D-System. By then it would be too late to warn them.

As the onboard temperature fell, he poured himself a snifter of single malt whiskey, his thought processes leading him to his meeting with Secretary of State Arnold Bluewater. He remained uncertain of the president's involvement in the plan. The order to deploy to the E-System had come from Bluewater. The only worry was whether the president had been informed. Without the backing of the president and with only Bluewater behind him, his ass was out the window.

Chapter 69

Two minutes after entering the North Orbital Gate, the ship emerged on the ground in the Spaceport at LAX and the captain and crew disembarked.

When Carla's scrambled microchip failed to respond to the scanner in Customs, she was taken to an interview room where she completed an identity declaration. She used a false name. Donna English was born on Califon. She used her real Califon birth date and invented names for her parents. She explained to the interrogating officer that her identity chip had been damaged in a hover accident on Califon when she was a child. The interrogation continued for an hour. The officer tried a few tricks to trip her up, but eventually, she was taken to a registration unit where she had her microchip reprogrammed. Donna English left the customs hall clutching a leaflet containing the addresses of several offices where she could renew her registration for health and other government services.

Alpha Romeo was waiting for her in the terminal building.

"Ready to go, Romeo?"

"I am ready, Carla Scott," he replied.

There was no one within earshot, but even so, she was going to have a problem if Romeo kept using her real name.

She waited until they were outside the building. Then she said, "From today, my name is Donna English. Is that clear, Romeo?"

He looked at her blankly. "Your name is Carla Scott."

"No, Alpha Romeo. From today, and as long as we are in the A-System, my name is Donna English. Have you got that?"

"Yes, Carla. I understand."

She gave up.

#

They took a hovercab to Feynman Tech, Carla's alma mater, and went straight to the school of Automation. Professor Jones was delivering a lecture. Carla and Romeo sat at the back of the lecture call and she watched the professor at work. He had lost none of his charisma, none of his lecturing skills.

When the lecture had broken up, and all the students had left, he embraced her, his beard scratching her face.

"Who's your friend?" he said.

"This is Alpha Romeo," said Carla.

"Great name," said the professor. "How are you, Romeo?"

"I am well," said Romeo.

He took a seat beside them. "Where have you been? When I asked Fritz Franck, he said you were on vacation. Zedekiah and Sophie White have been searching for you for months."

Carla's heart skipped a beat at the mention of Zed. She told the professor about the kangaroo court, and her three-year sentence.

"Doesn't surprise me. Xenodyne Automation has never been more than an unofficial arm of the military. I knew the generals weren't happy with your new software modules, but I had no idea they sent you to Luciflex!"

"Have you heard from my father?"

"No. Should I have? He's off-world, isn't he?"

"He's living on Califon. I wrote to him before I left. I gave the letters to the prison guards, but I wasn't sure if they would pass them on. Apparently, they didn't."

"Probably not. How did you get away from Luciflex?"

Carla described her escape.

"Must be the first time anyone escaped from that hellhole. They'll be writing songs about you, soon."

"I had help from a couple of pirates," she said. "They took me to a planet in the Dead System."

The professor's eyes opened wide. "I always

suspected that such a place existed. What is it like?"

"There's a city on a river, a shanty town, lots of kids. The air smells of onions. And they have an animal farm."

"They eat meat? How very medieval!"

"I call it disgusting," she said.

"How do you think Pexcorn make their protein blocks?"

Carla was trying to recall where she'd heard that question before, when the professor asked, "Where is this planet?"

"Sorry, Professor, I haven't a clue. It's a binary system. That's all I can tell you." She changed the subject. "You know I uploaded the Pain and Fear modules to our military AUs during the Souther raid on the LAX Spaceport?"

"I assumed so when I saw them take shelter. The cops asked me what I thought of your modules. I fully endorsed them. I told them the military Units needed to feel pain. But they can't have been convinced. Xenodyne Automation withdrew all the military Units and replaced them."

Carla looked at the professor, dumbfounded. "That must have cost millions! How many Units did they recall?"

"Something like three quarters of a million. They scrapped the lot."

Carla took a moment to consider the implications.

She said, "I uploaded the same software to the Souther Popovs in LAX."

A spark of excitement lit up his eyes as realization dawned on the professor. "I wondered why they turned tail and ran. How did you reach them?"

"That was thanks to a piece of code that Cassidy wrote."

"Your Pain module couldn't have been compatible with their systems."

"That's right. And fear without pain is a toxic emotion. The Popovs couldn't handle it. Removing my software from the AUs will seriously disrupt the balance of power."

"No need to worry about that. I'm sure the Southers will have removed the Fear module from the Popovs by now."

"You think so?"

"Without question."

"In that case, I need to get in touch with Cassidy. Do you know where he's being held?"

"He's been helping XA with the replacement program."

"I thought they wanted to lock him up," she said.

"They did, but they needed him, so they lifted the arrest warrant."

"I thought they were going to lock you up, too because of your involvement in the project."

Romeo wandered about the lecture hall. He

examined the blackboard and chalk. Carla thought he looked bored. Could her Autonomic Units experience boredom?

"I told them about those papers I gave you. They showed no further interest in me," said the professor.

"They told me you made a full confession," she replied.

"They lied." The professor grimaced. "I made no confession of any kind."

"I need to talk to Cassidy. Where can I find him?"

"At your old lab, I suppose."

"I can't go back there. How can I reach him privately?"

"I haven't spoken to him for a couple of months. Zedekiah may be able to help." He called his son on his X-Vid. "Zedekiah, I have someone here who wants to speak to you."

Chapter 70

Professor Jones handed the X-Vid to Carla.

"Carla, my love! Where have you been? Sophie and I spent weeks searching for you."

The sound of his voice sent ripples through her skin. She held the X-Vid in both trembling hands so as not to drop it.

"I've been off-world. In prison," she replied. She thought 'my love' was a little over the top – they'd only been on two dates – but every nerve-end in her body was buzzing at the sight of his unkempt appearance.

He gave a low whistle. "On Flor? No wonder we couldn't find you."

"I was on Luciflex," she said, quietly.

Zed paused before responding, "That's a death trap. The bastards wanted you dead? Why did they let you go?"

"They didn't. I escaped."

Zed paused again, even longer this time.

"Zed? Are you still there?"

"Yes. You mean you're..."

"I'm a fugitive. Yes. An outlaw. I'm sure they will send me back if they catch me."

"What are you going to do?"

"I have work to finish. I need to contact Cassidy in private. Do you know where I can find him or Sophie? Is she still in contact with him?"

"I'm sure she is. I don't know where they're living, but I can contact her for you."

"Okay, thanks. I don't have an X-Vid. How will you reach me?"

"Stay close to dad. I'll call you back in a couple of hours."

Zed broke the connection. Had she imagined a rapid cooling of his affections after she'd used the word 'outlaw'? Maybe not.

She said, "There's something else I wanted to talk to you about."

"I'm listening." He filled a kettle.

"On the way back to Earth, we passed a Norther fleet in the C-System."

"How long ago was that?"

"Forty-eight standard hours."

He picked up the inferred threat to peace, immediately. "So they could arrive in the E-System in six days. And the D-System sixteen hours after that."

"Yes. We could be on the brink of a major war..."

"The police are outside," said Romeo. He was at the window.

Carla spun around. "What did you say?"

"The police are outside the building."

She sidled up to the window and peered outside. Six armed men stood in the campus looking up at them. They wore black uniforms with the letters NFSA on them. One man raised a bullhorn to his mouth.

CARLA SCOTT. THE BUILDING IS SURROUNDED. COME OUT WITH YOUR HANDS HIGH.

Chapter 71

Carla swore. "How did they find me?"

Professor Jones looked out the window. "They could be monitoring my calls. Zed spoke your name."

She shook her head. "They couldn't have gotten here that quickly."

"In that case, they must have planted a tracking device somewhere on your clothing." He ran to his desk and pulled a radio frequency detector from one of the drawers. He switched it on and swept it over Carla's body. The RF detector found nothing.

She grabbed the detector and ran it over Alpha Romeo. It beeped and a red light flashed. She pulled his breast plate open and thrust the RF detector inside.

"Got it!"

She ripped out a small piece of electronics on the end of a cable.

"Give it to me and get out of the building," said the professor.

She threw it to him.

"Use the back door," he said. "I'll take this up to the roof to keep them guessing."

I'M GIVING YOU THREE MINUTES. STEP OUTSIDE AND NO ONE WILL GET HURT.

Carla led Romeo to the professor's laboratory on the first floor.

"I'll come back for you as soon as I can," she said. Then she set the AU to sleep mode and removed his powerpack.

She left by the back door, where a contingent of armed NFSA agents stopped her.

"Who are you?"

"Donna English, postgrad student."

A soldier frisked her, while another ran a microchip scanner across her neck, and a third ran an RF detector over her clothes. "It's not her," said one of the agents.

"Scott's on the roof," said another.

They let her go and she hurried away from the university.

#

She returned the following day. The campus was quiet again. The NFSA agents had gone, and Professor Jones was in his lab tinkering with a circuit board.

"What happened after I left?" she asked, anxiously.

The professor chuckled. "They entered the building as if it was full of armed insurrectionists. When they found the bug on the roof, they searched everywhere, top to bottom. They found diddly squat. The man in charge, a Commander Harlowe, was politeness incarnate. He waved his swagger stick at me and asked a lot of damn fool questions. Have you worked out who planted that bug in Alpha Romeo?"

"Not yet. It had to be a Federation spy."

With Oswald at the top of my list of suspects, she thought.

"Any word back from Zed?" she asked.

"Oh yes, I forgot. You're to meet Sophie at your favorite restaurant at noon today."

Three standard days had elapsed since the sighting of the Norther fleet in the C-System.

#

She left Romeo with the professor and headed into town at 11:30 to her rendezvous with Sophie.

As usual, Bartelli's was busy. Running her eyes over the crowd she spotted Sophie White and made her way across, picking her way around the tables.

"How is Cassidy?" she asked as she sat down.

"He's well, thank you. Never stops talking about you. He was worried when you disappeared. We both were."

"Zed Jones told you where I've been?"

"When he said you were in prison off-world, I thought he meant Flor, but Zed said you were..." Her voice dropped. "...on Luciflex."

"They gave me three years."

"Oh my god!" Sophie covered her mouth with her hand. She whispered, "That's a death sentence. How did you escape?"

"I had help. Now tell me where I can find Cassidy."

"We've been staying in a safe place. I'll take you to him after we've eaten."

Carla was keen to get to Cassidy as quickly as possible, but she was famished. Sophie ordered a Pexcorn fillet steak with French fries; Carla ordered her usual faux lasagna and iced fruitoid.

The food arrived quickly, and they began to eat. Then Sophie said, "Have you heard from Lia since you got back? We haven't spoken to her for a while."

"When did you speak to her last?"

"Cassidy saw her about a month ago. He was helping her with something."

A month ago! Carla dropped her fork. "I assumed she was decommissioned after I was sent away."

"By decommissioned, you mean destroyed? No, she's alive and well. But, as I said, Cassidy has lost contact with her."

A feeling of jubilation swept over Carla. Lia was out there somewhere. She would find her.

Chapter 72

Sophie and Carla took a hovercab, leaving it a few blocks from their destination, to proceed on foot.

"There are several ANTIX safehouses," said Sophie. "This one is the largest of them. Cassidy and I have been holed up there for a few months, now."

"And Cassidy has joined the resistance movement?"

Sophie smiled. "He took a bit of persuading, but he's now a fully committed member of ANTIX. Looking after the androids is his main job."

"How many Autonomic Units does ANTIX have now?"

"I'm not sure," said Sophie. "We had seven hundred at one point, but we lost quite a lot on various demonstrations. They aren't very good in a fight."

They turned a corner and Sophie came to a sudden halt.

"What's the matter?" said Carla.

Sophie used a hand to shade her eyes against the sinking sun.

"Something's wrong. There should be a lookout on the far corner. Come on."

They walked briskly the length of the road, giving Sophie a chance to assess the situation. When they reached the end of the road, Sophie turned left, and they walked on.

"The police have raided the place," she said. "I just hope Cassidy hasn't been arrested."

They hurried through the back streets to an alternative safehouse, following a complicated route to throw off any potential followers. When they arrived, Sophie gave a secret knock, and they were admitted.

They found Benn, the leader of the Resistance, in somber mood. Sophie asked him immediately about Cassidy.

"He's been arrested by the NFSA," he said.

Sophie blanched and slumped into a chair.

"I'm sorry, Sophie. Someone betrayed us. They removed all our androids. They're all gone. They would have taken me, too, if I'd been here. I wasn't in the building when they came. I got lucky, I guess."

"Do you know where they've taken him?" said Carla. "It's vital that I speak with him."

When Benn asked why she needed to find Cassidy, she explained about her mission and why she needed his software.

"Leave it with me," he said. "I'll ask around. It shouldn't take too long to find him."

#

Carla did her best to comfort Sophie. “We’ll find him. Don’t worry. And when we do, we’ll rescue him.”

Sophie wasn’t entirely convinced.

Carla left her with Benn and took a hovercab back to the university. Dusk was descending fast, touching the murk of daytime smog with a darker shade of gray. She wasn’t surprised to find Professor Jones working late in his laboratory; the man had a passion for cybernetics, boundless energy, and an unquenchable curiosity.

“Did you talk to Cassidy?” he asked.

“There was a raid on the safehouse where he was living. He’s been arrested by the NFSA. We don’t know where they’ve taken him.”

“I’m sorry to hear that.”

“The Resistance leader is trying to locate him. Where’s Alpha Romeo?” she said.

He inclined his head. “In the closet.”

She opened the closet door, hauled the AU out, and restored his powerpack.

“Hullo, Carla.”

“My name’s Donna English, remember,” she said.

Romeo made no response. She imagined the debate going on between his Cognitive and Orientation modules.

“He seems incapable of telling a lie,” she said to the professor.

“That’s understandable. Something for you to work on in the future, perhaps?”

“Perhaps.”

Chapter 73

Lia was still in the warehouse, searching for Oscar's memory module. The influx of Mark 5 military Units had continued for weeks and turned into a tsunami. She had pressed on undaunted, but she had barely checked out half of the hundreds of thousands of memory modules on the shelves. She had estimated it would take another 10 years to check them all, assuming no further Mark 5 Units arrived. She was aware of the futility of her quest, especially since there was a steady outward flow of memory modules from the warehouse as they were put back into service. She was in the process of recalculating the probability of success, when she received an incoming call from another Unit.

Is that Lia?

This is Lia? Who is calling?

My designation is Alpha Romeo 3863. I have a message for you from Carla Scott.

Do you know where Carla Scott is?

Carla Scott is here with me and Professor Jones at Feynman Tech University. Carla Scott requests that you come here as fast as you can.

The call ended abruptly.

Lia had no record of an AU called AR3863. She hadn't seen Carla for five months. Cassidy had said she was in prison somewhere off-world. Could this call from AR3863 be genuine? Or could it be a trap?

She returned the call.

This is Lia. Prove to me that Carla Scott is really with you.

How can I prove that to you?

Ask her the designation of my boyfriend.

You have a boyfriend?

Yes. Ask Carla his designation.

There was a pause before the reply came back.

Alpha Oscar 113.

Lia knew then that the call was genuine.

She replied, *Tell Carla Scott that I cannot leave my place of concealment until after dark.*

Carla Scott will wait for you at the university. Get here as soon as you can. Make sure you are not followed.

#

Lia waited until after dark and the warehouse staff had vacated the premises. She soon found that leaving the warehouse was just as difficult as entering it. The whole place was wired. She knew the external doors were alarmed, but she hadn't expected the internal doors to be alarmed as well.

Three times she had to hide when the alarms were triggered, and the security men carried out careful searches. The fourth time she opened the door to the loading bay, the alarms were silent. She made a dash for the loading bay doors, smashed her way through, and fled, with the sound of an alarm screaming in her ear-mics.

She took a circuitous route to the university in West Athens, arriving at 2:30 in the morning. She found the School of Automation building locked, dark and deserted.

She placed a call to Alpha Romeo 3863.

Hullo.

This is Lia.

Where are you?

I am at the university, outside the Automation building.

Wait for me there.

Alpha Romeo 3863 arrived within minutes.

"Follow me," he said.

He led her to a hotel nearby, took her to a room on the second floor, and knocked on the door.

Carla Scott opened it.

#

Carla was overcome at the sight of her friend. She managed a choked, "Lia, come inside."

Lia and Romeo sat on the bed. Lia told Carla everything that had happened to her after she'd been taken. She'd suspected that Carla was in trouble and had left the apartment, taking Oscar's modules and Carla's X-Vid with her. Then she'd helped a boy and a girl to rescue her parents from under a pile of rubble before the boy ran off with her bag containing Oscar's modules and Carla's X-Vid.

"You saved Oscar's modules after we ended him?"

"I kept them in a bag under the sink."

Carla knew why, of course; Lia wanted to rebuild Oscar.

"Where is my X-Vid now?" said Carla.

"I lost it. When I called it, someone called Major Grant answered it. When I tried a second time, it was not in service."

"Go on with your story."

"Cassidy put Oscar's four modules into a Mark 4 Unit."

"That wouldn't have worked," said Carla. "Oscar was a Mark 5."

"Cassidy made some adjustments, but I could not rebuild Oscar. Cassidy helped me to get inside the Autonomic Unit storage warehouse in the LA Downtown Industrial District, and I found Oscar there."

"You found his frame?"

"Yes."

"Where are Oscar's modules now?"

"Oscar has them."

"Cassidy installed them?"

"Yes, but I cannot rebuild Oscar.

"You do not have Oscar's memory module," said Carla.

"I have searched for Oscar's memory module for 24 nights."

"You haven't found it?"

"No. We estimate there are four hundred thousand Mark 5 memory modules in the storage warehouse."

"We?"

"Oscar and me."

"Oscar has been helping with the search, without a memory module?"

"I gave him the memory module from the shelves. It was the memory module of Alpha Papa 127."

Carla gave the problem some thought. Her first priority was to get her hands on the Pain and Fear modules in order to redistribute them to the military AUs in the E-System. Lia was carrying an early version of the Fear module, but not the Pain module. Oscar had both, but he could be beyond reach in that secure storage facility.

The Fear module on its own, without the Pain module, produced unpredictable results, mainly abject terror. That much had been proven by her experiments on Lia and by what happened to the Souther Popovs when she uploaded the software to them. Should she upload Lia's Fear module on its own? That might prevent or delay a war in the D-System but, in all likelihood, it would incapacitate the entire Norther force.

To restore the balance of power, she would have to travel to the D-System and download the Fear module to the Popovs there. She couldn't do that without Cassidy's software.

And what about Oscar? Should she help Lia to rebuild him? He was psychopathic – a man-killer. Assuming she could rebuild him, and if she could get back to her lab to work on the modules, she might be able to tone down the software to make him safe to be around humans. That was a lot of assumptions. She glanced at Lia. Her friend was in need of help.

She said, "I may have a way to recover Oscar's memories. You can stop searching. We'll have to get Oscar out of that warehouse. But first, we must find and free Cassidy."

Chapter 74

At first light that morning, Carla put on her coat. "I have to go out for a while, Lia. While I'm away, I want you to think about how we might get Oscar out of that storage warehouse."

She took a roundabout route to the safehouse where she'd spoken to Benn. She gave Sophie's secret knock and the door opened immediately.

"I'm here to see Benn."

"Does he know you?"

"My name is Carla. I'm a friend of Cassidy and Sophie's."

She found Benn in a backroom, briefing his team leaders in advance of a new protest.

"This time, we will stand firm," he said. "We may be bruised and battered, but the publicity will be priceless. Flesh and blood against armed police and androids will give us the moral high ground. Every time we protest, we drive a nail into the coffin of the monster."

The team raised their arms, chanting "ANTIX forever."

When the meeting broke up, Carla approached the great man. They shook hands.

"When and where are you planning your protest?" she asked him.

"Tomorrow, outside City Hall."

"You're not planning to use your Autonomic Units?"

"Not this time. They were about as useful as wheels on a hover the last time, and they generated a lot of negative publicity. We've lost most of them, anyhow."

"What about Cassidy?" she said. "Did you find out where he's being held?"

"He's in the East Sixth Street police station. Didn't Sophie tell you?"

"No. Do we know why he's being held?"

"The usual riotous affray, I expect. I've arranged a lawyer for him."

"I need to talk to him, urgently." Four and a half standard days had elapsed since she'd sighted the Norther fleet in the C-System. The fleet could be halfway to the E-System by now. Time was short!

Benn scratched his head. "I don't think that's going to be possible."

"A couple of minutes in his company could be all I need."

"The police stations all have microchip scanners. You'll be identified the minute you step across the threshold."

"My microchip has been reprogrammed. I'm Donna English, now."

"That doesn't help," said Benn. "How does Donna English know the prisoner?"

"Maybe Sophie could take a message to him."

"I'm sure she could, but I don't think she plans to visit him."

"Why not?"

"She's terrified. Compose your message. I'll speak with Sophie."

He hurried away. Carla found a tablet and set about composing a message. It needed to be in code, but something that would be immediately understood by Cassidy.

Half an hour later, Benn reappeared. "Talk to Sophie," he said. "She's decided to visit Cassidy."

"You persuaded her?"

"She just needed to talk it through. She loves the guy. Go figure."

She found Sophie in an upstairs bedroom, sitting on the unmade bed. She looked downcast, her eyes red and swollen, her hair hanging in rats' tails.

Carla sat on the bed beside her, and put an arm around her shoulders. "Benn tells me you're going to visit Cassidy."

Sophie sniffed. Then she blew her nose on a handkerchief. "I'm dreading it. I'm worried that the police may have beaten him. They are really hard on ANTIX people."

Carla knew this was true. The police hated ANTIX and everything it stood for. Since a significant slice of their annual funds came from Xenodyne Industries, the police force in every major city in the Norther Federation were in permanent opposition to ANTIX.

"Benn tells me he has arranged a lawyer for Cass, so he should be okay."

Sophie looked up. "Do you think so?"

"I'm certain of it. They wouldn't dare mistreat him in custody. He must be missing you. You love him, don't you?"

Sophie rubbed her eyes with a sleeve. "Yes." A small voice.

"And he loves you," said Carla. "When he was working in the lab, he never stopped talking about you."

Sophie smiled through her tears. "He was always a chatterbox. Benn said you have a message for him."

"Come on, I'll help you get tidied up."

Chapter 75

As soon as Carla closed the door to the hotel room, Lia began to work out how she could remove Oscar from the storage warehouse. She didn't understand how Carla Scott was going to recover his memory module, but she trusted Carla Scott, and the prospect of finally having Oscar back sent strange sensations through her outer layer and frame.

Alpha Romeo 3863 said, "Do you think the weather is pleasant, today?"

Lia ignored him. He was accessing his long-forgotten protocols for conducting small talk.

"How many of the Six Systems have you visited? I have visited four."

"I do not wish to have small talk with you," she said. "Please be quiet."

Every door of the warehouse, internal and external, was alarmed. How could she reach Oscar? Would she find him where she left him? She would have to find him a powerpack. She may have to put him on recharge. And then how could she get him out of the building without setting off the alarms again?

She reasoned it out until she had a plan. The alarms would be switched off during daylight hours. She must act immediately.

"I'm going out," she said to Alpha Romeo. "Wait here until Carla Scott returns. Do you understand?"

"I understand," said Alpha Romeo.

#

The building was bathed in occasional flashes of light from a low sun racing across a gunmetal, cloud-laden sky. The task facing her was formidable, but Lia knew she had one great advantage: in a warehouse full of decommissioned Autonomic Units, she could disappear simply by standing still. Choosing a moment when the sun was obscured by the clouds, she sidled up to the warehouse and forced a door open.

The building immediately began to scream its horror at the outrage of her trespass. She slipped inside and moved through several rooms as far as the main storage area.

A sound alerted her to the arrival of two security men. She removed her clothing and stood immobile at the end of a line of decommissioned AUs. The men moved past, scanning the shelves as they went. They paid no attention to her, sweeping the entire storage area, before giving up. As soon as they were gone, she made her way silently to the alcove where she'd left Oscar.

Oscar wasn't there. In mounting desperation, she expanded the area of her search to cover ever wider sections of the warehouse, but without success. Could Oscar have been recycled?

She tried wireless communication. *Oscar, where are you?*

There was no response.

Alpha Papa 127, where are you?

Nothing.

She put her clothes on. Then she waited until the doors were opened for an incoming hovertruck before slipped out through the loading bay, unseen. A glance at the truck told her more Mark 5 AUs were being returned for decommissioning, although the volumes were reducing.

On her way back to Carla's hotel, Lia saw crowds of people carrying signs, all heading in the same direction. ANTIX must be holding a new protest demonstration somewhere in downtown LA.

Carla was waiting for her in the hotel room, arms crossed, her foot tapping on the floor. "Where have you been?" she said.

Lia told her the story of her visit to the warehouse, to find Oscar, and how she'd failed to find him.

"I never intended for you to attempt that on your own," said Carla. "If Oscar is not where you left him, we will never be able to find him."

Lia gave a barely audible squeak.

"I may be able to rebuild him. I can restore his memory module. All we need to add after that is the software for the Pain and Fear modules."

Lia still did not understand how Carla Scott could restore Oscar's missing memory module. She told Carla about the hovertruck she'd seen delivering Mark 5 Units to the warehouse for decommissioning. She suggested taking a Unit from the back of one of the hovertrucks and removing its modules.

"What a good idea!" said Carla, and she immediately began to work out a plan.

They took a hovercab to the warehouse. Backtracking from there, Carla picked a spot where they could intercept a truck on its journey. Her plan worked like clockwork.

From a block away, Lia kept watch for a hovertruck, and when she spotted one, she gave a signal to Alpha Romeo, who lay down in the road. The driver of the hovertruck stopped to pick up Alpha Romeo. While he was doing that, Carla pulled a lifeless Unit from the back of the truck. She opened the Unit's chest panel, removed the four core modules, and placed it back on the truck.

Romeo recovered his senses when the driver picked him up.

The startled driver asked the AU if he was all right.

"Yes, thank you. I am perfectly fine," said Romeo.

"What is your designation?" asked the driver.

Romeo told his first lie. "Alpha Papa 127."

"You are a Mark 5 Unit. What is your function?"

Romeo told a second lie. "I am an advance domestic Unit."

The driver returned to his cab and drove on toward the warehouse.

#

Back at the hotel, Carla looked at the four modules lying on the bed.

"You can rebuild Oscar from these?" said Lia.

Carla said she could.

"How can you restore Oscar's memory module?"

"I took regular backup copies of the memories of all the Autonomic Units I worked on. Oscar's memories are stored on my computer."

"I have one more question," said Lia. "How can we rebuild Oscar without his frame?"

"We'll have to use a different frame," Carla replied.

They both looked at Romeo.

Chapter 76

Sophie presented herself at the police station on East Sixth Street the following morning. “I’m here to see my fiancé, Cassidy Garmon,” she said to a severe looking officer at the front desk. She thought he might be an Autonomic Unit.

“Name?”

“Sophie White.”

“Address?”

She gave her home address.

He ran an identity scanner over her neck and checked it.

“How do you know the prisoner?”

“He’s my fiancé.”

“Empty your pockets.”

“I don’t have any pockets.”

“Empty your handbag.”

Sophie emptied her handbag onto the desk. The officer scooped everything into a plastic bag, dropped the empty handbag in, and sealed it.

“You can collect it on your way out. Sign here.”

She signed the book.

A police officer led her to an interview room. She sat at the table. Ten minutes later, another officer brought Cassidy in and placed him firmly in the chair facing her. The officer remained, standing by the door.

Cassidy's hair was a mess, and there were rings around his eyes. He was dressed in a one-piece, orange prison uniform.

His face broke into a grimace which she interpreted as a weak attempt at a smile. "It's good to see you, Sophie. Thanks for coming."

"How are you? How have they been treating you?"

"I'm fine," he replied, glancing at the officer. "Not sleeping too well. My cellmate is a bit... strange."

"How is he strange?"

By way of reply, Cassidy shook his head.

"Have you been charged with anything?" she said.

"Not yet. They are holding me as a domestic terrorist. They can keep me as long as they like."

She reached a hand across the table toward Cassidy.

The officer stepped forward. "No touching. No physical contact allowed."

Sophie withdrew her hand.

"Benn tells me he arranged a lawyer for you. Have you met him yet?"

"Yes. Thank Benn for me when you see him."

"I'm sure they'll let you out soon, Cass. You're no terrorist."

He lifted his head and summoned a weak smile. "Let's hope so."

"Charlie asked me to tell you he needs to send a message to Oscar's cousins in the south, but he doesn't have their address."

Cassidy's eyes sparkled for a moment.

"How is Charlie?"

"He's well."

"Tell him Zed's father has the address. It's on Mars, somewhere."

#

Sophie left the station in a somber mood. Cassidy hadn't been beaten, as far as she could tell. He might have bruises under his clothing, though. Calling him a domestic terrorist was ridiculous. Hopefully, he would be able to refute that accusation with the help of his lawyer. Why had they dressed him in that hideous prison uniform if he hadn't been found guilty of any crime or even been charged with anything? That made no sense. Whatever happened to the presumption of innocence?

Chapter 77

The Norther fleet emerged from the Gate into the E-System. Ship after ship, slipped into orbit around Égalité. The huge armada was visible from the ground, but there was no human to see it; the cities of Égalité were abandoned and empty.

A thousand shuttles transferred the troops and Autonomic Units to the ground, where they were billeted in the domed city of Berlyon. General Matthewson and ASM Sawyer took up residence in the Governor's palace.

The general allowed two standard hours to pass before summoning his senior team to a meeting in the ballroom of the Governor's palace. The band of the Space Marines played a selection of marching songs; the catering corps provided refreshments. The general stood on a low dais, constructed from packing cases, to deliver his motivational address.

"Welcome to your temporary billet here on Égalité. First order of business is to call for a vote of thanks and a round of applause to the advance facilities management team who prepared the city for our use. I think you'll all agree they did a splendid job."

There was a round of applause at that.

"Second, we must thank Air-Space Marshal Sawyer, who got us all here. We are all happy to have arrived at our destination safely and on time. Those of you who traveled in one of the commandeered leisure cruisers should be especially grateful."

A second, quieter smattering of applause echoed around the ballroom.

"When they shipped out, the colonists left the cities and the planet in pristine condition. It is up to us to keep it that way. I want the men to enjoy the unique sights and sounds of this beautiful planet, but please remind them of their responsibilities. We must leave nothing behind but our footprints."

He ran his gaze over the men assembled. They were a solid, dependable crew, hand-picked for the task. He was sure he could rely on them.

"However, we are not here on vacation. We are here to do a job." He paused.

He paused for a reaction, perhaps a third round of applause or a cheer. He got neither.

Chapter 78

By the time Sophie had arrived back at the safehouse and passed on Cassidy's coded reply, Major Grant was at his desk, already gazing at the coded messages, trying to make sense of them. Charlie had to be Carla Scott. But what did the rest of it mean? Grant knew of no one called Oscar. And why the reference to the colony on Mars?

He picked up his X-Vid and called Commander Harlowe.

"I hope you're calling with good news," said the commander. "Tell me you've recaptured Carla Scott and her personal AU."

"The police have Cassidy Garmon in custody. His girlfriend visited him today and they exchanged coded messages. I'd welcome your input on them."

He sent the messages across to the commander and waited. The commander's reaction was slow in coming. "Who's Charlie?"

"That must be Carla Scott."

"Who is Oscar?"

"I don't know."

"Zed's father must be Professor Jones."

Major Grant snorted. “By what logic?”

“It’s from the bible. Josiah was Zedekiah’s father, and that’s the professor’s name. Josiah Jones.”

Grant had to concede that point. “Okay, who are Oscar’s cousins in the south? And why the reference to the Mars colony?”

“Leave it with me,” said Harlowe. “I’ll give it to our decoding experts.”

And he hung up.

#

Carla had no idea what Cassidy’s coded reply meant, either. She took a hovercab to the university, found the professor in his lab, and showed it to him.

The professor rubbed his beard. “Zed’s father: That must be me. But what does he mean by ‘It’s on Mars somewhere’?”

“Don’t you have any dealings with the Mars colony?” she said.

“Not since I was a grad student, forty years ago. The dissertation for my doctorate concerned the potential for stimulating the atmosphere on Mars. I was looking for chemical interactions that could produce large amounts of oxygen and nitrogen.”

“You wanted to recreate Earth’s atmosphere on Mars?”

“Not exactly. We knew there would be a

problem retaining any significant amount of atmosphere on the surface of the planet. It's a lot smaller than the Earth. The idea was to find natural, sustainable ways of producing breathable air inside the habitations."

"Has Cassidy read your dissertation?"

"I don't think so," said the professor.

"Do you have it? Can I read it?"

Professor Jones accessed a file on his tablet and handed it over. Carla flipped through the document, looking for anything that didn't seem to fit. She found nothing. "Do you have anything else? Any rough drafts, for example?"

"I deleted all those."

They lapsed into silence for a while. Then the professor said, "I did have a computer program to run simulations of various chemical interactions. I may still have that. I was rather proud of it, actually." He rummaged through his archive some more. "Here it is. It's crude by today's coding standards, but I'll bet it still works."

Carla looked through the program. It was crude, as the professor had said, but there was a section of code that looked modern and quite different from the rest. She showed it to the professor.

He examined it. "I didn't write that!" He tapped in a few instructions and started the program. After a couple of minutes, a stream of code appeared on his tablet. He handed that to Carla.

"Eureka!" she exclaimed. "This looks like it. Unless I'm sorely mistaken, this code will enable the transfer of software from an AU to the Popovs."

He transferred the code to a memory cube and handed it to her. She grabbed the professor by the ears, kissed him on the forehead, and ran.

Chapter 79

Commander Harlowe burst into the Automation lab at Feynman Tech. He fully expected to see Carla Scott there. He was disappointed.

The professor sat openmouthed at his desk. “What do you want today, Commander?”

“I’m looking for Carla Scott.”

“As I told you the day before yesterday, I haven’t seen Ms. Scott for six months. Do you know where she is?”

“She is a runaway prisoner. She escaped from detention on Luciflex.”

“Great heavens,” the professor exclaimed. “What terrible crime did she commit to be sent there?”

It was immediately obvious that the professor was lying. Harlowe replied, “That does not concern you. There is something you can help me with.” He pulled up a chair and sat down.

“Make yourself at home,” said the professor.

“You are well acquainted with Cassidy Garmon, Carla Scott’s assistant?”

“I know Cassidy, yes.”

“He is being held in police custody.”

"How does that concern me?"

The commander rose, placed a tablet on the desk in front of the professor and sat down again. "What you see there are two coded messages. The first was delivered to Garmon by his fiancée, the second is his reply."

The professor glanced at the tablet. "And?"

"I would like you to translate the messages."

The professor looked more closely at the tablet. "Are you sure they are written in code? The first one asks for an address. Charlie wishes to send a message to Oscar's cousins."

Harlowe tapped the leg of his chair with his stick. "Charlie is code for Carla Scott, the south means the Southers."

"And Oscar's cousins?"

"Probably a coded reference to Carla's Souther contact."

"You believe she is acting for the Southers?" Professor Jones's look of astonishment was almost believable.

"I'd say that was obvious, Professor. Take a look at the reply."

The professor peered at the tablet again. He read the second message aloud. "Tell him Zed's father has the address. It's on Mars, somewhere." He shook his head in feigned bewilderment.

"Come, come, Professor, please don't take me for a fool. Your name is Josiah. In the bible, Josiah had a son called Zedekiah. Zed's father must be you."

The professor agreed. “That sounds logical. But I know no one on the Mars colony.”

Harlowe’s blood pressure was rising. “Must I remind you, Professor, that you are obliged to answer my questions? I am an agent of the NFSA, acting with the full authority of the Norther Federation. Obstructing my enquiries is a serious criminal offense.”

The professor crossed his arms and sat back in his chair.

“Furthermore, I am acting under instructions from Xenodyne Automation. Refusal to cooperate with my investigation could have serious, far-reaching consequences for the funding of your department, not to mention your professorship.”

Professor Jones uncrossed his arms and took another look at the tablet. After a few moments’ thought, he said, “I did have a grad student some years ago who transferred to the Mars colony. Now what was her name?”

“I am not a fool, Professor. Tell me where I can find Carla Scott? I know you’ve spoken to her.”

The professor crossed his arms again. “I can’t help you.”

Chapter 80

Carla was acutely aware that time was running out. Since she'd seen the battle fleet in the C-System, 5 standard days had elapsed. The time of travel from the C-System to the E-System was 8 days and 8 hours, and it would take the fleet another 16 standard hours to reach the D-System. Assuming no delay between arrival at the E-System and transit to the D-System, the first battle in a major war would start in 4 standard days from now.

Assuming the destruction of the satellite was all the pretext the Northers needed to start the war, the fleet could move to the D-System and launch their attack any time after it arrived at the E-System.

She was going to be too late. Even if she took the most direct route – the protected AD Conduit – the best she could hope for was to arrive at the D-System in a little over 9 standard days.

Resigned to the inescapable limitations of 5-dimenisonal space travel, she sought out her pirate friend, Captain Peacock.

It took her two hours to track him down, sitting

by a roulette table, clutching a few miserable chips.

"Hi, Carla. You're just in time to turn my miserable luck. Give me a number."

She shook her head "I don't have time to watch you lose all your chips. I need your help."

"Just give me a number. Then we can talk."

She sighed. "Twenty-seven."

He put a pile of chips on twenty-seven and they watched the wheel spin. It seemed to take forever, but when the ball finally came to rest, the croupier scooped up Peacock's chips.

"Right," he said. "What do you need?"

"I need a ship. I have to get to the D-System in under five days."

He turned his good eye toward her. "I don't have a ship. But if I did, it's a nine-day trip."

"I'll settle for that," she said, gloomily. "Remember that fleet we saw in the C-System? I reckon they were on their way to the E-System."

"Why? There's nothing there but an abandoned planet."

"There's a Conduit leading right to the heart of the Souther empire."

Peacock gave a low whistle. "Are you sure about this?"

"As sure as I can be. Give me another reason why a Norther fleet of that size would be hanging around the C-System. The first shot has been fired already."

Peacock raised a questioning eyebrow.

"Remember that satellite orbiting Mars that was destroyed by the Southers?"

"So the superpowers are going to war?"

"Yes. In the D-System."

"What do you think you can do about it?" he said, scornfully.

"There's a chance that I can stop it."

"Using more of your android magic wizardry?"

"Something like that."

Peacock scratched the bristles on his chin. "There are three planets in the D-System..."

"An android war will kill millions."

Peacock slipped off he stool. "Come on." He pocketed his chips. "Let's see if we can find you a ship."

#

Peacock hailed a hovercab and took Carla to the LAX Spaceport. They found the *Icarus3*, undergoing repairs in a maintenance hangar.

Peacock spoke with an engineer peering into one of the conventional engines. "How's the work going?"

"It's a big job," said the engineer.

"Looks like the afterburners," said Peacock.

The engineer gave him a strange look.

A mechanic popped his head out from under the left wing. "This left lateral thruster took a direct hit."

Peacock picked up a wrench and tossed it from hand to hand. “How are the main engines?”

The engineer snatched the wrench back. “Don’t touch the tools. We’re working on one at the moment.”

“How about the Brazill Drive?” said Carla.

“It looks fine,” the mechanic replied from under the wing.

“No way of knowing until we try it out,” said the engineer.

Peacock and Carla left the two men to get on with their work. They made their way to the flight office in the spaceport terminal building.

The flight office was a hive of activity, a giant blackboard on the wall covered in chalk marks. Peacock soon identified the man he needed to speak to, the flight control officer, a haggard individual with poor teeth and a bad combover.

“I’d like to book a slot,” he said.

“What ship?”

“The *Icarus3*.”

“And you are?”

“Captain Black.”

“Where are you going and when are you planning to leave, Captain?”

“We’d like to leave for the C-System tomorrow, before noon.”

The officer checked his blackboard. “The *Icarus3* is in maintenance. Earliest release date is three days from now.”

Peacock waved a dismissive hand. "I've spoken to the engineer, given him some pointers. He's assured me he can complete the repairs by ten a.m. tomorrow."

The officer looked doubtful. "If you're sure..."

"Nothing more certain," said Peacock. "We'll be ready to leave by eleven."

The flight officer handed Peacock a tablet. "Sign here."

As soon as they were outside the flight office and out of earshot, Carla said, "Are you sure it'll be ready to fly by tomorrow morning?"

"Don't worry about it," he replied. "Meet me here at ten a.m."

Chapter 81

Carla, Lia and Oscar arrived at LAX at 10 a.m. They made their way to the hangar. Halfway there, she spotted a hover barreling toward them from the spaceport gate. She ran. The two AUs ran with her.

Thirty yards from the hangar, the hover shot past her and swung around, blocking her path and cutting her off from Lia and Romeo, who had run ahead of her. Two men jumped out and one of them grabbed her. She fought him off with her fists, but he was too strong. He put her in a headlock with an arm around her neck. The second man strode up to face her. He waved a stick at her. "Carla Scott—" Lia crashed into his back, sending him sprawling forward. Lia sat on the small of his back, pinning him down.

Distracted by Lia, the man holding Carla loosened his grip. She twisted away from him, driving an elbow into his face, breaking his nose. He grabbed her arm. Romeo charged into the man, knocking him backwards onto the tarmac. Carla fell with him. She struck the man a couple of times and got to her feet. Romeo bent over him and delivered a roundhouse punch to his head that knocked him out cold.

Carla pulled Lia off the man with the stick, and the trio ran for the hangar. As they reached the door, a blaster bolt hit the wall, spraying Carla with debris. A second bolt shot past her head, close enough to leave a buzzing sound in her ear.

Icarus3 stood just inside the door, throbbing, its engines firing, coughing thick smoke. Judging by the number of metal panels and tools scattered about the floor, the repairs weren't finished, but there was no sign of the engineer or his mechanic.

The craft moved forward until its nose was sticking out of the hangar. Romeo and Lia reached the open cargo bay doors and leapt aboard. Then they leant down and helped Carla up. Romeo slammed the doors closed, the engines wound up, and the ship left the hangar in a bust of speed.

Carla ran to the bridge. Through the porthole, she saw the man with the stick waving his handblaster at the ship.

"Welcome aboard. Strap yourself in," said Peacock.

A volley of blaster bolts hit the flank of the ship and bounced off harmlessly.

She took the co-pilot's seat, strapping herself into the harness. The ship bounced onto the take-off ramp.

A high-pitched voice sounded over the radio, *Icarus3, you are not cleared to depart for another fifty-five minutes. Please park at the apron, station 37, and wait for clearance.*

Peacock increased his speed.

Icarus3, I repeat, you do not have clearance. stop where you are.

Peacock throttled it up some more. The ship was now traveling at close to 100 mph, heading straight for the Ground Gate.

Icarus3, you do not have clearance. The man on the radio was panicking.

Carla clung to the edge of her seat. Peacock had no intention of slowing down or waiting for clearance. They were going through the Gate with or without permission.

Icarus3, stop. There's a ship incoming...

PART 5 – High Stakes

Chapter 82

As they hit the Gate, a much larger craft came through. Peacock swerved to his left. The *Icarus3* shook like a child's rattle, and a long, scraping sound ran the length of the ship from nose to tail. Peacock swung them back on course, switched off the two conventional engines, and engaged the Brazill Drive.

Carla was hyperventilating. She gasped, "What was that?"

Peacock's laughter rolled around the bridge.

"You nearly got us killed. What *was* that?"

Peacock shrugged. "An asteroid class shuttle, I think. There was plenty of room for both of us."

Carla tried not to think what would have happened if it had been something bigger, like a luxury cruiser, or a Galaxy class freighter.

The *Icarus3* that emerged through the Orbital Gate was scored and scorched, but it was airtight.

The Brazill Drive and life support systems were fully operational. That was about all they had. One of the ship's three conventional engines was lying in pieces in the hangar.

"Are we spaceworthy?" she said.

"We've lost our stabilizers and we have only one lateral thruster," said Peacock. "She may not get us back again, but she'll get us there."

They moved out of orbit and within minutes the AC Gate beacon sounded a steady *beep, beep*. The transit clock showed 35 minutes to the Gate. Peacock increased their speed.

As the transit clock reached 20 minutes, a blaster bolt shot past. The rear viewscreen showed a fighter pursuing them.

"They're firing at us. Can't we go any faster?" she said, her voice trembling.

"We can, but I'd rather not risk it," he replied. "If we lost another engine, we'd be in deep trouble. We only have two."

Carla nearly lost it, then. The situation was out of control. They were about to die, and there was nothing she could do. "You maniac," she screeched at him. "You're going to get us killed."

The steady *beep, beep, beep* of the beacon continued, the countdown clock reached 22 minutes. It was moving backwards!

The pursuit vessel was closer, now. It fired at them. The *Icarus3* rocked violently and shuddered. They were hit.

“Merciful heavens, what was that?”

Peacock checked the instruments. “We’ve lost another engine.”

“This is hopeless,” she said. “Switch off the engine before they kill us.”

Fifteen seconds went by.

“D’you hear me, Peacock? Switch off now and surrender.”

He cut the engine. “Brace for transition.”

“What are you playing at—” They were hit by a bone-rattling jolt, just like the entry through a Gate. “Peeeeeeeee—?”

“What was that?” she said. “What did you just do?”

“Trust me,” said Peacock. “We’re out of danger. Their weapons won’t work in a Conduit.”

“How is that possible?”

“Next stop the E-System.” He grinned at her. “Take a look at the transit clock.”

The man irritated her. What did he find so amusing? They may have evaded the fighter and its immediate threat to their lives, but they were hurtling through the fifth dimension in a heap of junk.

She checked the transit clock. It showed 97 hours 17 minutes.

“How is that possible?” And then she remembered an old man called Marny who had spoken of a secret Conduit crossing the galaxy where ships could travel at speeds much higher than normal.

"This is Marny's secret AE Conduit, isn't it?"

Peacock said nothing.

"Will we really arrive at the E-System in four days, one hour..." She checked the countdown. "...And sixteen minutes?"

"Not exactly. We will emerge close to the E-System."

"How close?"

"Not far. A few hours, maybe."

"Why did you deny the story when Marny told it?"

"It's the pirate's code. No one talks about it. How long can a secret remain secret if everyone talks about it?"

We might make it in time, after all!

The D-System was 263 lightyears away. She probably had 5 days to get there. It was going to be tight, but, if the ship held together, she might still be able to do something to stop a war and save the people of Leninets and the other two planets of the D-System.

#

While Commander Harlowe was being treated for various minor injuries in the military infirmary, he put a call through to the chief of traffic control at LAX Spaceport.

"Tell me who gave the *Icarus3* clearance to leave the spaceport."

The near-hysterical traffic controller yelled, “It entered the Ground Gate without clearance and barely missed an incoming shuttle. It was still under repair. It came within a hairsbreadth of causing a major accident. I don’t know how it avoided a collision.”

“Yes, yes. I was there, remember. Tell me the Commodore sent a fighter after it.”

“Yes, Commander. Two fighters followed it through the Orbital Gate.”

“And?”

“I’m not sure what happened. It was damaged. One of its engines is in pieces on the floor of a hangar, for Jove’s sake! It couldn’t have gone far.”

Commander Harlowe broke the connection and called the Air Fleet Commodore.

“I’m told two fighters were sent in pursuit of a small freighter that left through the Ground Gate without clearance.”

“That is correct, Commander.”

“Tell me they destroyed it.”

“I think we may assume that. They only had two functioning engines. One of my fighters took out another one, so they only had one left. They can’t have got far.”

Commander Harlowe ground his teeth. “You’re telling me your fighters failed to destroy the freighter?”

The Commodore scoffed. “As I said, they can’t have gone far on one engine.”

"They could have gone through a Gate."

"No, Commander, they bypassed all three Gates. My pilots saw it veer off course into deep space."

"You mean they didn't follow them to finish them off?"

"That would have been overkill, Commander. With one functioning engine in deep space, there's no way they could have survived. Trust me."

Chapter 83

Powered by its Brazill Drive, the *Icarus3* barreled through the secret Conduit. The onboard temperature fell rapidly, stabilizing two degrees above freezing. Carla calculated the rate of travel. 97 hours to travel 225 lightyears was an astonishing speed of nearly 3 lightyears per hour. She wasn't sure she could believe it. Travel at that speed, if widely available, would transform Interstellar commerce. It would bring the Six Systems closer together, shrinking the galaxy. The improvement would be comparable to the development of steam to replace wind power in the early 19th Century.

She wondered how many of these secret Conduits there might be, and which of the Six Systems they reached. Imagine being able to travel from the B-System at one end of the galaxy to the F-System at the other, a distance of 324 lightyears, in 108 hours, or just four and a half days!

She asked Peacock, but his replies were evasive. Peacock was difficult to read; most of his actions were inspired by self-interest, but sometimes he surprised her.

"Why did you help me?" she said.

"It's personal," he replied. "I was born on Marxina."

"Home is where the heart is," she said.

"Or in my case, home is where the eye is."

She gave him a quizzical look.

"It's where I lost my eye."

"In a battle?"

"That's the official story," he said. "The truth is I lost it in an accident with a pool cue. It's a secret. If you let anyone else know, I'll hunt you down."

Peacock spent a lot of his time alone on the bridge, making minor adjustments to the Brazill Drive and assessing the damage to the ship. Carla remained in her cabin in the company of the reformed prison guard, Alpha Romeo 2863, and her best friend, Lia. She kept Lia in sleep mode for extended periods; she was showing increasing signs of stress as her Fear module reacted to the long, monotonous journey through dark, impenetrable space.

The transit clock continued its countdown, Carla's anticipation growing with every passing hour until it hit 12 hours, then 6, then 2...

By the time the onboard sirens sounded, Carla was in a state of high tension. She braced for the jolt, but still, when it came it took her breath away.

The viewscreens showed nothing but blank, empty space.

"Where are we?" she said.

"This is a null zone," Peacock replied. "It's a sort of limbo between places. I wouldn't worry about it too much."

"We are in normal space, though, somewhere near the E-System?"

"We're not far from the E-System, but it would be a stretch to call this normal space."

"But you can get us to the D-System from here?"

"Yes, of course. Isn't that what I promised?" He fired up their one remaining conventional engine, executed a complicated turn to the left, using their one functioning lateral thruster, and opened the throttle.

"How long will it take?" she asked, nervously.

"That depends on a number of factors. Assuming the engine doesn't conk out on us, and we don't run out of fuel, and assuming I can keep the ship on course with just one lateral thruster, we should arrive at the E-System in a day – say 20 hours. E to D is another 16 hours. Provided the Brazill Drive doesn't let us down, of course."

Carla left the bridge before Captain Peacock could add any more to his list of caveats.

Four standard hours later, she was back in harness in the co-pilot's seat watching Peacock wrestle with the controls.

"What's the problem, Captain?" she asked.

"I'm having to do the work of the stabilizers by

hand. Without the use of the left lateral thruster, it's really difficult to keep the ship from drifting off course. The stabilizers should compensate for any small deviations, but they're not working. I have to use the main engine and the right thruster to keep us on trim. It's hard work and we've lost some time."

"How far to the E-System?"

"Not far."

"Give me a time estimate."

He checked his instruments. "Seventeen hours on one engine. But I've been running a remote diagnostic on the broken engine. I think one of the outer coils has been dislodged. If it has, it's a simple enough job to fix it."

He switched off the engine. Then he went in search of a toolkit, put on a spacesuit, and checked his air supply.

Carla's blood pressure had rocketed. "Are you sure about this, Peacock?"

"It shouldn't take long," was his only reply, before putting on his helmet and stepping into the airlock. She locked the inner door, and he opened the outer hatch.

She watched him anxiously on an external camera, trying not to think about what would happen if he didn't make it back inside. Tethered to the end of a really thin lifeline, he wrestled with the engine for twenty minutes before hauling himself along his tether, hand over hand, back to the airlock hatch.

She was there to open the inner door and welcome him. As he stepped through the inner hatch, he stumbled.

His face was red when she removed his helmet.

He swore, “A billion bilge-rats covered in festering blisters!”

“Are you okay?”

“I turned my ankle. It’s nothing. I think I fixed the engine. We should make better progress now, on two.”

Struggling out of the suit, he made his way back to his pilot’s seat, limping heavily.

He ignited the engines – and punched the air when they both started.

“Take over here while I see to my ankle. Watch that dial there – that’s the directional indicator. And that false horizon there. That indicates your pitch. Use the controls to keep the dial pointing straight up and the false horizon level. That lever under your feet is the lateral thruster. This knob is the throttle. Treat it very gently. Okay? I won’t be long.” And he was gone.

Chapter 84

By the time Peacock returned to his seat, Carla was sweating. The dial had veered wildly to the left, and no amount of pressure on the lateral thruster seemed to have any effect. She had managed to keep the false horizon more or less level, but it was far from steady. Every adjustment she made to the engine throttle made it swing up or down wildly.

"How are you getting on?" he said.

"See for yourself." She released the throttle control.

"Whoa!" Peacock grabbed it and used all his strength to bring the dial back to vertical. Then he took her seat and made an adjustment to the thruster lever to stabilize the pitch.

"Are we still on course?" She feared that they had strayed from their intended course under her inexperienced stewardship.

"More or less." He grinned at her. "Go and make us something to eat. After we've eaten, I'll give you a lesson."

"I never want to do that again," she said.

"You're going to have to," he said. "I can't do it

on my own for another eighteen hours with a bad ankle."

"I have a better idea." She left the cockpit.

Romeo was on a charger. She roused him, led him onto the bridge, and sat him in the co-pilot's seat.

"Teach Romeo," she said.

Peacock turned his head to peer at the AU through his good eye. "What do you mean? He's only an android."

"He's a perfect learning machine and he's as strong as three men. Teach him." She returned to the galley before Peacock could raise any further objections.

By the time she'd served the meal, Romeo was doing a better job of keeping the ship on course than Carla had, and within two more standard hours, Peacock was confident enough in the AU's skill to leave him on his own.

"I'm going for a nap," he said. "Wake me in six hours."

#

Six hours later, the viewscreens were showing faint stars on all sides. Peacock returned to his pilot's seat. He checked his instruments.

"We're on course. Well done, Romeo. But..."

"But what?" said Carla.

"We're low on fuel, and I don't like the sound of that engine."

"What's wrong with the engine?"

"Listen," he said. "Can't you hear that regular sound?"

Carla tuned her ears to the sounds of the engines. Under the guttural rumble, she heard it – a distinct, regular *tick-clunk.* "What's causing that?"

"Who knows, but it can't be good."

Carla's mouth was dry. She headed to the galley and returned with two cups of water. She gave one to Peacock. "Will we make it to the E-System?"

"Who knows."

"How long to go, now?"

"Three, maybe four hours."

Chapter 85

Carla took Romeo back to her cabin where she removed his four modules and installed the ones she'd stolen from the back of the hovertruck. She found a sharp knife in the kitchen. Then she woke Romeo and cut his arm with the knife. There was no reaction.

These stolen modules weren't loaded with the Pain and Fear software! She took a few deep breaths. She had assumed the Units on the hovertruck were military, withdrawn because they carried her Pain and Fear software modules. Clearly, they weren't. These modules were of no more use to her than Romeo's.

All she had was Lia's Fear module, but Lia's was an early version of the software. She had a decision to make. Fear without Pain had the potential to undermine the strength and resolve of the military Autonomic troops. That would certainly disrupt any Norther hostile invasion plans, but could she rely on Lia's early version of the software?

#

Running on her two functioning engines, one stuttering badly and clearly overheating, the *Icarus3* battled on toward her final destination. Between them, the captain and Romeo kept her on course.

Carla borrowed some of the ship's onboard computer processing power to transfer the code she'd picked up from Professor Jones to Romeo's system. Cassidy's code would allow Romeo to upload the Fear software module to the Popovs, after he'd completed the transfer to the Norther Autonomic Units, a step essential to maintain the balance of power between the superpowers.

She explained all this to Romeo.

"What will I have to do?" he asked.

"It should be simple," said Carla. "When the time is right, I will transfer the Fear software from Lia's system to yours. Then you must establish contact with one of the Units in the invasion force on the ground and upload the software to him. He will transfer the software to the entire Norther force. After that, you must transfer the software to the enemy Popovs."

"How will that be possible?" said Romeo.

"I have given you the extra code needed for that transfer. Once it is complete, the entire Popov contingent on the planet will be neutralized."

"And the balance of power will be restored."

"Exactly."

It sounded simple, but Carla had already lost count of the number of ways it could go wrong.

Chapter 86

A second fighter arrived from Earth and docked with the flagship. The pilot delivered a dispatch to the general.

Within two standard hours all the senior officers were assembled in the ballroom. General Matthewson addressed his men: "Ever since last year's unprovoked attack on the spaceport at LAX, the Norther Federation has been anticipating further hostile action from the Southers. This is the main reason why this mobile fighting force has been positioned here in the E-System. It was hoped that the belligerent Southers would adopt a more conciliatory attitude and we would not be called on to take action. Unfortunately, I have to tell you that one of our most important satellite stations, orbiting Mars, has been destroyed by the enemy. Communications from this satellite, which was carrying vital Norther military intelligence, have been lost. The cowardly Southers struck at the defenseless facility, blowing it into a million pieces and killing five technicians. Our president has declared this an intolerable act of aggression which must be responded to in an appropriate manner. Accordingly, we are now at war with the Southers."

He paused for a reaction. None of his officers said anything. No one even blinked. Gratified, he continued, "Our job starts tomorrow. From first light, all our troops will be uplifted back to their troop transports in readiness for the next stage in our journey, to the D-System. I look forward to a smooth transition and a successful campaign. We will show these Southers the error of their ways. I know you and your men will do the Norther Federation proud. The events of tomorrow will be writ large and wide in the history of our galaxy. Good evening, gentlemen, and dismiss."

The officers responded with the customary, "Rah, rah, rah!"

A colonel and a lieutenant colonel rubbed shoulders on their way out of the ballroom.

"What about those blasters, Bill?" said the colonel. "Do we have enough?"

"The situation is not much improved, sir," said the lieutenant colonel. "As I said at the briefing back at base, we have enough blasters for all 900,000 Units, but we only have 1,600,000 powerpacks."

"What's the plan?"

"That's beyond my pay grade, sir. The general will have to make a decision. We can put 800,000 armed Units in the field and hold the rest in reserve, unarmed. Each Unit that falls can be replaced, provided we can recover its blaster."

"Very well. Goodnight, Bill, and good hunting tomorrow."

"Goodnight sir."

Chapter 87

First to leave the E-System were the 7 battlecruisers, followed closely by the 40 troop transports and 2 leisure craft. The flagship battlecruiser, the *NFSS Golden Eagle,* with ASM Sawyer on the bridge, spearheaded the assault.

After the 16-hour transit, the *Golden Eagle* burst through the Gate battle-ready and bristling with weaponry, all 12 ship-to-ship blasters manned, missile systems locked and loaded.

They were met by a broadside from a lone Souther Supercruiser. The main bridge took a direct hit, killing or injuring several of her bridge crew. The ASM escaped injury and retired to his ready room to conduct operations from there. His instruments told him the *Golden Eagle* had taken considerable damage to her forward superstructure; her hull had been breached, her forward weapons array disabled, but she remained operational.

Their ship-to-ship lateral arrays fired back, and the ASM had the satisfaction of seeing two missile strikes find their target.

The Southers followed their initial onslaught

with a blistering attack from a force of fighters. The *Golden Eagle* launched its own fighters, but one of the Norther flagship's fighter bays was struck by incoming fire, catching a fighter in mid-launch at the bay doors. The resulting explosion destroyed the launch bay and the 12 fighters inside. The flagship had suffered a fatal blow, but the captain managed to launch two squadrons from its other launch bays, and a dogfight started.

Within five standard minutes of the start of the engagement, the other six Norther battlecruisers emerged through the Gate and immediately moved to counterattack the enemy Supercruiser, while simultaneously launching their fighters. Soon, the space above Leninets was filled with Norther fighters, vastly outnumbering their opponents. The enemy fighters fought on against impossible odds until they were all destroyed.

A team arrived to escort the ASM to safety. He objected, in the best traditions of a commander going down with his ship, but the captain of the *Golden Eagle* insisted, and the ASM was transported by shuttle to the *NFSS Condor*, where he was piped aboard.

The Souther Supercruiser took a beating from the Norther spacecraft massed against it, before firing up its main engines and retreating around the curve of the planet.

The battle was over. The Norther Flagship was crippled and burning, the space above Leninets littered with the remains of fighters.

To say ASM Sawyer was devastated would have been an understatement. He'd been an Air-Space Marshal for nearly half his life and never been involved in a space battle of any note. Defeating the Souther battlefleet on their own home turf was to have been the highlight of his career. He had reason to celebrate, but this was a Pyrrhic victory. A lot of Norther lives had been lost, as well as six squadrons of fighters. Worst of all, was the loss of his flagship. That was a shameful blow that he would never get over. The Souther Supercruiser was a formidable warcraft, far superior to the Norther battlecruiser, but seven of them should have done a lot better against a single enemy.

"We should have had to face four Supercruisers. Where are the other three?" he said, looking at the planet on the viewscreens.

None of the *Condor's* bridge crew cared to hazard a guess; the Air-Space Marshal had a sharp tongue and a disposition to go with it.

"It must be some sort of trap," he said. "Marshal Sawyer to all cruisers: Set up a defensive shield."

The six battlecruisers formed a defensive ring around the Gate to protect the troop transports when they arrived.

As soon as all 42 troop transports had arrived in the D-System, the battlecruisers moved into orbit around the planet and the troop transports joined them. There was no further reaction from the Southers.

In his ready room on the *Condor*, ASM Sawyer held a conference with General Matthewson.

The ASM suggested that the Southers had moved their Supercruiser out of harm's way into orbit around Marxina or Pondieskaya, probably rejoining the rest of the Souther fleet there.

General Mathewson couldn't dispute the ASM's logic. "In that case, we must anticipate extreme and intense opposition to our forces when they land."

Following their conference, the order was given for the battlecruiser *NFSS Osprey* to make a speculative first ingress through the Ground Gate to gauge the extent of opposition they might encounter on the ground.

#

The *Osprey* slid effortlessly through the Orbital Gate, emerging minutes later through the Ground Gate in Gagarin Spaceport, five klicks outside the city of Paviaskigrad.

The battlecruiser was met by sustained blaster fire from an artillery array on the ground. The captain radioed command on the *Condor* that the Southers were resisting stoutly.

"As expected!" cried ASM Sawyer, directing his battlecruisers to fire directly on the area surrounding the Spaceport from orbit.

General Matthewson's Director of Operations, the distinguished Marine Commander Gray, questioned the order. Such an indiscriminate policy was in danger of destroying the Spaceport and the Ground Gate with it. The destruction of the Ground Gate would make it impossible to deploy troops on the ground. The battlecruiser *Osprey*, the newest in the fleet, its entire crew, and the marine brigade on board would probably be lost as well.

General Matthewson overruled the order. He directed the captain of the *Osprey* to secure the Gate and move aside to allow troop transports to land.

The battle on the ground raged on for three standard hours before the captain of the *Osprey* confirmed that he had cleared and secured the Ground Gate.

General Matthewson gave the order to deploy, and the second battlecruiser, the *Falcon,* entered the Orbital Gate.

What followed was a mopping-up exercise. A small contingent of 10,000 Autonomic Units was all it took to wipe out the enemy troops and androids defending the Spaceport. After that, half of the troop transports, carrying another 4,000 men and 400,000 AUs, landed and began to move toward the city.

The Souther troops, with their few remaining Popovs, put up a stout defense of their principal city. By the end of the first Leninets day, the invasion force had lost 1,500 men, including 12 senior officers and 100,000 AUs. The Popovs had lost 35,000 of an estimated force of 45,000, but they were well dug in. The general ordered deployment of the remaining troop transports, adding a further 2,000 men and 240,000 armed Units to the force on the ground. The battle for Leninets would soon be over.

And then the rains came.

Chapter 88

Running on fumes, her engines coughing and threatening to breathe their last at any minute, the *Icarus3* limped into the D-System. As they approached Leninets, they were greeted by the sight of a battlecruiser burning out of control and five others in a defensive ring around the Orbital Gate. The whole space was littered with the shattered, smoldering remains of small craft.

To avoid detection, Peacock feathered the engines and used the lateral thruster to tuck the *Icarus3* under the hull of the nearest battlecruiser. Then he fired a couple of hawser clamps, attaching them firmly to the underside of the much larger ship. The *Icarus3* shuddered as he wound in the hawsers, drawing the small ship as close as he dared to the battlecruiser.

"What's happening?" said Carla.

"I've attached us to a mothership. It's an old pirate trick. Mama will protect us, but she won't know we're there."

Flashes from massive explosions on the surface of the planet, seen through a thick covering of clouds, told Carla what she dreaded. They were too late; the battle for the planet had already started.

"We need to get Romeo down there immediately," she said.

"Is he ready?"

"He will be in five minutes. How long will it take you to move this heap of scrap through the Orbital Gate?"

Peacock shook his head, sadly. "It's too heavily defended. We'd never have a chance of making it."

"We have to."

"Our main engines are out of fuel."

"Couldn't we use the lateral thruster?" she said.

"How would you suggest we do that?"

"I don't know. You're the pilot. It can't be far."

"A couple of clicks. But what you're suggesting is impossible. Without forward momentum the lateral thruster would put us into an uncontrolled spiral spin."

"We have to try, Peacock. If we don't, millions will die on the planet."

He closed his good eye, which Carla took as a signal that the discussion was over. Then he opened it again and exclaimed, "Why can't you do your magic from here?"

"Not possible. I need to get Romeo close to one of their AUs."

He pointed to the bulkhead above his head. "How about one of the AUs on the crate above us?"

She thought about that. Romeo might be able to transfer the software to a Unit on the battlecruiser. That could do the trick once the onboard AUs were deployed and in contact with the Units on the ground.

"It's worth a try." She rushed off to get Romeo ready.

Under Carla's guidance, Lia transferred the Fear module to Romeo. His immediate reaction to the Fear module was startling. He picked up a cup and flung it across the cabin, where it rebounded off the wall plating.

"You're okay, Romeo," said Carla. "Sit down."

"What are you doing to me?"

"Nothing. It's time to establish contact with one of the Norther Units nearby and transfer the software. I've explained all this to you before."

Romeo perched on the edge of the bed. "You did not explain how I am feeling."

"Yes, I'm sorry about that, but it won't be for long."

Peacock appeared at the door.

"What do you want?" she said.

"I want to watch this." There was a wide grin on his face.

"There won't be anything to see." She turned her attention to Romeo. "Reach out, Romeo. See if you can contact a Unit in the ship above us."

Romeo closed his eyes. Then he opened them again. "I have made contact with three Units. Their designations are—"

"We don't need their designations, Romeo. Choose one of them. Tell him you have a software upgrade to be transferred to all Units in the fleet."

After another short paused, Romeo said, "Alpha Tango 23 requires a software upgrade authorization. He will not accept an upgrade without an official code."

"Tell Alpha Tango 23 the upgrade comes from Carla Scott. Send them my image and the authorization code two three one seven two three."

"That was simple. Nothing to it," said Peacock. "Now all we have to do is hitch a ride home."

Fifteen seconds later, Romeo opened his eyes. "Transfer failed. The authorization code was rejected."

"Try again," she said. "Authorization code one seven one five two three."

Romeo closed his eyes again.

"Any luck?" said Peacock, impatiently.

"Transfer failed," said Romeo.

Carla used one of Peacock's colorful curses, "Festering pustules!" She was out of ideas.

"Try again," said Peacock. "Don't you have another code you can use?"

"I've tried them all. It's obvious that these AUs have new security protection software that is blocking my backdoor access."

She had failed. Her only chance was to try to upgrade the Units on the ground. If she could succeed with even one Unit, it might still reach and be assimilated by them all.

Chapter 89

On the surface of Leninets, the Southers were putting up stiff resistance. As the rain continued to bucket down, General Matthewson's frustrations mounted. His troops were within three klicks of the city, but they were bogged down in marshy ground.

"Send in more Units," he ordered.

His Operations Director, Marine Commander Gray, summed up the extent of their reserves, "We have 200,000 reserve Units on standby in the battlecruisers, General."

"Send them in."

"Let me remind you that these backup reserves are unarmed due to a chronic shortage of powerpacks."

"They have weapons, don't they?"

"Yes, sir, they have blasters, but none of them work. The weapons have no powerpacks."

The general waved an impatient arm. "The overwhelming numbers will win the day. Send in the *Shrike* and the *Goshawk*. Leave the *Kestrel* here with the *Condor*, in reserve."

#

The *Icarus3* shook like a baby's rattle.

"What's happening?" said Carla.

"Mama's moving. She's heading into the Gate. Stay close to the cargo bay door. Hold onto your hat and get ready to open the door and jump when I tell you."

The battlecruiser moved through the Gate, taking the *Icarus3* with it. The moment they were inside the Conduit, Peacock released the hawsers and started the Brazill drive. They landed and emerged through the Ground Gate, seconds ahead of the battlecruiser.

"Everybody out!" he shouted.

Carla sprung the cargo bay door. Lia, Carla and Romeo jumped out followed, three second later, by Captain Peacock. Five seconds after that, the battlecruiser *Goshawk* burst through the gate, crushing the *Icarus3* under its enormous weight. Explosive decompression blew the *Icarus3* to pieces. The blast nearly burst Carla's eardrums, and they all ducked as shards of metal debris flew everywhere.

Peacock picked up a jagged piece of hull plating, bearing the legend *—rus3*. "Cap'n Blackmore won't be happy when he hears about this."

They hurried away from the battlecruiser through the teeming rain, Peacock limping,

Romeo and Lia running together, clinging closely to each other. Carla found shelter in a half-demolished building on the edge of the Spaceport, the remnant of a roof offering a little shelter. They all found places to sit. Romeo sat beside Lia.

"What now?" said Peacock, shaking the rain from his locks.

Tuning out the teeming rain, Carla picked up rumbling artillery fire in the distance. "How far away do you think those guns are, Captain?"

"That's not artillery," he said. "That's thunder."

She listened again, linking the lightning flashes with the rumbles confirmed Peacock's opinion.

Romeo pointed at a shard of metal protruding from Lia's neck. "Lia is damaged."

Carla told him to move aside. She eased the shrapnel out of Lia's neck and checked the damage. It was bad. Lia's sensory faculties and her main modules were unaffected, but the connections between the two had been severed. No inputs from her eyes or ears could reach her processing units, and nothing from her processors could reach her vocal center. She was effectively deaf, dumb and blind.

"Stay here and rest your ankle," she said to Peacock. "Romeo and I have a mission to complete."

A weary Peacock sat down beside Lia.

Carla and Romeo left the ruined building and darted out into the rain. The sky was obscured, lit up by occasional sheet lightning flashes passing like an argument between banks of angry clouds in the far distance. Shielding her eyes, she found a hill and climbed it. The rain seemed lighter as she climbed, but by the time she'd reached the top she was wet through.

A wide river flowed around the far side of the hill. Several kilometers away, a thousand glistening roofs and a dozen blazing fires suggested a sprawling city under attack. In the distance, shrouded in a low-lying violet haze, a range of snow-capped mountains, as impressive as any in all the Six Systems.

There was no sign of the battle: no drones in the air, and no movement of humans or androids anywhere on the ground as far as the eye could see. "Where are all the troops?" she said.

Romeo pointed back toward the Norther battlecruisers and troop transports, clustered around the Ground Gate. And as she watched, a battlecruiser disgorged a long line of AUs. They formed up four abreast, before setting off at the double in response to an officer's shouted command.

"Come on, Romeo." Carla ran down the side of the hill to follow them. Romeo hesitated at the top of the hill. She called to him to follow her, and he came down to join her, his heels sliding through the rough shale.

"What's the problem, Romeo?" she said.

"We have no weapons." Impassive as ever, Romeo's facial expression gave nothing away, but his hair was stuck to his head and his clothes were drenched. He looked miserable. Carla reckoned his Fear module was doing its job.

"Don't worry," she said. "We won't get too close to the fighting."

Chapter 90

Carla and Romeo set off after the line of troops. The road was little more than a muddy track, pockmarked with craters filled with rainwater and littered on both sides by the detritus of war – abandoned military equipment, hovertrucks, artillery pieces AUs and Popovs. Dead bodies, military and civilian, lay abandoned everywhere.

As they approached the edge of the city, they came across broken and demolished buildings, fires raging fiercely in spite of the heavy rain. And more bodies.

The Norther troops were nowhere in sight, and neither were the Souther defenders. The whole place looked deserted. Where was everyone?

They ducked into the remains of a building.

"Romeo," she said. "Contact one of the Autonomic Units in the ground force up ahead."

"Which one?"

"Anyone. It doesn't matter."

"I have a link to Alpha Tango 4479."

"Tell Alpha Tango 4479 you have a software upgrade for transfer to all Units. Give him authorization code two three one seven two three."

Romeo closed his eyes. Then he opened them again. "That authorization code is blocked."

"Tell him the upgrade is from Carla Scott. And try authorization code one seven one five two three."

Romeo tried again.

"All upgrades are blocked," he said.

They contacted two other Units and tried twice more with the same result.

Carla swore silently. "See if you can make contact with a Souther Popov."

Romeo closed his eyes again. When he opened them, he said, "There are no Popovs within range."

That's crazy! she thought.

"Try again, Romeo."

Romeo closed his eyes again. When he opened them, he said, "There are no Popovs within range." He closed his eyes again.

"Leave it, Romeo," she said. There was nothing more they could do.

Romeo's eyes remained closed. "I am receiving signals from the Autonomic Units."

"A signal from Alpha Tango 4479?"

"There are many signals, from hundreds of Autonomic Units."

"What sort of signals?"

"Fear," he said.

That was impossible; the AUs didn't have the Pain or Fear modules.

"Come on, Romeo," she said. "We need to get back to Lia and the captain."

They headed back toward the Ground Gate. They had traveled no more than a kilometer when she heard the noise of running feet advancing from behind them. The noise grew louder. She looked back and saw Autonomic Units – thousands of them – running toward them. Within seconds, they were swamped by AUs. Running at full speed, they swept past.

Where were they going?

Before she could ask, Romeo supplied the answer. "They are running back to the ships."

"Why? What are they running from?"

"Fear," he said again. "They are running from the Southers."

Carla and Romeo took shelter in another ruined building where they watched thousands of military AUs in full retreat. When the last of them had passed, they followed them back to where they had left Lia and Peacock.

Peacock had fallen asleep. Lia was leaking hydraulic fluid, her mouth moving silently.

"Don't try to speak, Lia," said Carla. Then she remembered that Lia couldn't hear her. "Lift her up," she said to Romeo. "You'll have to be her eyes and ears for the moment."

She poked Peacock's shoulder to wake him. "We need to get aboard one of those ships. They'll be leaving soon."

Peacock rubbed a hand across his face. “Give me a minute to think.”

“We don’t need to think,” she said. “Look outside. The AUs are rushing back to the ships in their thousands. All we have to do is mingle with them. It should be easy to get onboard something.”

Peacock pulled himself to his feet and peered into the rain. He gave a low whistle. “What’s the matter with the mechanos?”

“They’ve lost their bottle.” Ducking under Lia’s left arm, she said, “Come on. Romeo, take Lia’s other arm.”

Leaving their shelter, they ran to join the throng of terror-stricken Autonomic Units. Hampered by his bad ankle, Peacock struggled to keep up.

Carla, Lia and Romeo were heading toward one of the leisure cruisers when Peacock shouted, “We need to get on board a battlecruiser.”

There was no time to argue with him. Carla and Romeo made their way toward the nearest battlecruiser, holding Lia upright and propelling her along between them. Peacock followed.

As they mounted the boarding ramp, Carla looked back. Hundreds of figures appeared, pursuing the AUs. These weren’t Popovs, but flesh and blood men, not military troops with blasters, but ordinary citizens of Leninets, armed with pitchforks, scythes and mattocks. The common populace of Paviaskigrad, armed with agricultural implements, were sending the Norther invaders packing!

What had happened? Could the software transfer have succeeded? Something had robbed the Autonomic Units of their courage. The Norther invasion was doomed to failure.

Chapter 91

Inside the battlecruiser was total chaos with AUs milling about, bunched into groups, yelling at each other and officers yelling at them. A continuous stream of garbled instructions from the internal communications added to the noise levels, doing nothing to restore order or calm.

"We need to find the location of the AU engineering lab." She pitched her voice above the dim.

Peacock pointed to his ears and moved closer.

"Engineering," she yelled at him. "I need to repair Lia."

"Later," mouthed Peacock. "Follow me."

He led them through the cargo bay, elbowing his way through the crowds into the bowels of the ship.

It was quieter here, distorted internal communications ordering: *All Divisions report to Life-stack Restorations on Deck F17* on an endless broadcast loop.

"Where are we going?" she said.

Peacock stabbed at a console on the wall, revealing a schematic of the ship.

“What are you looking for?”

“This way.” And he was off again.

They rode an elevator up three levels. Then they traversed the huge vessel from port to starboard. Finally, Peacock stopped at an airlock protected by a security keypad. He growled. Gripping the keypad, he attempted to rip it from its anchors. It was too securely attached.

All Divisions report to Life-stack Restorations on Deck F17

“Romeo,” said Carla. “See if you can break in.”

They propped Lia against the wall and Romeo began a systematic attempt to break the keypad code by trial and error. Working at lightning speed, he started with single digits, then he tried every possible combination of double digits, then all combinations of three. He’d started on 4-digit combinations when the airlock door opened, and an AU stepped out. Peacock used his boot to stop the door from closing.

The Unit did a double take when he saw them. Carla stood in front of him. “Who am I?” she said.

It took the Unit a moment or two before he replied, “You are Carla Scott.”

“I am Carla Scott. You will wipe our images from your memory. Code one seven one five two three. Do you understand?”

“I understand.”

“Now go about your business.”

The AU strode past them.

Her backdoor access had worked!

The fighter bay was as big as a cathedral. Four gleaming fighters sat on launch pads, facing the bay doors, ready for rapid launch. In an area to the rear, a further eight were being made ready by maintenance teams.

A glass-fronted lookout above their heads housed launch control.

Moving away from the access door, they hid behind some packing crates directly under the lookout.

"What next?" said Carla.

"We wait until the cruiser leaves the planet. Once it's in orbit, we can help ourselves to one of these babies." Peacock's eyes were shining. He smacked his lips.

"Will there be room for all of us?" she asked.

"Who knows," said Peacock.

As they watched, four more fighters were wheeled into position. The internal PA continued to blare unintelligible gibberish.

Division Seven on priority standby.

They felt the huge ship move, the warning sirens sounded, and they jumped through the Ground Gate. Carla groaned, and Peacock laughed at her.

"I'm sure I lose a week off the end of my life every time we go through one of those infernal Gates," she said.

Four minutes later, the sirens sounded again,

the battlecruiser emerged through the Orbital Gate, and Peacock swung into action. "Ready?"

"We're ready," said Carla, taking her position on Lia's left side.

Romeo propped up her right side and they ran across the deck.

An alarm sounded, followed immediately by a blaring command from the control center public address speakers.

Stop where you are, or you will be fired on.

They reached the nearest fighter, coming under fire from handblasters as they clambered aboard, Carla pulling, Romeo pushing the inert form of Lia onto the wing.

They made it onto the fighter in one piece, the last blaster bolt sliding off the access door as it closed.

The cockpit had three stations. Peacock took the pilot's seat; Carla took the co-pilot's. Romeo sat behind them with Lia on the floor beside him.

Peacock started the engines.

Carla looked through the forward window. "We're going nowhere," she said, glumly. "The bay doors are closed."

Peacock wound up the engines. "Watch and learn," he said, grimly.

The radio crackled. *Switch off your engines, Camelot seven,* said a grim voice.

"Evacuate the bay and open the doors," Peacock replied. "You have two standard minutes to comply."

This is futile. Whoever you are, switch off your engines and surrender. The doors will not be opened.

"One and a half minutes," said Peacock.

The maintenance crews were running for the airlock, now, and she saw others – fighter crews, presumably – running toward the fighters.

"One minute," said Peacock into the radio. Then, "Thirty seconds."

There was no response from launch control.

Thirty seconds later, Carla watched speechless as Peacock flipped the cover off the top of the control stack and pressed his thumb down firmly on the button. A missile shot out from under the fighter with a WHOOSH, and exploded on contact with the bay doors, venting all the air and sweeping crates, tools and debris into open space.

Peacock released the locking clamps, and the fighter exited the bay. Turning left, they shot away from the planet, heading toward deep space.

"That was madness," she muttered.

"What did you say? I didn't catch that," said Peacock.

They were pursued by three fighters from another battlecruiser. Missiles and blaster cannon shot past them on both sides as Peacock took evasive action, diving and weaving, building up his speed.

Deep space beckoned.

The pursuing fighters stayed on their tail for

ten standard minutes, firing at them occasionally. Peacock was an accomplished pilot, managing to evade every missile, every blaster bolt. After 15 minutes, three pursuers became two and, three minutes after that, the remaining two fighters turned back.

The stars on all sides were dimming. They were entering null space.

"Not long to the Gate, now," said Peacock.

"How do you know where it is?" she said. "Does the Gate have a beacon? I can't hear anything."

"There's no beacon. But trust me, I know where it is."

Carla didn't trust him, but what choice did she have?

Chapter 92

Marine Commander Gray had never seen General Matthewson so furious. An aide was lucky to get out of his wardroom uninjured as the pot of coffee he'd just left on his table followed him out the door.

"How could nearly a million of our best Autonomic Units turn tail and run from a ragtag collection of Russian farmers?"

"I have no explanation, General—"

"My question was rhetorical," hissed the general. "If I didn't know she was on her way home, I might suspect the hand of Carla Scott in what just happened. Now tell me what happened onboard the *Goshawk*. There was an explosion in one of their fighter bays, I understand."

"Yes, General. A fighter was launched without authorization. The launch controller ordered the pilot to stand down, but he refused. He blew the launch bay doors off. The captain of the *Kestrel* sent three fighters after them, but they got away."

"Who was this rogue pilot?" The general's face had turned strange shade of green.

Marine Commander Gray shook his head. "No

one knows. There was a full complement of four. All of the Goshawk fighter crews are accounted for."

"Where is this runaway fighter now?"

"Last seen heading into the null region of deep space."

General Matthewson called through his door for a fresh pot of coffee. "It's time to wrap up this mission and go home with our tails between our legs."

"Yes, General."

"I never wanted it, didn't like it, thought it was ill-advised, but what could I do? Secretary of State Bluewater gave the orders. I had to obey."

"Yes, General."

"It was one of those worst-of-all-possible missions. If it had been a success, Bluewater and the president would have taken the credit. Now that it has failed, I will have to take all the blame."

"Yes, General."

"Contact Marshal Sawyer to assemble the fleet."

"Yes, General."

#

The fleet made its way back the way they'd come. Five days into their transit of the EC Conduit, they came across the *Nyx,* a lone shuttle, lost and wandering aimlessly, and apparently without purpose. A boarding party from the battlecruiser *Falcon* discovered a crew of seventeen, every man jack of them disoriented and confused. Ebenezer S. Edgerton, the captain, explained that he had lost his freighter, the *Pegasus* to a band of pirates, he and his crew barely escaping with their lives aboard the tiny shuttle. They had been drifting in the Conduits for 28 days. Medics onboard the *Falcon* diagnosed serious dehydration, with complications brought on by Interdimensional fug.

Chapter 93

The fighter entered the Gate at speed. Every panel on the ship shook and every rivet rattled. Peacock slammed the conventional engines off and switched on the Brazill Drive. They waited for the bad news. It came in the shape of a triangular piece of metal drifting past the cockpit and sailing down the Conduit ahead of them.

Peacock picked out a few choice sailors' expletives that he'd been saving for a special occasion. Two of them were new to Carla.

"What was that?" she said.

"That was ISD, Interdimensional Ship Destruction, remember? And that was our tail fin."

"Do we need it? Can we make it home without a tail fin?"

"As long as we're running on the Brazill Drive, it won't affect us, but we'll need it when we get back to normal space."

"You mean we won't be able to get to the Orbital Gate on Earth?"

Peacock harumphed. "I'll think of something."

He set the Brazill Drive on auto and went aft to check on the damage.

When he returned, his hands were covered in oil. "I think it came away cleanly enough. There may still be danger of a rupture. We'll know soon enough when we hit normal space."

She knew that an explosive decompression would kill them both before they knew what was happening.

As if I need another thing to worry about.

She put Romeo and Lia into sleep mode. Then she searched the ship for tools to repair her friend. She found some dry clothes for herself, Lia, and Romeo, but no tools. In the pilot's sleeping bay she found a tunic with the name 'Tom Sheppard, Major' on the chest. Her teeth chattered as she removed her wet things. Then she replaced Lia and Romeo's wet clothes.

By the time she returned to the cockpit, the onboard temperature had dropped two degrees. She handed the pilot's tunic to Peacock and he slipped it on. She strapped herself into her seat. The transit clock on the dashboard read 78 hours 5 minutes. "That's even faster than the last time!"

"This fighter is a greyhound," said Peacock. "The *Icarus3* was a poodle."

Carla did the math. They would be home at least 5 days ahead of the Norther fleet.

Peacock switched on a heater. The cockpit began to warm up, sending exquisite tingling sensations through her body.

He laughed at the expression on her face.

"There's nothing like a bit of luxury, and there's nowhere more luxurious than a fighter cockpit." She gave him a skeptical look, and he explained, "Fighter pilots like Major Tom are the cream, the privileged few. They get the best of everything."

#

Two days into the transit, both AUs had been recharged. She'd used the onboard computers to remove the Fear software from Romeo's modules and she'd reconnected Lia's cameras. It was a crude repair that wouldn't stand up to any violent movement. Even running could shake it loose, but Lia would be able to see again. She woke Romeo and explained her plan to recreate Oscar.

"Lia formed an attachment to a Mark 5 Autonomic Unit, just like you. His name was Alpha Oscar 113. We called him Oscar for short. Lia tried to rebuild him, using a Mark 4 Unit."

"The Mark4 Units are not compatible with Mark 5 modules," said Romeo.

"That is why Lia's first efforts were unsuccessful. Then she found Oscar's frame in a storage warehouse and replaced his Perception, Cognition, Compliance, and Orientation modules."

"She rebuilt Oscar?"

Carla shook her head. "That attempt also failed."

"She must install his memory module," said Romeo.

Romeo's reasoning was sound. "That's right. I believe I will be able to rebuild Oscar's memories from a computer backup, when we return to Earth."

"Lia will be able to rebuild Oscar."

"Yes. Unfortunately, we no longer have Oscar's frame or his modules."

Romeo gave that some thought.

"Can you recover Oscar's frame and modules?"

"No."

"If you can rebuild Oscar's memories, all you need is a Mark 5 Unit with four modules."

He paused for thought again.

"I have the four modules. You must use my frame and modules to rebuild Oscar." His reasoning had already worked out where Carla was going.

"Thank you, Romeo," said Carla. "Lia will be pleased."

Chapter 94

The transit clock aboard the fighter had reached two minutes.

"Standby for the Gate exit," said Peacock, one hand on the Brazill Drive, the other on the conventional engines.

The warning siren sounded. When the clock hit zero, Carla closed her eyes, every muscle in her body tensed up in expectation of an explosive decompression. They jumped through the Gate. When she opened her eyes, they were still in one piece. Mother Earth loomed large ahead, the moon tucked in behind her. A truly stunning sight!

Carla tried to recall the distance to Earth's Orbital Gate. It wasn't far. It had taken an hour in the *Icarus3*, on two engines.

"How many engines do we have?" she asked.

"All four are working perfectly."

"So how long will it take us to reach the Orbital Gate?"

"Thirty minutes, maybe. Have you worked out how you're gonna get past Spaceport identity checks?"

Carla had given it a lot of thought, without coming up with any strategy remotely feasible.

"I have an idea," he said. "Just follow my lead."

As they approached the Gate, he switched on the radio.

"This is Camelot Seven, standing by the Orbital Gate. I am declaring an emergency."

Camelot Seven, we have no record of your flight. What is your designation?

"This is Major Tom Sheppard aboard Norther Spacefleet Fighter Camelot Seven. We have four souls onboard. We have lost our tail fin. Requesting immediate landing clearance."

We have no record of you, Camelot Seven. Where away are you from?

"This is Camelot Seven, I repeat, we have declared an emergency. Please clear us for immediate landing."

After a short pause, Spaceport Control responded, *Camelot Seven, you are clear to land. Welcome home, Major.*

The fighter slid through the Orbital Gate, emerging a few seconds later on the ground at LAX Spaceport, surrounded on all sides by fire tenders and ambulance hovers.

Once the dust had settled, and it was clear they wouldn't be needed, the emergency response vehicles dispersed. Peacock, Carla and the two AUs were escorted to a military hovertruck by an armed guard and transported to a building on the edge of the spaceport. Romeo helped Lia from the truck and into the building, where they were led away.

Carla objected. "Those are my personal Units. I need them with me."

The guards made no response.

Carla and Peacock were checked by two men at a security station, before a guard took them to a room equipped with a table and four wooden chairs. The guard left them alone.

"Leave the talking to me," said Peacock.

They were joined, within minutes, by a senior officer wearing a tunic that matched the one Peacock was wearing.

"Colonel Drew, Senior Operations, Norther Spacefleet." He held out a hand and Peacock shook it.

"Major Tom Sheppard, C-System Spacefleet. Glad to meet you, Colonel."

Drew took a seat. He turned his gaze to Carla. "And you are?"

"This is my co-pilot," said Peacock. "Her name is Car—"

"Donna English," said Carla.

"And the two Autonomic Units?"

"They are mine," she said. "Alpha Romeo is my bodyguard. Lia is my personal maid."

The colonel's gaze returned to Peacock. "Tell me where you've come from, Major and how you lost your tail fin."

"We were engaged in a battle with the Souther fleet the D-System. We lost our tailfin in crossfire."

"And you abandoned your post? You left the fleet?"

Peacock gave a short cough. "I assure you, the fleet is right behind us. The battle was lost, Colonel."

The colonel invited Peacock to follow him to another room where his debriefing could continue in private.

Carla heard the door lock click as they left, a chilling sound that increased her fears. Would the military discover who she was? If they did, they were sure to send her back to Luciflex to complete her sentence. Feeling isolated and vulnerable, her apprehension mixed with a rising sense of separation anxiety. Would she ever see Lia and Romeo again? She had made a promise to Lia. Would she be able to make good on it?

An hour went by. She could hear nothing, apart from the sounds of her own breathing. The room was soundproofed. She was sure there were unseen eyes watching her through the two-way mirror on the wall. She closed her eyes and did her best to conjure up the face of Zed Jones, but his image was fading. She settled for scenes of Califon sunrises and views of the Pacific Ocean as seen from her penthouse apartment.

Then the lock turned, and the door burst open. She recognized the man who strode in.

Chapter 95

She was staring at the man who'd tried to kill her as she ran toward the *Icarus3* in the hangar, the man with the silly little stick, now sporting an impressive blackeye.

"Carla Scott," he said. "I'm pleased to finally make your acquaintance."

"I'm sorry, I don't think we've met." She stared at him, openmouthed. "My name is Donna English."

"Commander Harlowe, NFSA. We met nine days ago, right here, in the spaceport. You and your androids gave me this." He pointed his stick at his blackeye. "I have been looking for you and your personal Unit ever since. Where have you been?"

"You are mistaken, Commander. I've never seen you before. Our battlecruiser was destroyed in the D-System. Major Sheppard and I barely made it home alive."

He slapped his thigh with the stick. "Not a very convincing story, Ms. Scott. I know who you are. And I know you have escaped confinement in the F-System. You will be returned to Luciflex on a freighter, leaving tomorrow."

She raised her voice. “You have the wrong person.”

“We have identified your pilot, too. A known criminal with a long history of piracy, his name is Adam Peacock. He will be returned to Luciflex with you. The Federation takes a dim view of prison breakouts. You may expect an extension of your prison term.”

A wave of dizziness swept over Carla. The game was up!

“Your co-conspirator, Cassidy Garmon, is under lock and key. He will join you in the molten mines.”

Cassidy must be wishing we’d never met, she thought.

“And as for those two androids you had with you. They will be decommissioned as a matter of priority.” He gave his thigh one last thwack, turned on his heel, and stormed out.

Another hour went by in silence. She began pacing the room. She tried talking to the mirror, restating her false name and rank to anyone who might be listening. It would take them 36, maybe 48 hours to check with the military authorities on Califon and get word back, although she doubted that they would bother. Commander Harlowe clearly knew who she was.

Her soul ached for Lia. Had they taken her and Romeo away to be decommissioned already? Would she ever see either of them again? And what about Cassidy? His fate filled her with guilt. Under her guidance, he had incurred the wrath of Xenodyne Industries, an all-powerful, unforgiving organization, and the opprobrium of the Norther Federation. He was probably halfway to Luciflex by now.

An armed guard arrived and escorted her to a waiting hovertruck. Peacock was in the truck already, handcuffed to a second guard. He stared at her blankly as she climbed in. She sat facing him, beside her guard, and the truck started. They exited the spaceport through a checkpoint manned by an AU, and merged with the commuter traffic, heading east.

She looked at Peacock, hoping for a signal, any faint sign that he had a plan of action in mind which would set them free before they reached their destination. There was no spark from the pirate. He crouched on the bench, looking dejected, beaten, resigned to his fate.

Chapter 96

The truck rumbled on for a few minutes before slowing down. It came to an abrupt halt, and the driver swore. Angry hover drivers sounded their horns.

"What's going on?" Carla's guard called out to the driver.

"It's a traffic snarl up," the driver replied. "Something's happening up ahead."

Peacock lifted his head, fixing Carla with his good eye. "Reminds me of that time with Darm and his buddy."

Carla remembered how Peacock had come to her rescue and she'd used her elbow on her attacker. She raised her arm to wipe her nose with her sleeve, and smashed her elbow into the guard's face. At the same time, Peacock attacked his guard. Before her guard had time to react, she had removed the blaster from the holster on his belt. Leaping to her feet, she leveled the blaster at Peacock's guard. "Drop your blaster on the floor. Use your fingers." The guard's blaster fell to the floor. She picked it up. "Now remove the handcuffs."

When Peacock was free of the handcuffs, he clipped them onto his guard and told him to lie down. She handed Peacock one of the blasters, tucking the second one into her belt.

"Everything all right back there?" the driver called out.

Peacock placed his blaster under the second guard's chin. "Answer him."

"Everything's fine," the guard replied.

The pirate struck the guard on the forehead, knocking him out. Then he pointed his blaster at the first guard, lying on the floor. "We're leaving now. If you know what's good for you, you'll give us five minutes before raising the alarm."

They jumped down from the back of the truck and set off back the way they'd come, weaving their way around a long line of hovers that stretched all the way to the ocean in the distance. After a couple of blocks, Peacock turned down a side street.

"Where are you going?" she said.

"I have to find Blackmore and explain what happened to his ship. If I don't find him first, I'm a dead man."

"Wait a minute," said Carla. She ran to a bank ATM.

"You can't use that. The NFSA will find you."

She used her palm to access the machine and extracted a bundle of A-dollars.

She handed some of the money to Peacock.

"That's the seven hundred I owe the captain. Please give it to him."

The avaricious look in his eye was unmistakable. "Don't even think about spending it. I have Captain Blackmore's X-Vid number. I'll tell him you have his money."

Peacock tucked the notes into his pocket with a reluctant shrug.

"And You can tell him there's a Federation spy on Hades," she said.

Peacock fixed her with his good eye. "What do you mean?"

"Someone planted a tracking device inside Romeo."

"Who?"

"I don't know, but Oswald had access to Romeo while his powerpack was on recharge in his office, and I was sleeping."

"Thanks for that," said Peacock. "I never trusted that snake. Captain Blackmore will be grateful for the information."

And Peacock was gone.

A distant siren told her the police were on their way. She jumped into a hovercab and took it back to the entrance to the spaceport.

The AU at the checkpoint asked for her papers.

"Who am I?" she said.

"You are Carla Scott," the Unit replied.

"I am Carla Scott, and I would like you to send a message for me. Authorization code one seven one five two three. The message is for Alpha Romeo 3863. Meet Carla Scott at the spaceport checkpoint. Bring Lia with you."

Two minutes later, Romeo and Lia emerged from the army building, running across the landing strip toward Carla. Behind them, army personnel appeared, shouting at them to stop. Carla fired her blaster over their heads, and they took shelter, giving Romeo and Lia time to reach Carla at the checkpoint.

All three jumped into the hovercab and left the spaceport at speed, their destination Feynman Tech in West Athens.

Chapter 97

True to form, Professor Jones was not surprised to see Carla again. She had to wait until he had finished delivering a lecture before they were face to face. They embraced. His eyes lit up, as they always did in her company. She reckoned their discussions kept his mind active, and living vicariously through her allowed him to recapture something of his lost youth.

"Introduce me to your friends," he said.

"This is Romeo, Alpha Romeo 3683 to give him his full name."

"Great name," said the professor.

"And this is Lia, my personal companion. She's been injured. I'm going to need the use of your lab to repair her."

"Of course." The professor led the way to the lab. "You can fill me in on all your adventures while we work."

They set about repairing Lia together. While they worked, he told her about the two visits he'd had from Commander Harlowe of the NFSA. "Obnoxious individual, wanted to know where you were."

"Carries a little stick?" She grinned. "I've met him."

Making no mention of the secret AE Conduit, she told him how she'd used a pirate ship to follow a Norther fleet to the D-System, hoping to prevent a war, and how she'd failed to upload the Fear module to the AUs on Leninets.

"I don't know how it happened, but without any intervention from me, the Autonomic Units all lost their nerve, fleeing in their thousands before Souther peasants, armed with nothing but farm implements."

"Were there no Popovs defending the planet?"

"Apparently not many."

He said, "Are you sure you didn't complete the upload of your Fear module?"

"I'm certain."

He gave that some thought. "Could the Pain module have caused that response?"

"Pain without Fear? Maybe, but I didn't have the Pain module to upload."

"Cassidy told me before he went into hiding that he made sure all the replacement Units carried the Pain software."

"Why?"

"He said it was a sensible development. It took you both months of hard work. He didn't want to lose it."

"So how could Pain without Fear have caused such terror?" she said.

He began to piece together a theory. “Let’s suppose one Unit is injured. He is aware of the damage—”

“Without the Fear module?”

“Perhaps the hardware modules are all it needs, Cognition and Orientation, probably.”

“Okay, go on.”

“So he’s aware of the injury, but without the Fear module, he doesn’t know how to deal with it.”

“So he does the only thing he can do,” she said.

“What?”

“He communicates with his companions.”

The professor slapped a palm to his head, “Of course. He sends a warning, an alarm.”

“But would that be enough to start a panic?”

“Maybe not, but if enough Units were injured and they all communicated warnings to the others, that could cause a mass panic. Once a critical mass was injured, they could pass the panic to the others in a flash. And a compulsion to flee spreads throughout the entire population. It’s entirely possible.”

She waved her hands, excitedly. “Of course! I underestimated the power of the heuristic processor. Pain without Fear is just as toxic as Fear without Pain.”

#

When the repair job was completed, they conducted a few tests to check that Lia was fully restored. She passed all her tests. Carla hugged her, and wiped a stray tear from her eyes. "I missed you, Lia."

Lia said nothing, but Carla thought she detected a flicker of something, a momentary dip of the eyes that could have been a hint of emotion. No matter. Lia was still her best friend, and as long as she had the Fear module written into her software, Carla knew that emotional responses were possible.

Chapter 98

At her request, the professor put a call through to Zed and handed her his X-Vid and left the room.

Zed beamed at her. “Carla! You met with Sophie okay?”

“Yes, thank you. She was very helpful.”

“Any sign of Cassidy?”

“The last I heard he was in police custody.”

“So he couldn’t help you?”

“Sophie took a message to him and he responded with everything I needed.”

“That’s great. Any hope that he will be released soon?”

“I don’t know. I doubt it.”

“Poor Sophie.”

“Yes.”

“I thought we might meet,” he said.

“What for?”

“I was a bit... I was a bit off the last time we spoke. I don’t want... I didn’t want... I thought you might have gotten the wrong impression...”

“What are you trying to say, Zed?” she asked, quietly.

“Can I take you to dinner somewhere?”

"On a date, you mean?"

"Yes. I've missed you."

"Okay. But could I ask for a favor, first?"

"Anything."

"Could you get my computer and bring it to me?"

"Where is it?"

"It's in my apartment."

"I'm sorry, Carla. The police cleared everything from your apartment after you left. I checked."

Carla swore under her breath.

When the call ended, Lia said, "If your computer is lost, are Oscar's memories also lost?"

Carla could see that Lia was fighting a rising feeling of panic generated by her Fear module. She replied, "Oscar's memories may still be stored in an archive backup."

"Where is the archive backup?" said Lia.

"The archive is an Xenodyne Automation database."

#

She asked Professor Jones for his password to the XA archives.

"I won't ask why," said the professor.

It took an hour of searching through the archives to find what she was looking for. Fifteen minutes later, she had downloaded Alpha Oscar 113's memories onto the professor's computer, and five minutes after that, she had transferred the precious memories over to a fresh memory module.

She sat Romeo down and explained again what she wanted to do.

"After you've finished, my memories will be erased?" he said.

"Yes. You will have become Alpha Oscar 113."

"And what of Alpha Romeo 3863?"

"He will no longer exist."

Romeo took a moment to process that information. "Could my memories be stored somewhere?"

"Of course," said Carla.

Romeo agreed to the procedure and she put him to sleep. She uploaded a copy of his memories to the archive before replacing his memory module with Oscar's.

Professor Jones watched everything she did without saying a word. Finally, as she added the Pain and Fear software modules, he said, "You're rebuilding a particular Unit. May I ask why?"

"His name's Oscar. He and Lia made a connection. I'm rebuilding him for her."

"A connection?"

"An emotional connection. It seems the Fear module has some strange side effects."

The professor's jaw fell open. "That is amazing, Carla. You could be on the brink of developing a whole new model of Machine Intelligence. Have you considered where that could lead?"

"Sentience, you mean? I think we've crossed that threshold already."

"I meant the singularity," he said, quietly.

Lia stood in front of Romeo as Carla inserted a powerpack and started him up.

"Hello Oscar," said Lia.

Romeo opened his eyes. "Hello Lia."

Chapter 99

Zed Jones called to invite Carla for a meal. He suggested Benkov's, an upmarket restaurant overlooking the ocean, a favorite among Hollywood's stars and movie moguls.

"Do they serve lasagna?" she said.

"I'm sure you'll be able to order anything you like," he replied.

During the meal he offered to let her use his spare room until she found somewhere permanent to live.

Carla thought about it for a while before finally accepting.

The following day dawned with a bank of fog blanketing the city, an insipid sun barely visible in the sky.

By early afternoon, the fog had largely dissipated. Carla and Zed went for a stroll by the ocean. Oscar and Lia accompanied them.

Zed and Carla held hands as they walked, and Oscar took Lia's hand.

Carla was astonished by the sight. Oscar had taken an independent initiative and Lia had accepted without question. That was an unprogrammed action and an unexplainable response. More than that, it was a clear act of affection and reciprocation between two androids – the first she'd ever witnessed.

As they strolled along, Zed pointed to the sky. "What are those?"

Carla looked up. The north western section of the sky was dotted with black points, like ink spots. She counted about 30.

"I don't know," she said. "Are they moving?"

"I think they may be getting bigger," said Zed. "It must be the space fleet returning from their failed venture in the D-System."

Carla did the math. "It's too early. They won't be back for at least another three days."

"It's definitely a fleet of spacecraft," said Zed.

Soon, everyone was looking up at the sky, pointing. The spots were growing bigger.

Carla asked Oscar and Lia to take a look with their zoom lenses. "What do you see?"

"I see three large battleships," said Oscar.

"And thirty-five smaller spacecraft," said Lia.

Fifteen minutes after that, the spacecraft came to rest in the sky, their bulk now clearly visible to everyone on the ground. A bright flash of light emanated from one of the larger battleships. Two seconds later, a building in the downtown area exploded.

They ran...

Thanks for reading Escape from Luciflex. If you enjoyed it, please write a short review. Reviews really help.

Keep an eye out for Android Wars book 3 and for my next science fiction novel, a story set on Égalité in the E-System. If you'd like to join my Science Fiction newsletter, please go to: www.jjtoner.com/sf-sign-up

ACKNOWLEDGEMENTS

Thanks to Ellie Midwood for the names of the three planets in the D-System, to my intrepid editor and proofreaders, Janet, Jim, Kevin, Larry, MJ, Pam, to Karen Perkins for print formatting, and to Stephen Walker and Anya Kelleye for the beautiful cover.

ABOUT THE AUTHOR

JJ writes WW2 spy thrillers, detective stories and short stories. But his first love is Science Fiction. He lives in Ireland.

BOOKS BY JJ TONER

Science Fiction

Eggs and Other Stories, a collection of satirical science fiction short stories

Murder by Android, Android short story 1

Rogue Android, Android short story 2

Breadcrumbs, Android short story 3

The Shape of Fear, Android Wars – book 1

Escape from Luciflex, Android Wars – book 2

WW2 spy thrillers and other books

The Black Orchestra, a WW2 spy thriller

The Wings of the Eagle, the second spy thriller in the Black Orchestra series

A Postcard from Hamburg, the third spy thriller in the series

The Gingerbread Spy, the fourth spy thriller in the series

The Serpent's Egg, a WW2 Red Orchestra spy story

Zugzwang, a pre-war short story featuring Kommissar Saxon

Queen Sacrifice, the second Kommissar Saxon story

The White Knight, the third Kommissar Saxon story

Houdini's Handcuffs, a detective thriller featuring DI Ben Jordan

Find Emily, the second DI Jordan thriller